DEAD WORLDS
UNDEAD STORIES
VOLUME 6

EDITED BY
ANTHONY GIANGREGORIO

OTHER LIVING DEAD PRESS BOOKS

DEAD WORLDS UNDEAD STORIES VOLUME 6

750

Table of Contents

LOVE PREVAILS

DANE T. HATCHELL

It was the screaming in the distance that led them off their chosen path. There were four of them—two married couples. The sanctuary of their urban community had buckled under the onslaught of the walking dead. The community ultimately had become a beacon, calling the flesh-eaters with the smell of fresh meat. The battles had gone in the favor of the living for many months. There was even hope that the living were winning, and that the walking dead's numbers would finally begin to dwindle. But day after day they came, to be slaughtered by the hundreds with gun shots to the head. Eventually though, food supplies for the weary warriors ran out. Being too weak to fight, one fateful night all hope was lost, and the men, women and children of the tiny town died in agony.

"It's a living man and he's calling for help," Kara said, concerned, directing her statement to Keith, her husband.

"It may be too late for him. We might walk into a situation we can't get out of," Keith said. He was concerned for Kara's safety first. Above all else, his main existence was to protect her.

"Kara's right, Keith," Jill said and looked toward, Steve, her husband. "You know it's the right thing to do."

Keith realized they were right and signaled them to head down to the valley below. The trek was steep, and a line of pine trees hid what lay ahead. Each of the men carried a shotgun, tricked out for maximum ammo capacity. Steve slipped a couple of times, his eyes looking more at his surroundings than where he was walking.

Finally arriving at the trees, now at least they could steady their descent by grabbing a hanging branch along the way. The screams for help weren't getting louder, even though they were getting closer.

"We're wasting energy, I think we're too late," Keith said.

"We've come this far and I see a stream over there to the left," Kara said. She knew he wouldn't challenge her. The group slowed their pace as the trees gave way to a clearing.

The bright sunshine illuminated a grassy area about a hundred yards away; the source of the screams had been found.

Keith pulled out a pair of binoculars from his backpack. There, tied to a pole, was a man that looked to be in his thirties. His clothes were torn and his face was bloody; black turkey vultures were feeding on corpses around him.

"Looks like some kind of set up," Keith said, taking his eyes away from the binoculars. "I don't like it, we should leave. Zombies didn't do this, we should leave right now." Keith read the indecision on the faces of the others and raised the binoculars for another look. Two living dead were making their way to the man, as the screams for help continued. Keith thought this would be the end for the poor soul. There was too much distance between them to help. A feeling of guilt rolled over him as he continued to watch, but he managed to detach himself from the gruesome reality he was witnessing.

When the zombies were about twenty feet away from the fresh meal, a thicket not far away rattled and two men with twelve foot spears and another two men with swords appeared, whooping and hollering. The spear carriers ran at full force and lanced the ghouls in the chest, driving them to the ground. The sword carriers followed close on their heels and brought the shiny blades of steel crashing through the grinning skulls of death. It was over quickly, and by their yells of triumph, the warriors were proud of their victory.

"Wow, guys, did you see that?"

"It looks like that guy is bait and it's some kind of sport for those people. We need to get out of here," Steve said anxiously.

The women stood in silence, waiting for someone to make a decision.

"Right, let's go. We should get some water and then make our way back home. The stream is heading the same way we're going, and maybe we can find a better path to get back than the way we came." Keith turned to lead and everyone fell in line as Steve maintained the rear. No one noticed the screams again, the sounds of the river, and their own breathing drowning it out.

The stream was about twenty feet wide and was extremely clear. The water was moving at a brisk rate and small fish were feeding near the bank. Each person knelt down next to the water and Keith scooped out a taste with a small plastic cup. It was cool and fresh tasting, more so than the bottled water they had survived on during the beginning of their journey. He passed the cup to Kara, removed his canteen from his pack, and filled it. Everyone drank their fill and topped off their canteens; Steve refilled the one gallon container he carried in his pack.

"Hello there!" a voice from behind called out in a friendly manner.

Keith whipped around, his shotgun leveled and pointed at a lone man standing just a few feet away as Steven did the same with his gun. The man was wearing a set of blue overalls and a red shirt. A Remington 870 hung unthreatening on a sling over his right shoulder.

"Well, now. There's no cause for that," the man said.

"Jesus, man, you scared me half to death. What're you doing sneaking up on us like that?"

"Wasn't sneakin', just makin' my security rounds. Names Pete, Pete Zeller."

Keith thought a moment, looked at the others, then lowered the shotgun upon seeing that Steve was in a ready position to use his if necessary.

"Sorry, I'm just a little jumpy....you know. My name's Keith Sims and that is my wife Kara." He pointed to Steve and Jill. "And that's Steve Mitchell and his wife Jill."

"Well, I'm please to meetcha. Where're you folks from and where're you headin'?"

"We're from Bakersfield, about three hundred miles away according to my GPS," Keith said. "I guess the dead were running out of food in the cities and they started hitting us. We could see the writing on the wall and got the hell out of there before the dead won. I really don't know what's going on there now. We're heading north, to a remote an area as we can find. We plan on living off the land and surviving as the pioneers did, until the dead all disappear or we all die trying." It was a plan, and the only hope that Keith and the others knew of.

Pete nodded once or twice as he listened to Keith's tale and then said, "Your story isn't much different from mine, or from others in our little 'tribe'. This area, the hills and the mountains, have kept us hidden from any major attacks so far. We've come together and built a workin' society. Not everyone can care for themselves, there's old people, children, heck we even have dogs and cats. Perhaps you and your wife and your friends there might like to come have a visit, maybe even stay. We would sure welcome two new couples."

"Thanks, buddy, but I don't think so. A large group of people is sure to attract the undead sooner or later," Steve said. "We just went through that, and we like our chances out in the wilderness."

"I understand, friend, but I recommend you leave the way you came," Pete said.

"Yeah, why's that?" Keith asked.

"Well, you keep followin' the stream and you'll be gettin' into some thick brush. You'll have to use a machete to hack your way through it."

Keith looked at his crew and then further down the stream; it did look lush with greenery.

"Okay, guys, what do you think?" Keith asked.

"We were making good time before we took that detour. It's not that far back and we don't know what lies ahead. Let's backtrack," Steve said.

"Well then, fellas, I'll lead the way for ya," Pete said and started forward at a brisk pace. The crew secured their gear and followed behind.

Something was bothering Keith about what Pete said and he raised a question. "Hey, Pete, how do you know this is the way we came?"

Pete stopped walking, turned around, and gave Keith and the others a big smile.

"Well, because we've been followin' you."

Before the four travelers could so much as move, from behind them the sound of four pump shotguns loading made the situation clear. Steve's face went blank and he slowly moved his left hand towards his gun.

"Wouldn't do that if I were you," Pete warned calmly, his shotgun still hung on his shoulder casually.

"What do you want?" Keith asked with disgust in his voice, pulling Kara closer to him, Steve doing the same with Jill.

"Nothing, nothing really," Pete smiled. "We just don't want you to make the mistake of goin' out there all alone. Just come on and visit us for a spell. If you don't like it, you can leave. Now, let me hold on to those guns for you so we don't spook anyone along the way, all right?"

"Oh, Keith, what are they going to do with us?" Kara whispered softly into his ear.

"I don't know, honey, but I'll protect you. You know that I'll always protect you."

"Now see here, little missy, don't go to frettin' none. There's food and ammo and music, we'll make you feel at home. Just follow me and we'll be there in no time."

Though his tone was friendly, the four men with guns trained on them said there would be no debate and they headed off once more.

The trek was mainly made in silence, the path they traversed leading up a rocky hillside. The village was constructed mainly from logs and branches, rocks and dried mud and grass. Countless skeletons from destroyed zombies were piled on the perimeter, a massive large funeral pyre waiting for a match. In other places the bones were strewn about the ground like fallen branches after a bad storm. The odor of decay was prevalent.

"This is awful," Kara said.

"Helps mask the smell of the livin', you'll get used to it," Pete said. "You won't even notice it after a while."

"Look, just give us the fifty cent tour and let us get on our way. You said you would let us go," Keith demanded.

"Well, can't let you go until you see the Chief," Pete said. "Bronson is his name; he's the leader of our little tribe. Real fine man, really, really strong, too."

Pete led them down the main path to the village; it took a while for the imagery to set in. The small cabins were adorned like a shop of horrors with human bones. Human femurs were tied together, forming crude fences with skulls smiling on top of the posts. There was a man working a crude plow made from an automobile bumper, digging a ditch. Two living dead were harnessed to the front and a pole extended in front of them with a human arm dangling from a rope. Three men with guns were at watch to make sure nothing got out of hand. Two young boys were 'sword' fighting with what looked like ulna bones. A middle-aged woman was pounding skeletal remains into smaller pieces and a young girl was using a mortar and pestle to grind it to powder to be used as fertilizer. The cabins were very small and very confining from the looks of them. There were fires here and there and people were meandering about doing chores, not paying much attention to the four new arrivals.

Kara noticed that the few old people they walked by didn't even bother to look up from their work. It was like they were trying to go unnoticed or afraid of being seen. There was no way to gauge how many people lived in the small village, but from the number of cabins, it couldn't be over a hundred. Passing out of the main village, a group of about twenty could be seen in the distance. They were overlooking the same valley where the man was tied to the pole. Someone in the group noticed Pete and the four new arrivals approaching, and Bronson was quickly alerted.

Bronson was a large man over six foot three and a muscular two hundred and fifty pounds. A full beard and long hair concealed his age well. Next to him were two women that obviously were his companions. One was tearful and stared at the ground; the other was smug and stood possessively by his side.

"Hello, Pete! A fine day it is that you've found four new friends!" Bronson bellowed while approaching the group. "Welcome my friends! Welcome to New Paradise. I'm Bronson and I'm in charge here, and who might you be?"

"I'm Keith, my wife Kara, and that's Steve and his wife, Jill. We're from Bakersfield and just passing through. We're not staying, and wouldn't be here if we didn't have those guns pointed at our backs." He gestured to the four men still behind them.

Bronson thought for a moment, his brow creasing, then said, "You wouldn't be here unless you were trespassing near New

Paradise." He tilted his head to the right. "You may have led a bunch of the undead our way if we didn't stop you." He walked closer to Keith. "The way I see it, *you* have endangered us. If you did lead them here, then you need to be here to help us fight them off."

"We weren't followed and we didn't know we were trespassing, so just let us go," Steve said.

"Sorry, friend, it doesn't work that way. You'll stay as long as I say. And I say you leave when I feel that a chance of a new attack has passed," Bronson said.

A moaning yell came from the crumpled body tied to the pole in the valley below, his anguished voice echoing on the wind.

"Bronson, please..." his tearful companion asked in a soft broken voice. "Please stop this, please end his suffering now."

Bronson turned his back on Keith and walked over to the two women. He stopped and wiped the tears from the crying one's face. She looked up at him with big watery eyes, and said, "It's over, you won...I'm yours...please end it now."

Bronson grabbed the back of her neck and gave her a deep kiss, grinding his lips against hers. He let her go and gave a hand signal to someone down below. Pete motioned for the group to move forward and the crowd parted for the newcomers to view. From a gate not far away, a lone zombie walked forward with his arms and hands bound behind his back. A mixture of eight men and boys were on each side, carrying twelve foot spears as they prodded the lumbering ghoul towards the tied man. The zombie snarled and gnashed its teeth as it moved towards the prey in front of it.

The man was semiconscious and the commotion of the approach snapped him into a fearful alertness. His screams were dry, and at such a high pitch that it could be mistaken for a woman's. The lumbering ghoul fixated on the screaming man and quickened its pace as much as atrophied muscles would allow.

"No! No!" the man screamed as the zombie tore off a mouthful of his cheek, chewing the flesh with its yellowed teeth. The screams continued; a mouthful of nose and lips, then a chunk of neck. The screams finally stopped, but the ghoul was allowed to continue to feed. Keith couldn't believe what he was witnessing; at the level humanity had fallen in such a short time.

"This is just sick, what's the matter with you people?" Keith asked in disgust.

"Ahh, well, as if you're one to judge. This was justice; this was his doings, not ours," Bronson said with an intense look at Keith.

"But you said you're in charge, so the responsibility lies with you. You could have stopped this."

"He broke the law, and it's by my words that the laws will be kept."

"What did he do to deserve this?" Steve asked.

"He lost the challenge."

"Lost what challenge?" Keith asked.

"For control of the tribe; the challenge to be the leader. I beat him fair and square, as witnessed by many others, there was no dishonor involved. I won, he lost. His woman is mine, his possessions are mine. If I'd lost, it would be me tied to the pole feeding the undead."

Kara looked at Keith and whispered, "We need to leave here, Keith."

"Shhh, don't worry, honey. Let's not overreact, it'll be all right, just give me some time," he said.

Jill was huddled behind Steve, who said, "Look, this is your justice, not ours. We don't belong here, let us go."

"I say when you leave...unless you want to challenge me," Bronson raised his voice and glared at Steve who felt his bowels quiver a little, not able to find the words to reply. The angry scowl on Bronson's face softened when he finally noticed Jill standing by Steve's side. He hadn't noticed how pretty she was before. Nice skin and soft features, pretty green eyes and a trim figure.

Bronson smiled at Jill, "Maybe you should check with your wife first. If you lose, she's mine." He turned around and walked a few feet from the crowd. "Listen up! Listen up! It's time to get back to work and make sure enough food is prepared for the night. Jason and Jeremy, go on over..."

In the far distance, a horn blew, and all stood still in silence. The count and cadence of the sound signaled an attack was coming.

8

Bronson glared at Keith, "Now, you see? You did lead them here. Pete, give them their guns back and everyone load up and get to your positions."

One of Bronson's girls told Kara and Jill to come with her. Bronson barked that all the women were to stay together. Keith looked at Kara and nodded for her to go with the woman. With protest, Kara moved along with Jill pushing her forward.

"The long range horn signals there's around fifty of them to the southeast, Bronson said. "Keith and Steve, we go out in groups of five. We'll split you up, follow your group leader. Don't worry about the women; there'll be men guarding them."

Six groups of five loaded up and headed out. Each group kept about twenty yards apart and traveled in a wide line. Keith concentrated on matching their pace; he didn't want to slow the group down. About a half a mile from the village, the first shots rang out. It was a group on the far left that made first contact, and the remaining groups moved to flank the undead. More shots were fired and Keith thought he could make out the approaching zombies in the distance. He was warned not to shoot until he was certain of a head shot.

The zombies were being mowed down left and right. Keith stopped, took aim, and brought one down. He felt a certain satisfaction, a sense of belonging. Maybe he judged these people too fast, maybe he and the others should stay. In no time the zombies were put down and the group began to head back to the village. Two hours had passed since they had first set out.

Keith met up with Steve on the return trip; Steve had killed two. There was a lot of backslapping and retelling of how the kills went down. One man claimed that he got two heads with just one shot. As the group approached the village, everyone was there to greet them. But rather than being received with congratulations, they were met with somber faces.

Two men made their way to Bronson, "We have some bad news to report."

"What, did we lose someone? Was the village attacked?" Bronson demanded.

"No, the village is fine. I....don't....Rebecca...Rebecca and Teri are both dead."

"Dead, how?" Bronson asked.

"Teri stabbed Rebecca...Rebecca grabbed a gun and shot Teri. Teri died instantly...Rebecca an hour later."

Bronson looked down and shook his head from side to side. "Damn fools." He turned quickly and walked away. Pete was heading in a different direction and Keith headed him off.

"Pete, why isn't Bronson upset about two deaths? He just lost his two women."

"Rebecca, she was new. Teri, well, he's had her over half a year. Probably tired of her shit by now."

"So, what, they're just nothing more than possessions? He's what, the king around here? He just takes what he wants?"

"Now, look, Bronson doesn't take anything. Any woman that's his, he's earned. It's our way, the way of our tribe," Pete defended.

"Okay, whatever."

"Say, Keith, you and Steve carried your own weight back there. Sure would be nice if you guys stuck around a while," Pete said, changing the subject.

"Thanks, and to be honest with you, I've been considering it. I don't know though, I don't think Kara likes it here," Keith said.

"Tell her to give it some time. Hey, Ben's boy Leroy is coming of age tonight. You and Steve have earned a seat...we serve beer on special occasions."

"Beer? You guys still have beer?" Steve asked.

Pete chuckled. "Not beer like you're thinkin' of. We make it out of cane that grows wild here. It has enough sugars to ferment and packs a pretty good punch. The party cranks up after the women and children go to bed. Just us men, and you can watch Leroy come of age."

"I'll check with Kara," Keith said.

Pete looked at Keith disappointedly. "The men will expect you to be there." Without waiting for a reply, he turned and walked off, leaving Steve and Keith to contemplate his last statement.

The women of the village prepared one of the cabins for the four new additions. The cabin was about twelve by twenty feet and wasn't much good other than getting out of the weather. Four sleeping bags were provided along with a low, narrow table just high enough to place their legs under.

When it was time to eat, they were led to a communal area for a meal of deer and fresh potatoes. They met several of the men who had gone out to defend the village, and they all shared stories of home. The conversations were cordial, and the individual tales of horror each had experienced over the last few months wasn't shared. A bell was rung which signaled the clean up and retirement of the diners. Jill was handed a candle by one of the women; she lit it with the use of a torch and the four made their way back to their cabin.

The candlelight danced before them, illuminating their faces as they sat around the small table. Keith was hesitant to speak as there were more questions than answers. Time though, wasn't on their side.

"I know we've been through a lot today, but we should make some decisions now," Keith said. "The positives are that there's food, shelter, and protection here. The negatives are the form of 'government' by which this village is run. The questions are as follows. Are we accepted members of this clan or are we deceived prisoners?"

"They've given us our guns back, they must trust us," Steve offered.

"What can two guns do against a hundred? We can't fight our way out of here. They're not taking that big of a risk," Kara said.

"Still, there's safety in numbers...I feel safer in this village than I did on the run. Except...except...I don't know about Bronson. I...didn't like the way he was looking at me," Jill said softly while looking down at the table. Steve hugged her and smiled, comforting her.

"I have to admit that Bronson's a strange man. Have you noticed how he tries to project power in every situation?" Keith asked. "I guess it's how he must maintain his authority, ruling through intimidation. He's a natural born leader, though; the battle today was smooth and methodical. He even made us pick up our shell casings so they can be recycled. He doesn't miss anything and he doesn't delegate much authority." Keith's voice indicated he was leaning to wanting to stay.

"The woman and children are put up for the night and there's a minimum of security because of that party," Kara said. "If we don't trust them, we need to leave now, if we can get far enough away before they discover we're gone, then they may not think we're worth chasing. But I don't know what to do...Steve, Jill....what do you think?" Kara didn't need to ask Keith.

"I don't want to move too fast, I'm okay with giving this some time," Steve said.

"I...I think so, too," Jill added.

Steve nodded. "I think that Keith and I should go to the initiation, bond some more with the other men. Gain some trust and learn whatever more we can. The beer may loosen their lips. We'll watch ourselves, and if we don't like what we see, and if the guys get plenty tight enough on the beer, we can leave early in the morning."

"Yeah, good plan. If they have too big of a head, by the time they realize we're gone they won't have the legs to go after us," Keith said.

"Keith, do you think Jill and I will be safe here?" Kara asked.

"Look, you have two shotguns and the door has a lock on it. Don't let anyone else in but us; I think this is our best plan," Keith told her.

The two couples finalized the details if an early escape was to be attempted. The men stood watch as the girls went to the bathroom one last time before the men would leave for the initiation. With kisses and hugs and mutterings of "Good luck", the men headed out to join the party.

With the faint strumming of a guitar floating in the air, Keith and Steve made their way towards the party. Several large fires were burning and the sounds of laughter were getting louder as they approached. The two men were a bit unprepared for what they found.

There were three wooden posts embedded in the dirt, set ten feet apart, and across from them another three posts. To each post was tied a writhing, gnashing member of the living dead. Past what resembled a gauntlet, was another zombie that was suspended by individual ropes on each wrist and each ankle. But this one was hanging down with the front of its body parallel to the ground, suspended about three feet above the earth. Its body formed an 'X' and it was swinging back and forth as it tried to free itself.

The party was going strong with no one paying any special attention to the unholy creatures. When the two men walked up, a dancing and happy middle-aged man handed them each a cup of beer, tipped his hat playfully, and danced away. The two looked at each other and sniffed the home brew, then took a sip.

"Not bad," Keith said and Steve gave a smile of approval.

"You boys took your time gettin' here," Pete said. Unknown to the two men, he had been on the lookout for them. "Not much time to get a buzz on before the show."

"You know how it is, just making sure our wives are comfortable," Keith said.

"Whatcha think? Pretty good stuff?" Pete asked.

"It does warm the insides," Steve chuckled.

"Well, there's plenty of it, but you guys need to come on over with me.....it's about to begin."

The guitar playing stopped and the merriment turned to a muffled hush. The men positioned themselves behind the upright corpses tied to the posts, standing side by side to one another. Bronson appeared from out of the crowd with a drum made from deer skin. He stopped just a few feet from the suspended zombie's face. It was a woman and she fixated her hunger on him, teeth clacking on empty air. Opposite and away from Bronson, Ben and his son, Leroy, arrived at the front of the gauntlet. Ben's body was draped in layers of deer skins, and around his neck, strips of leather were wound thickly. A two foot blade was grasped tightly in his right hand.

Bronson brought down the open palm of his hand with a loud thump, and repeated the beat four more times. He made a slight nod towards Leroy, and bellowed, "From the womb!"

Leroy walked up to the first gnashing corpse and slowly offered his neck to the animated jaws. The ghoul gnawed at the leather, unable to penetrate the thick material. Leroy backed away, raised his blade, and chopped off the head with three meaty blows. A cry of approval burst from the crowd as Leroy walked to the opposite side and stood in front of his next test.

Bronson continued, "To the weaning!"

Leroy again repeated the offering of his neck to the next rotting corpse, followed by lopping off its head to the cheers of the crowd. He then went to the next snapping death on the opposite side.

"Through puberty!"

Again Leroy repeated the ritual.

"To life's meaning!"

Again.

"The final stand!"

Again.

"To live or die a man!"

Leroy walked up and slowly offered his pursed lips towards the last one bound to a post. The head of the zombie strained its bonds as it chomped wildly for a taste of human flesh.

Leroy finally took a step back and laughed loudly. Grasping the blade with two hands, he jammed the knife into its eye, twisted to slice the brains, then withdrew it to then finish off the ghoul with a chop to the neck. The crowd howled in unison, clanking mugs and downing drinks.

Leroy slowly unwrapped the strips of leather from around his neck, then pulled off each deer skin until he was exposed and naked. The crowd started to chant, "Ride...ride...ride...ride..." Leroy walked behind the suspended living dead woman. Standing between her thighs, he reached down and massaged his penis. The crowd continued to chant in a slow cadence, "Ride...ride...ride..."

Leroy spat on his hand and rubbed it on to the head of his shaft, then stuck it in her.

Bronson began pounding the drum in rhythm, "Ride... ride...ride..." The zombie doubled her efforts to free herself. Leroy held on to her thighs tightly, his hips thrusting to the beat, and to the chants. Petrified vocal cords found life as she screamed in what resembled a hoarse rage. Leroy grabbed the back of her hair and pulled tightly. His thrusting rhythm increased and the chants and drums followed.

Keith and Steve were frozen in shock, unable to tear their eyes away from the unbelievable scene. It was unnatural, it was defiling to the human soul. But it also carried a power that neither man had felt in some time: dominance!

It was an inner feeling that the living could prevail against the dead, not just struggling to stay alive or fearing what the next moment might bring. The living dead were like any other enemy man has faced over the course of history. They could be defeated, not by luck, but by strength! By the strength of the living showing them no quarter. If mankind had any chance of survival, it had to be this way.

Leroy picked up his blade and pulled the zombie's hair back as hard as he could. He placed the sharp edge against her pale throat and sliced deeply as his loins quivered in release. He worked the blade back and forth, panting shallowly. When the last bit of skin broke free, he turned around and held her head high in one hand and his blade in the other. Another burst of cheering sounded, and his father brought him a robe and covered him.

Leroy was now a man.

The party was starting up again, with more beer flowing for everyone. Keith and Steve drank without care; there were no thoughts of leaving tonight. Keith was wondering how they would go about explaining the sodomizing of a zombie to their wives.

The bodies of the destroyed zombies were unbound and carried away to be added to the piles of bones outside the village. Soon enough though, the men started feeling the weight of the day and the alcohol in their systems. The fires were allowed to go out, and everyone made their way back to their cabins.

"Well, it was different, that's for sure," Keith said to Steve who could only nod in agreement as they made their way back to their cabin.

Kara opened the door when Keith and Steve knocked; she had been asleep. Jill was still snoring softly and nothing was said by the men about the night's events. Kara was content that they had both made it back and didn't feel like talking. Keith was glad to be back with her, and cuddled closely next to Kara as he drifted off to sleep.

The morning brought energized hope to the two couples. They had awakened in a village full of people working together to prosper, not just to survive. People were stirring about, preparing for the communal breakfast. Several of the men were obviously hung over, but were putting their best foot forward.

Breakfast consisted of oatmeal and canned peaches, with plenty of fresh water to wash it down. The villagers were polite to them but seemed preoccupied with their daily duties of cooking, cleaning, and planning for the next meal.

"Well, if we're planning on staying, then we're gonna have to pull our weight," Keith said.

"Agreed," Steve said. "We need to learn all the rules of this place so we don't have to constantly be told what's going on. You and I can start with helping on perimeter watch, unless you'd rather help with the farming."

"Jill and I can help in the kitchen, we'll see how our talents are needed as time goes by," Kara said, accepting they were staying.

"Okay, then let's go find Pete and get this show on the road," Keith said.

On the way from their cabin, the two couple were greeted by Pete and two other men. They carried guns but they hung non-threatening from their shoulders. Keith realized that the only time he hadn't seen Peter with a gun was last night at the party; perhaps he was the chief officer.

"Mornin' folks, you four are lookin' good," Pete said with a polite smile.

"Thanks to your wonderful hospitality," Jill said. "The cabin, the food, we truly are in your debt."

"Everyone has their part here; we all work and give to one another so that we can all get along. In fact, Bronson would like to meet with you to find out if you're stayin' or leavin'."

"When?" Keith asked.

"How's about now?"

Keith looked at Steve and the women; a quick nod of approval was given and they followed Pete. Keith realized quickly they were headed to the ridge overlooking the valley where the man had been tied to the post on the day before and he didn't see the reason why. Pete and his two buddies were leading the way, and they never so much as looked back to see if the two couples were keeping up. Keith didn't feel threatened, but he didn't like the feeling his gut was giving him.

Bronson was with a large entourage of men, gathered around him as if they were taking instructions. Perhaps their daily or weekly duties were assigned this way, Keith wondered. Approaching Bronson, Keith also noticed that the body had been removed from the valley below, and the headless zombies were also gone. Bronson turned around and greeted the couples. "Friends, it's good to see you here this fine day."

"We're glad to be here, and our thanks to your hospitality," Steve jumped in before Keith had a chance. If they were staying, Steve didn't want to be overshadowed by Keith.

"Good, good, glad to have you with us." Bronson turned down his welcoming voice. "Yesterday you didn't want to stay with us. I admit, I did use my authority to force you to stay. I thought it would be for your own good, and I was right. Wasn't I?"

"Yes...yes, you were," Steve said with the others nodding.

"Well then, you see there's a need for force sometimes but it also comes with fairness. And I leave your future in your hands. You're welcome to stay with us, become a part of us, learn our ways, and obey our laws."

"That sounds good to us all. We welcome the safety and support of the men and women of this village. We pledge our allegiance, and want to be held to the same standards as everyone else in the community," Steve said.

Bronson looked away from Steve and at the faces of the others. "You all agree with him?"

Each responded with a, "Yes."

"Fine! Fine! Then it is settled." Bronson turned to the men around him, raised his right fist, and they all shouted in unison. He then turned his attention back to Steve and said, "Now that you're a part of us, and that I'm now your leader, I'll be taking your lovely wife for my own."

Steve's face turned white and sank into an immediate frown. "What do you mean?"

"Your wife, Jill, I want her."

"Oh, no, we're not gonna play that game," Keith interjected. Beside him, Jill and Kara were stunned.

"This doesn't concern you," Bronson snapped at Keith. "My word is law, and I say the girl is mine."

"No, she's mine, and I guess we made a mistake, so we'll be leaving now," Steve said with a shake in his voice.

"You won't be leaving....and I accept your challenge!" Bronson barked.

"Challenge? What challenge? I said we're leaving now," Steve said.

Steve, Keith and the women huddled together for protection. Several men standing by Bronson leveled their guns toward the two couples. Someone shoved a gun into Steve's back and pushed him towards Bronson, who separated from his men and walked to meet Steve.

"Defend yourself! You dare challenge me! If you want to make the laws, then you must defeat me!" Bronson slammed two open palms into Steve's chest, to knock him down. Bronson outweighed Steve by fifty pounds easy.

"Stay down...if you know what's good for you," Bronson warned.

Steve could hear the other three screaming for Bronson to stop it, but Steve knew it wasn't going to do any good. Never once did he think that his life might come to an end from a living man, not since the dead began to walk.

Bronson was bigger and stronger and Steve knew he had to outsmart him somehow. He got up and brushed the dirt from his hands and slowly walked towards Bronson. "Look, we don't want any trouble, please, just let us leave."

Without a hint of his upcoming action, Steve took a quick step forward and delivered a roundhouse kick square to Bronson's solar plexus. Bronson bent forward, heaving for air, and Steve gave him a jump kick to the left side of his face. Bronson spun around and landed on his hands and knees, spitting blood. Steve was unsure what to do now. He knew he didn't have a chance if Bronson got his arms around him. Steve ran up and slammed his foot down on Bronson's backside, causing him to lunge forward and fall flat on his chest. Steve hurriedly ran to his right side and began kicking Bronson's ribs, hoping to break some or at least puncture a lung.

Bronson timed the kicks, made a quick turn, and caught Steve's foot. He twisted it, sending Steve to the ground. Bronson jumped onto Steve so they were face to face and smashed his left forearm onto Steve's throat.

"You son-of-a-bitch, you're gonna die," Bronson hissed through clenched teeth.

Screams and protest came from Steve's companions but he lost any hope that they could help him. His face was turning a deep purple, and he felt that consciousness would soon leave him. Bronson was almost eye to eye with him, spittle and blood dripping out of his mouth. In a last act of desperation, Steve forced his way up and bit down hard on Bronson's left ear. Bronson yelled like an animal and pushed down harder on Steve's throat, which only caused his ear to tear and more pain to fill him.

Bronson twisted himself off of Steve and stood over him; Steve could do nothing more than lay there, breathing heavily. Bronson's ear was hanging by a thin bit of flesh and blood dripped down his chin. He walked over to Steve's left leg and put his foot on the knee. He lifted Steve's foot until a small pop was heard, Steve screaming, his body offering no protest. Bronson then kicked Steve in his side, a few times as Steve moaned weakly with each kick.

Kara was in shock and Jill had her face in her hands, crying, unable to look. Keith knew that Steve was going to die, and that their safety wasn't guaranteed. The eyes of his captors were on the fight and Keith knew it was now or never to try something desperate.

The nearest man had his back turned and was just three feet away from him. Keith lunged forward and snatched the gun from the man's hand then took a forward roll, ending upright on one knee. Bronson was just about to deliver the death blow to Steve with a kick to the head when the gunshot rang out.

The round hit Bronson near the heart and sent him reeling backwards. Keith had just enough time to get behind Pete. "Nobody moves, I'll kill him, too."

Before anyone could react, a horn sounded out nearby. One long, continuous blow, and it was getting louder.

19

"Oh my God," Pete choked out.

As if the two couples no longer existed, Bronson's men ran towards the village as fast as they could.

"What the hell's going on?" Keith demanded.

"They're comin', and it's a bunch of 'em. Get that damned gun out of my back."

Jill ran over to Steve, who was lying unconscious with his eyes closed and swollen. She felt his neck for a pulse and touched his face, fearing the worse. Her eyes glanced up and sheer horror flooded her entire body. Down in the valley and climbing the ridge, were scores of the walking dead. She started patting Steve on his cheek, begging him to wake up.

"Damn it, boy, the war is on. That was the immediate perimeter alarm, let's go."

"Why didn't we get more warning?" Keith asked.

"Hell, I don't know, I guess the sentry got eaten, now let's move it!" Pete raced towards the village.

Kara screamed, "Keith!" and pointed towards Steve and Jill. The first of many, two zombies were stumbling towards them. Keith was about to shoot but he was afraid of hitting Jill. Kara screamed for Jill to run, but she was still trying to get Steve on his feet. More of the dead had made their way up by the time the two ghouls had Jill in their pale hands and another had fallen onto Steve. Jill's dying screams made the hairs on the back of Keith's neck tingle.

"Keith, save me! You said you would protect me!" Kara cried.

"I will, I will, I promise! Let's get back to the village!" Keith's last memory of his friends was of a zombie with his head buried in Jill's neck and another feeding out of Steve's stomach. Shots could be heard up ahead, and the two ran to join the rest of the village.

The men had taken strategic positions and were making each shot count. The women and children were aiding in reloading spare guns and exchanging them for the empty ones. Keith made his way to the firing line and unloaded his gun on targets, taking down six of the walking dead. A fresh gun was handed to him and he took out five more. Body after body fell to the ground, shots ringing without pause. The dead kept coming, unending, and their approach grew thicker in numbers. Tens, hundreds, a thousand, were on the march, an ocean of savage carnivores, a virtual tsunami of rotting corpses.

Keith realized that all his newfound hopes for mankind were for nothing. He was fooled into believing that the living had a chance. The dead had left the cities in search of food; there was no place to hide. They would roam the entire world until the last piece of living flesh was eaten.

The dead were approaching in overwhelming numbers; the living had to give up ground or die.

"Keith! What do we do?" Kara cried out.

"Let's get back to the cabin!" Keith yelled and grabbed her by the arm, running along with others that were retreating. The dead were starting to pour into the village; there would be no escape. Keith and Kara burst into their cabin and quickly locked the door. He loaded his gun and Kara made sure hers was ready to go. The window was boarded shut but cracks revealed the terror their ears could hear. The living were being overwhelmed, totally outnumbered. Women were being ripped apart; children were snatched up and eaten.

"We're trapped," Kara whispered.

"Our best chance...our only chance, is to wait and see if they move on. Maybe they'll eat their fill and leave," Keith whispered, not wanting to be heard by the dead. Kara stood close and sobbed, "Please...please, Keith...I don't want to die..."

The shooting had nearly stopped and not long after the cries of the living grew silent. Peering out of the cracks of the cabin wall revealed the street thick with the living dead. There were more than Keith could count, more than he imagined could ever be possible. There were knocks on the cabin walls, with sounds of shuffling and moaning. The door handle moved slightly, making a mechanical clicking sound, followed by knocks from several fists meeting the door.

Keith and Kara stayed silent, holding their breath and praying for a miracle as they huddled in the corner. The door handle moved again, and then it moved continuously. There was a bang against the door and it gave way a little, bent by the weight of the hungry ghouls outside. Keith stood ready, praying the door would hold. The mass of dead flesh pushed harder. Keith pushed the table between the door and the wall. The moaning from the zombies became louder; they could smell the living within.

The lock gave way, and the door slammed open halfway to be stopped by the table. Keith fired, dropping the first rotting face he saw. Again he fired, and again, and again. Kara handed him her loaded gun and began reloading the empty one with bullets from her pocket. Keith dropped every body that was at the door until the dead were stacking up in the doorway. Body on top of body now blocked the opening and he held his fire. He could hear the rest outside, but they were no longer trying to enter.

Were they giving up, did something distract them? Did a wall of dead zombies somehow act as a barrier to the living dead?

Minutes passed, seeming like hours. There was movement outside, and the dead body on top of the pile was pushed off, followed by the next one and the one after that, until Keith put a meatless face in his open sites and blew another head off, and another, until the door was blocked again. But it continued, the dead were being shoved away and Keith kept stacking them up. Kara looked out of the cracks in the cabin to see there were just as many undead as when it started.

"Keith, I don't want to die," Kara whimpered. "You said you'd protect me from them."

"And I will, honey, I will."

"No, you can't, it's over. But you can spare me the pain of being killed by them. It's time, Keith, do it now."

He looked at her to protest and realized she held an empty box of bullets. She looked at him with big brown eyes and tears running down her cheeks. "You can still save me, Keith."

Keith realized there were only three bullets left and a lump grew in his throat.

"Please...I love you." Kara pulled the muzzle of the gun towards her head. The ghouls were busy pulling the bodies away, and Keith knew time had finally run out.

"I love you, Kara," he said, kissed her softly, and as she closed her eyes, tears streaming down her cheeks, he pulled the trigger. "I did it...I kept my promise...I saved you."

Keith turned back to the door to see the head of another zombie come into view. He pulled the trigger and blasted it backward.

LOVE PREVAILS

He glanced at Kara slumped on the floor, her beautiful face now a mangled mess, and sat down beside her. With her limp hand in his, he placed the warm muzzle of the gun into his mouth, tasting the cordite as the metal burned his tongue.

Closing his eyes, he squeezed the trigger.

GUNFIGHT AT THE 9TH CIRCLE K FROM HELL

RICHARD MOORE

John raised the brick over his head and hurled it at the window.

The sound of breaking glass disrupted the silence of the night. The concrete brick tumbled a few times across the floor inside, chewing up the linoleum. When the shards of glass and debris had settled, nothing followed. The burglar alarm was dead, just like the street lights. Just like everything. John returned to the pickup truck and Rachael reached in, then handed him one of the mallets that were kept in back.

I took a last drag from my cigarette. There was something surreal about being back at the Circle K on Chandler and McQueen. A year ago, I'd lived just a few blocks away, an average Joe with a wife and kid I loved and a mortgage. I would usually stop by the Circle K on the way to work to buy coffee and the Mesa Tribune.

Now, purely by chance, here I stood twelve months later, breaking in at two in the morning to raid the store's dusty shelves of its liquor and cigarettes. I'd been another man back then, with no concept of the living Hell I'd soon find myself in, or the atrocities I'd have to commit just to stay alive.

To hell with the past, I told myself. *It's dead. Let go of it.*

I tossed my cigarette to the ground and stamped it out, then lifted a mallet from the truck bed and followed John and Rachael toward what remained of the window.

The three of us knocked in the shards around the edge of the frame, making it safe to climb through into the store.

"Any survivors in here?" John called when we were inside. "Is there anyone alive in here?"

Silence. There was nobody inside the store.

Outside it was a different story. I heard distant groans and moans.

We made our way deeper into the darkness, our flashlights moving ahead of us, searching out the counter and the fully stocked shelves behind it.

"Surprised nobody thought to loot this place before," John said, his eyes appraising the liquor and cartons of cigarettes. "Place is a goldmine."

I pulled a roll of heavy-duty trash bags from my jeans back pocket. The cigarettes and liquor that came in plastic bottles went into the trash bags. John found some boxes behind the counter and set about loading them with the liquor in glass bottles, while Rachael and I went back to the truck to set the mallets and trash bags in the bed.

We heard John before we saw him, feet crunching on broken glass, the bottles in the box he carried jingling against each other. He climbed out, stepping through the opening we'd made.

John said, "Looks like somebody's happy to see you, Rachael."

There was a long, slow, whispery groan behind us. We turned around. The zombie, who was naked from the neck down, moved at geriatric speed towards us. On his head, he wore a swim cap and goggles, and his arms moved continually, as though performing the breast stroke, making me think he must have been swimming at the YMCA or a gym when the zombies got him. All his limbs were intact, but even from here bite marks on his arms and legs were visible, chunks of flesh missing. That wasn't all that was visible. Somewhere along the way he'd lost his swim trunks.

"Oh my God!" Rachael shrieked and pointed at the naked zombie. "Now I've seen it all. That stiff's got a stiffie!"

The circumcised head of the zombie's erect penis bounced against his stomach with every shuffling step he took. There are some things that are wrong to laugh at but you laugh anyway. This was one of them. The zombie couldn't possibly know the three of us were laughing at him, but as he got closer, a frown formed, and for a moment I thought he was remembering, like it's been said some of them can from time to time. Then I realized the real reason for the frown. What little he did know, no longer made any sense. What he'd thought was food—meaning the three of us— wasn't food at all, or at least that was what the instincts he now functioned on told him.

"Ah," Rachael cooed. "Poor guy must be horny. What's wrong, big boy? Can't find yourself a nice zombie girl to take care of that thing for you?"

The zombie groaned, seemingly in response to Rachael's question.

John set the box in back of the pickup and removed a bottle of Johnny Walker Red. He gulped it down like water, his Adam's apple bobbing on his scrawny unshaven neck. When he'd swallowed half the bottle's contents, he screwed the cap back on.

"Tell you what, big boy," Rachael called to the hard-on zombie. "I'll give you one free shot. Get it in, and I'm all yours. Let's see if you can remember how to do the pussy stroke."

We watched in total disbelief as Rachael hiked up her skirt and pulled down her panties, then bent over the lowered tailgate.

Rachael's eyes met mine, and I saw a flash of gleeful insanity in them.

"Now that's not funny, Rachael," John said. "You pull them panties back up this second."

"Come on, big fella," Rachael said, ignoring John. She wiggled her ass, and I figured since she was showing it off I might as well get a look.

The zombie plodded across the parking lot toward us. I could see others behind it now, moving in from the street, attracted by all the noise we were making. In a few minutes we'd be overrun with them.

"Rachael!" John cried.

Ignoring him, Rachael stuck her ass higher in the air. "Come on and give it to me, big boy."

I knew she was doing this to provoke John. They were one of those couples who seemed to delight in finding ways to piss each other off.

"She's fucking nuts," John said to me and shook his head. "I swear to God, the woman has lost her goddamn mind."

"She's just drunk," I said.

We all were. We were drunk all the time.

"Come on, big boy," Rachael said again, for some reason finding this hysterically funny. "Come to Mama."

The hard-on zombie, who was just a few feet away from her now, suddenly lost its frown. Its gaze fell on Rachael's ass, breast strokes gradually decreasing in speed. It opened his mouth, and another of those whispery groans escaped cracked leathery lips, followed by a thread of drool. The drool landed on the tip of its dick. Maybe a trace memory kicked in, because all of a sudden it was going for it. The zombie lunged. I'd never seen one move so fast. Before Rachael knew what was happening, its hands were on her ass, spreading her cheeks, then his dick went in between them.

Rachael screamed "Get him off! He's up my ass! Get him off!"

The sight of the zombie thrusting away was so unbelievable that for a few seconds John and me could do nothing but stand and gape.

Then our senses returned. John gripped the bottle of whiskey by the neck and rushed in, smashing it on top of the zombie's head. I went and got one of the mallets from the truck bed. When I returned, whiskey was running down the zombie's face and bits of glass were stuck in its swim cap. But it was still thrusting and groaning, its mouth hanging slack and tongue lolling out. It must have got a taste of the liquor and not liked it, because its face scrunched up like the ghoul was sucking on sour candy.

John saw me coming with the mallet and moved out of the way. I raised the mallet and hit the zombie as hard as I could, right in the center of the face. The zombie toppled, and a second later was on the asphalt, looking up at the stars in the night sky, ruined flesh and fragments of bone all that remained of its nose.

I looked around. There were at least ten more zombies in the Circle K's parking lot now.

Rachael yanked up her panties and fixed her skirt. She staggered over to the naked zombie on the ground. His hard-on hadn't flagged, not in the least.

Rachael yelled at the creature, "Of all the fucked up shit that's happened to me, that just about tops it all."

"Well, that's what you get for playing stupid games," John said

"Come on," I said. "Let's get what we stopped for and get going."

Rachael grinned at me, and again I saw a flash of madness in her eyes. She got down on her knees next to the zombie's head, then removed his swimming goggles and put them on. Next she scooted down to his groin area.

"Rachael," I said. "What the hell do you think you're doing now?"

"Getting what we stopped for," she said, leaning in.

"No fucking way, Rachael! John, do something..."

John shrugged. "Well, she's right. I mean, it ain't nice, but she's right."

He got down on his knees next to the zombie's head and leaned in, his mouth closing over the zombie's right eye. Eyes were not my personal preference, but John had a real thing for them. I watched as he chewed through the eyelid and sucked at the eyeball, his teeth gnawing, working to pry the eye from its socket. Several of the other zombies stood still, looking down at them, trying to make sense of what was happening but unable to comprehend.

They were not the only ones looking at something they couldn't comprehend. Some places were just off limits. When I saw what Rachael had in her mouth, saw what her teeth were biting through, I had to turn away.

I went to the truck and got a bottle of vodka. Keeping my back turned, I forced it down.

John was right. Rachael was insane. But then, which of us wasn't?

What I knew of my own madness began with a public announcement, assuring everyone a cure to the zombie epidemic had been found. They asked people to volunteer for testing, promising they'd be well rewarded. When only a handful came forward, John and Rachael amongst them—the names of test subjects, including my own—were randomly chosen by computer.

The vaccine seemed to work at first.

Thinking we were the same as them, the undead ceased to see us as their food source. And even if one of us should somehow be bitten, the vaccine killed the virus, safe-guarding us against infection. Confident the vaccine was a success, an immunization program was quickly implemented. Too quickly, as it turned out.

Three weeks later, the first to receive the vaccination realized something was wrong. We suffered from depression, then mood swings and insomnia. Then we couldn't keep down any food. It was shortly after all this that the cravings started. Cravings that soon became impossible to deny. Those who'd received the vaccination, some two thousand in all, obsessively focused on one thing–to feed on the rotting flesh of the living dead. Day and night we could think of nothing else. And so, we left the safe zone voluntarily, knowing what we craved could never be found behind its fences, choosing instead to fend for ourselves out here in the lost lands.

Accepting what I'd become wasn't easy but being around others who were similarly afflicted seemed to make it more bearable. At least until their self-loathing or fragile mental states became too much to take. Then I moved on, traveling and feeding alone for as long as I could stand it. Sometimes, when areas were impassable by car, I'd walk with the dead for days on end, never seeing another living soul.

For six months I'd lived that way; moving from one group to another, staying with them a week at most, wary of discovering the extent to which their addiction had damaged their sanity. I'd been with John and Rachael for five days, and decided as I finished the vodka, I would not be with them for a sixth.

There was everyday commonplace madness, the madness to which I'd become accustomed, and then there was outright lunacy. What Rachael had done fell into the latter category. I would not risk my own fragile hold on reality by remaining near somebody capable of doing what she'd done. If I'd had the strength, I would have fled that very second. But they'd already begun, and I simply wasn't strong enough to refuse the call of my addiction.

I turned to the sound of them eating. The smacking of their lips and the slurping sounds they made fully awakened my hunger. Knowing it would wait no longer, I set the empty vodka bottle on the ground and went to join them, pushing past the zombies milling around the pickup.

John and Rachael had moved on from the hard-on zombie— who was now missing that particular body part, along with his eyes, nose, and most of the flesh from his face–to another. Rachael held down a plump zombie woman dressed in a business suit, while John opened her up with his knife. Rachael forced her arm into the dead woman's stomach, all the way to her elbow.

"For you," she said, yanking loose the intestines and holding them out to me.

I got down on the ground and accepted her offering. The intestines were cold and slimy and foul with putrescence.

Just the way I liked them.

* * *

"Zombie bastards!" a voice cried out followed by gunfire.

None of us had heard the vehicle approaching until the gunshots began.

Submerged in the deeps of a trance-like orgasmic bliss, we'd been unable to wake to the danger we faced until it was upon us.

It was easy to see why those firing at us from the windows of the RV mistook us for zombies feeding on people–instead of the other way around. While I'd surrendered myself to the pleasure of gobbling down the plump zombie's intestines, John had gone to work on the eyes, this time using his knife to pry them loose. Rachael meanwhile, had forced her entire head and neck through the opening in the dead woman's stomach, and was in there eating the internal organs.

The RV pulled into the Circle K's parking lot, tires screeching as the driver slammed on the brakes. Insignificant details filtered through into my mind. On top of the RV, I saw speakers mounted beside a sign board, the face of some long forgotten politician grinning down at me, making me think the vehicle had long ago been used for political rallies.

Rachael pulled her head free of the zombie's stomach; goggles still in place, face and hair sodden with fetid internal juices; strands of meat riddled with maggots hung from her mouth. I looked around, still chewing intestines, my mind so numb to everything else that at first all I could do was sit there and watch as we were attacked.

Four men jumped down from the RV, two from the cab up front and two from the side door. All were bearded and dressed for colder weather than the desert in May. If they were from Arizona, they must have traveled down from the north, where sweaters and leather jackets might still be needed at night. The sight of their guns awakened my fight or flight instinct, the sensation of transfer from one mind state to another akin to sticking a wet finger in a wall socket.

At one time I'd been in their shoes myself, and knew why they'd stopped. The broken window of the liquor store and what looked like zombies feeding on the living might mean people were still alive inside, barricaded behind a door.

The mistake they made was in thinking they'd be safe so long as they kept their distance and eliminated the fifteen or so zombies across from where they stood. Even though we no longer needed to protect ourselves against the living dead, all three of us kept up the old habit of making sure we were always armed.

The scent of fresh flesh caught the attention of the zombies surrounding us. At once they turned, then headed for the men as quickly as their stiffened legs would carry them. This created a barrier of sorts, obscuring us from the men's eyesight. While the men were occupied with delivering headshots to the zombies nearest them, the three of us reached for our weapons.

John whipped his gun from his shoulder holster, aimed, and fired. Two gut shots dropped the first of the men to the ground. Rachael fired three times. For a moment, I couldn't see for all the zombies blocking my view. Then one of them moved and I had time to see a man falling to his knees, one hand clutching his chest as blood squirted out between his fingers. My own gun, a Glock 17, seemed to magically appear in my hands. When I saw my shot I took it, never so much as hesitating. The bullet hit the man in the right leg, and I heard him scream as he went down. The last of them realized where the shots were coming from, and I saw the anger in his eyes, saw him raise his gun and aim it at me. Then he was gone, disappearing from sight as the zombies reached him, his lone death scream soon becoming a chorus as the flesh-eaters moved in to devour the two we'd injured.

The dead must have been ravenous, for the screams didn't last very long. Then all that remained were the sounds of them feeding.

* * *

I'd never been responsible for anybody's death before, and I tried to convince myself that under different circumstances—which is to say if I'd been in my sane mind instead of my conscience-free feeding state—I would have thought twice before firing.

"Christ," I whispered, lowering my gun to the ground. "What did we do?"

"Kicked their fucking ass is what we did!" Rachael said, and when I looked at her, she was once again grinning insanely, her face and hair still wet from being inside the zombie's stomach, and still wearing those stupid goggles.

John let out a triumphant whoop and hauled her to her feet. He raised a hand and Rachael gave him a high five. Their lips met, a sloppy, greasy kiss that left John's face smeared with the juices dripping from Rachael's mouth.

"Did you see that?" Rachael asked, raising the goggles off her eyes and onto her forehead. "Even with these things on I got the bastard right in the heart. Right in the fucking heart."

"Beautiful shot, baby," John said. "Knew you was good, never knew you was that good."

"Just like old times," Rachael laughed. "Like that one time back east, before all this, when I got that guy..."

"Right, right," John interrupted. "You mean the time you took that zombie out from way across the other side of the field. Hell of a shot."

Back east.

There were no zombies back east. The Eastern states had been blocked off, their borders protected by the might of our military, electrified fencing erected long before the zombies from the west ever reached them.

Rachael nodded slowly, realizing she'd slipped up. "Right... That's exactly what I mean."

They didn't need to tell me what I already knew. I could see the truth in their eyes. Rachael and John were killers. They'd been killers long before the dead ever walked the earth.

Rachael nodded toward the RV. "Let's go see if they have anything we want."

"Good idea," John said.

He held out his hand and pulled me up from the ground.

"Be right with you," I said, turning toward the truck. "Gonna grab us something to drink."

"See if you can find some bourbon," Rachael called, pushing through the zombies blocking her way.

John hurried to catch up, then leaned in towards Rachael and whispered something to her. She nodded, looking over her shoulder at me.

I rummaged through the box in the truck bed, pretending to look for bourbon. Frantic, I searched my pockets with my free hand for the keys to the pickup. My pockets were empty. I'd been the one driving, so where the hell were the keys? Searching my pockets a second time, I remembered they were in the ignition.

"*HEY, YOU, BY THE SIDE OF THE TRUCK!*" an amplified voice boomed, and I damned near crapped my pants. "*HURRY UP WITH THAT GODDAMN BOURBON.*"

I looked around and saw John and Rachael in the RV's cab, both laughing at the expression of terror they saw on my face. John was holding a microphone. He handed it to Rachael and her voice drifted from the speakers attached to the RV's roof. With heartfelt sincerity she sang: "*PEOPLE...WHO EAT PEOPLE...ARE THE LUCKIEST PEOPLE...IN THE WORLD.*"

That set them off laughing again.

I forced a smile and gave them the finger, then went back to rummaging through the box of liquor. From the periphery of my vision, I saw them both stand up and head into the back of the RV. Knowing it was now or never, I raced around to the driver's side of the pickup and climbed in.

When I heard the gunshot I ducked low, my hand frantically searching for the ignition key.

More gunshots, two this time, yet somehow I was still alive.

I turned the key and the engine roared. As I reversed, my eyes instinctively went to the rearview mirror. What I saw was so unexpected that I hit the brakes and twisted around, looking out the back window to see if it could really be true.

John staggered down the RV's steps, one hand cradling what was left of the right side of his face, the other pressed to his chest.

Rachael followed behind him, also staggering, also wounded, both hands failing to stem an arterial geyser spraying from her neck. John teetered on the last step, swaying back and forth. The zombies crowded in, drawn by the commotion, their heads raised as Rachael's blood rained down on them, pattering their faces.

I saw one of them lick a drop of blood from his lips. A frown, almost like he was deliberating over whether or not it met his approval appeared, then he turned away, losing interest. Rachael took another step and lost her footing. She fell forward, collided with John, and the pair of them tumbled together to the ground. Neither of them moved after that, but just laid there bleeding out.

The zombies moved away, their attention returning to whatever scraps remained of the men who'd initially attacked us.

There was obviously somebody inside the RV, somebody armed, and that was all the more reason to leave right now. But before I could, the RV's side door crashed open and a gray-haired old man stood at the top of the steps with gun in hand.

"How you like that, you zombie-eating freaks?" he yelled, looking down at John and Rachael. "Didn't figure on old Bill hiding out in the latrine, did ya? I heard all about your kind on the radio. But I never believed it, not till I seen it with my own eyes." Old Bill spat, aiming for Rachael and John's lifeless bodies. "Goddamn sickos. Good riddance to ya."

Old Bill squinted, looked across the parking lot into the pickup's back window, and right into my eyes. He raised his gun and took aim. If it wasn't for a timely distraction, I would have been a dead man.

I've never known exactly how it is a zombie can tell the difference between the living and the dead; and nobody had ever explained how the vaccine worked to make them think I was one of them. But they knew old Bill was alive right from the second they spotted him. What remained of the naked swimmer we'd first fed on was the first to reach the steps of the RV; the rest following close behind.

"Oh Jesus, son," I heard the old man cry. "You ain't got no penis!"

Old Bill fired his gun and the naked swimmer's head exploded. His swim cap went flying–along with the top of his head—into the throng of zombies clambering over each other to get at the old man.

"That's cause I fucking ate it," a voice that was unmistakably Rachael's yelled. "And guess what, old man? Now I'm gonna eat yours, too."

I saw her push past the zombies gathered around the steps, tossing them aside.

"Just so long as I get his eyes," I heard John say. "Never had a live man's eyes before. Never craved 'em. Not until now."

It was impossible. They were dead. Had to be.

And then I realized *dead* is exactly what they were. It had seemed there could be nothing worse than the side effect we'd all suffered as a result of the vaccination. But being condemned to feed on the living dead was nothing compared to this.

"Noooo!" the old man wailed. He fired two shots at close range, right into Rachael's chest. The bullets didn't even slow her down. She grabbed the gun from his hand and threw it away, then kicked his legs out from under him. Old Bill landed half-in and half-out of the RV.

When I saw Rachael tugging at the old man's fly, and John leaning in with his knife to pry loose his eyes, I put the pickup truck in drive, turned the wheel, and floored it.

* * *

John moved fast for a dead man. He ran full speed across the Circle K's parking lot, chasing the truck as I tried to flee. When I saw him dive for the passenger side window, I screamed. He crashed through the glass and landed on his elbows, his legs still outside the truck and kicking up and down. I screamed again, much louder this time, when I looked at him. One half of his face grinned at me. The other half was a bloody mash of raw flesh and shattered bone.

"Going somewhere, partner?" John asked.

And that was when I lost control of the wheel.

* * *

After I hit the wall, John and Rachael dragged me from the truck and brought me here, into the Circle K's stock room. They must not have been thinking straight. They were so focused on making sure I didn't escape that they forgot all about the old timer in the RV, but the sound of the RV's engine starting and pulling away reminded them. Cursing, John and Rachael ran out after it. When they came back in, they were bickering, blaming each other for letting Old Bill give them the slip.

Rachael's vocal cords were damaged and everything she said came out in a hoarse whisper. A flap of torn flesh on the side of her neck flopped down as she spoke, and she quickly fell into the unconscious habit of tucking it back in. John's jaw no longer worked very well, relegating his pronunciation capabilities to those of a four-year-old. It was like watching a sit-com set in the heart of Hell, with me supplying the laugh track.

I didn't laugh for long though. Not once they got started.

I'd always thought I had a pretty high tolerance for pain. I guess until then, I must have never really experienced how pain could truly feel.

* * *

There's not much left of me now. They took my arms, my legs, my eyes, my ears, my tongue, and, Rachael...that sick bitch...she took my...my...

Best not to dwell on it.

I lay here now, back from my death, replaying memories, trying to keep my mind off the hunger. It's no use. The hunger is all that lives in me now; the need to satisfy my appetite the only pain I'm capable of feeling. A few zombies have wandered in, but I no longer have any interest in them. Death helped me kick that habit.

Now I'm ready to start a new one.

I just hope it won't be long before somebody finds me. Somebody alive. Somebody who'll lean in close, just for a second—that's all I need—just long enough to open my mouth and sink my teeth into their warm flesh.

BORN IN A DEAD WORLD

DANIEL FABIANI

A syrupy breeze pries open my eyes, the room swirling double fold around me. I stand within a barrage of stained white tile. My feet planted firmly, I'm staring curiously. Faded crimson lines are smeared across the bathroom wall in vertical, horizontal and diagonal patterns; the landscape formed is that of a spilled red life.

I scan the area, and see bits of balled-up skin, like polyester lint, and hair piled in sludgy clumps as if a group of cats heaved them up. A lone eyeball looks at me with query from below, a hellhole of frozen blue in its center. Threads of dark optic nerve swagger from behind it like tadpoles out of water.

A cautious wave of animosity reveals itself beneath my skin. Uncontrollable thoughts demand satiety from the pit of my stomach; they implore with an iron grip and cling to bones for answers. My mind is grandiose with famine, with inquisition, and it supplies me the strength I need to press forward.

My fingers reach my nose to sniff and I'm able to see their garish state. Wincing from the sting of bleach to my senses, I close my eyes and the lids scrape against them. My fingers reach inside my mouth and slide over my pallet like an exploring, dry tongue; sandpaper comes to mind. The familiar sour taste is like spoiled milk. But the alien taste buds in my mouth allow me to enjoy the foreign flavor of rot.

The quiet in my home is crucifying; my ears rage from the pang outside. A transcending, cosmic expansion of insanity is unable to contain itself within my mind; wonder consumes my brain.

Where is my family?

The bathroom darkens as electrical power shows the last of its face like an intermittently beating heart, dying to the clamor outside my walls. It obscures my true vision, makes peripheral sight impossible. I can only see straight ahead.

A rumble pushes me to the toilet as if side-swiped by a diesel truck. My knee slams into it; a hard and marble fulcrum. I can make out its white exterior and sticky smears glistening. But I don't know what to make of this. All I can think of is some kind of food.

My stomach churns in vicious cycles, initiates a swimmy feeling in my head and a sparking, tender throb in my heart. Voracity slowly envelops my mind, deprived of the saccharine, copper-tinged flavor of blood. The shed of gore around me is proof that an ungodly presence has scoured the insides of my home. And I still don't know where my family is.

My legs move and take me away from the bathroom; I don't control them. The stride is robotic, and as my head turns to find the door, I am already walking out, the destruction clear. My body enters the hallway with arms outstretched and rigid, as if they want to choke something; fingers curled and prepared to grasp unwilling flesh to present them with my gift. I sense vacillation, the wanting to tear into cold dead skin, the need to massage its phlegm-like consistency as the prodding fingers of a pathologist would. But I also feel I need to pass this gift instead—to not give into hunger.

I move out of the hallway, witness devastation from a myriad of fresh bullet holes. Circular patterns of charcoal blight the wall, a black spiral of no return, and some glow a dying orange reminding me of cigarette burns. I walk heedfully, my stomach gurgling the way like a despot; the thin lining rages with gastric juices—hunger, hunger, hunger. I can taste it all over, feel its slippery spirit; my senses brim with creeping death. I trudge toward the closest thing that my body can find.

I strictly remember it being July. But why am I so cold? My bones shake like a wet cat under the gelid breaths of a Canadian December. Claustrophobia comes to mind; it feels as if I'm locked in a refrigerator, nothing more than some fat piece of deli meat. I'm trapped in this body. My arms are gray with age and they rake the walls like a despondent prisoner thriving to out himself. Fingernails rip furrows deep into the languid wallpaper and tear away from the fetid flesh of my body. My hands are shriveled like severe arthritis and my fingers draw lines up and down the walls.

I see no trace of veins throughout my limbs; no healthy circuitry of red or blue. I feel no eagerly pumping heart to feed warmth to my shaking corpse. I only see hollows of blood vessels;

brown, withered, drifting to the surface of my ashen complexion like dead flower stems. My hands have been sucked of life, prune dried and crusted, as brittle as baby blue robin's eggs. My arms are battered with scabs, leaking unhealthily and ripped as if a cold sore split from smiling lips.

I am in the living room now, which seems to be intact. The beige velour loveseat is in its resting place in the corner of the room. The coffee table is broken through the middle and a nefarious set of glass teeth glisten like the grin of a vampire. Something lays in its center...an arm? Yes, a woman's arm. The fingernails are oddly clean, the polish is fresh indeed, but the forearm is splinted as if gnawed upon by weak jaws.

The ripped flesh is clean at the base by a force I can not fathom, and then a familiar strength builds within me as drool bubbles down my chin for this piece of meat. It falls to the floor with a smacking sound and the smell reveals to me that this is my wife's arm. I have licked and indulged on these beautiful fingers time and time again. I have already savored the sweat that has poured from her slick body, so I must keep searching. But my body does not listen to my mind. It is its own leader.

My stomach speaks to me once again as her hand reaches my lips—my cankered tongue. It enters my mouth like sweet lady fingers and I crunch the bones as if it's sacred ivory, the shards creeping down my throat. It scrapes away, holds back no destruction to my dead esophagus. She still tastes heavenly though; better by blood than by lust or love, if she only could have been granted this gift.

I throw the arm to the side as my body craves something new. Moving again, regardless of the failed attempts from my brain, I am led into the kitchen. There I'm educated on the reasons to my chill as daylight struggles to be seen through the small broken window. Beams of a risen sun desperately try to cut through black smog of bone and ash like a yellow blade, but fails as the odd mist continues to suffuse a cumulous cloud of charred flesh.

The rest of my wife lies here without dubiety. Freshly split wounds trail red and thin across her face, accentuating the flesh of a once stunning woman. My head bends down to her, at the smell of blood. Her eyes are open, sunken in and calm; the right socket empty. The origin of that lone eye I saw in the bathroom is now identified.

She is still beautiful: even in the wake of her demise. Her body's the temperature of a wine cellar as my tongue slides over her pallid clavicle. Cool liquid issues from her ruptured intestine down by her groin, resembling sewage drain seeping blood and feces. My hands grab for her neck now, craving delicacy, her temple the soft spot in a baby's skull. Something is telling me to pass this gift on.

I peruse her slim throat, my tongue scabrous, heavy and parched. The atrophied veins are limp beneath, her skin paper thin—sallow. My teeth sink into the rubbery flesh, tear it wide and expose the dry, cracked tissues beneath. She doesn't react, only lays there as death winnows from her wounds and takes my offering, my alliance to her, and the love that will keep us together forever.

She still smells of the many perfumes I have given to her as gifts. Her cheekbones are solid, but have sunk within the hollow of her slack, yawning mouth. Her entire face has taken a shape of extreme terror—or of reluctance.

The jagged cuts along her face taste ripe, as my tongue wriggles around and laps at the wounds. I drop her back to the floor, her face heaped in the soapy blood of my former wife.

There is a disturbance outside and my head twists itself toward the kitchen window. My eyes discover an aimless mass of bodies springing forth from the overcast as if in stampede.

They turn in circles stupidly, faces contorted, eyes black and shining as obsidian stone, like a cat's nighttime glare. They seem to be confused by the limbo of the outside world, and do not know where to run, where to hide, what to eat. The bodies are physically similar to mine, but they bestow a gratuitous mouth in exchange only for simple and supple flesh.

I need to give the gift.

A crowd of innocent people run betwixt the slew of hungry dead. The beasts of famine run for them, faces in permanent frown. Their skin is archaic looking, hollows taking the in place of nostrils; black burning stars for their eyes. They seek no remorse and are unified in the need for meat, the utter cannibal-urchin within them.

And this is no ordinary light. My eyes see a dull shimmer of daylight wanting to break through the black haze; the haze that has quickly enveloped my town like a sandstorm. The lack of heat from the ensconcing sun has set the terrible chills, tremors running through me. The massive gray blanket of soot has covered all things life-giving.

The sky is folded into layers like a patina of metal and ash, the hand of the heavens begging for breath by forcing that pitiful yellow light through the fog. They cry pools of bone dust upon the soulless bodies, their gripping hands, their perpetually vacant faces. Hark; the heavens have no place here.

The kitchen radio blares a broadcast, the longest day with "*no tomorrow,*" according to news prompt. And as more volcanic waste plummets from above in wet torrents of dust and destruction, the blood of the risen continue their stroll and search for food.

What I catch through the window is not worry nor indifference, but my own reflection. Through the broken pieces of battered glass, I see my own bane form. Dark indentations have mushroomed over my eye sockets as well as the bottom of my face. Bite marks from tiny, ravenous mouths have indented my skin and to raise the flesh into a greenish tint as if tainted with toxic saliva. The cartilage where my nose should be is rotted to a shriveled flap of skin, reminding me of bruised fruit.

My teeth are bridges of brown decay that lay pairs of wasteful, jutting pieces of calcium in my mouth, the lips dry, cracked and bleeding. My head of rich ebony is now one of depleted baldness, bleach white and clammy. The skin atop my head falls to the side as I tilt sideways and reveals a cranium as pale as the moon. My eyes are the same dull, mindless caverns surrounded by starving black tissue like the rest of the beasts before me.

I disband my wanton reflection and put my fist through the window. I move toward another part of the house in need of food and feel for anything, my fingers leaving a thin residue on the granite topped counters as if the tips bleed pus. My walk is insouciant, devoid of character; my mind only focused on food. But the formerly pulpous sack that was my brain wants only to quench this defiance of character, to pass this gift to the unwilling.

Up the stairs and around the hallway where the bullet holes have created their own form of wasted wallpaper, my body takes me. The path to the upper quarter is beaten, ravaged of life and elation. There are boot prints in the floorboards now weakened by massacre. The banister crumbles to wood chips beneath my feeble grip. I nearly topple over, but my limbs are rigid and don't bend like those of the living.

This vessel that controls me sways oppositely like the leaning tower of Pisa, as if preemptively aware of the banister's ratty condition. I make it to the top floor and a puddle of congealed blood leads the way to my daughter's bedroom; the gray light outside sparkles with flame once again. Clouds of terror sift their way through the blockade of grit and echo into my home. The maroon path glows like a nightlight from the spread of fire outside. I pass this mess, my feet streaking in the wetness all around me, to enter Helena's bedroom.

In New York City, most things are dark, milk chocolate colors of exquisite marble or linoleum. Helena never accepted that notion of drab colors for her own bedroom. From the day she was able to sleep on her own without the comfort of her mother's pink and milk ridden nipple, Helena would yell at the mere sight of darkness. She would scream and pillage my ears until I showered her in light.

I decorated her room accordingly with light-colored furniture, white walls, and a warm colored carpet. But now everything is dusted in darkness. The walls are black with death and the carpet is stained with spilled scarlet life. I turn toward the bed to look for Helena and see the swamp-soaked sheets before me; fecal matter in the center like a liver spot. Two light brown eyes, a watchful pair, have been carefully scooped from their sockets and placed at the edge of the bed: they roll off as another shock wave shakes the house.

The great oak vanity stands alone in the battered room and I turn to it. Scratches and gun shots have transformed this place of outer beauty into a dump yard. My feet bring me closer to it and I see the waist-long hair dangling atop the vanity like an old, dirty mop.

A rancid scent wafts into the cleft of my nose, the stink of new death, of fresh fear. I place my dirty fingers on the wet seaweed of hair and the clumped strands part easily. The hard pieces pull away and I graze my palm across her arid white skull, drained completely of vitality.

It is like woodchips unto my fingertips. Then my lips rest upon her scalp and are bitten by the rot that emanates from it. A parasite the size of an adult cockroach creeps out of the morass of her hair and its lengthy, curious antennae proffers something to me like a friendly gesture, but I ignore it and turn my attention back to my daughter.

It scuttles away on thousands of little legs as Helena's body jolts in what resembles rigor mortis. I reach down for her neck, scrape away the wall of rust-colored blood and groan as my teeth grab for the lifeless crease of her throat. My tongue enters the parted wound and explores its whereabouts, searching for a vital vessel. And as if my tongue was of magic, my spit of the gods, spidery shocks motion her back to life like an external automated defibrillator.

She rises haphazardly and crooked; her spine not of conscious control. Helena's face freezes at the mirror fogged with blood and slabs of gore. She meets my own insidious stare and hisses; the peeled flesh of her cheek pulsates as fish gills do in water. Her eyes are tiny black flames, searching, curious; and now she has the gift.

Helena stands fully, removes scaly hands away from the top of the haggard vanity. Fingernails snap away from her tenuous grip, they release the same fetor that lingers beneath my own skin; the thickness of sulfur during low tide. Gummy substances drag along the surfaces of everything she touches. She bleeds the same red saliva from her fingertips as do mine. Now she is fully upright, standing before me with a tilted head and a furious, predatory grin upon her face. I know it well.

Joining in the same voracity I have woken to this morning, we move along in silence. No words are needed in this unison of deathly living. We scurry away to where we need to be. Helena's lips, ripped straight from her face, reveal the sickly, decayed flesh beneath her once rosy complexion. They are slick with red and stringy globs of skin.

We look more the same as I stare her down. Her perfect girl's nose is now the same basin-like cavity containing the few drops of blood left within us. Helena's eyes are black caverns, seeking, her mouth open and heart wrenching. She meshes in completely with the rest of her extended family beyond the very prison of the house.

Our minds make decisions together, holding invisible hands, bestowing apparitional judgments. Our hearts begin a rhythm of a predetermined destiny, beating in time with our barren stomachs. The electricity within us churns our thinning innards, spins the dead threads of our blood vessels and pumps energy into our circuitry of forgotten life. Our journey is toward the dying light, against the wall of bone dust and the harmony of the dead.

The journey back down the stairs is crucial to our survival. We must fend for dinner or there shall be no life for us. After all, the dead are best fed by the living. We all walk a path down to the kingdom of the fallen one way or another, so why not speed up the process?

Back in the kitchen, Helena moves toward her mother, and shamelessly laps at the dark spread of blood on the linoleum. She heaves at the flavor, the dryness of death injures her throat, but yet she continues. My wife lies still as Helena feasts upon her fingers.

The snap of the thumb on her lovely hand is the finale of ingestion. Helena loves the taste, I can see it in her rabid eyes; the same eyes that beckon the one thing I have come for—meat. But exit is imminent, this gift shall be spread. She stands dutifully, as if knowing to leave, her eyes bleeding for the darkness of the outside world. Helena's mind is inquisitive, like the curiosity of a thousand adolescences, all looming impatiently within the iced cadaver of her heart.

I study her piously; inquisition is the key to victory. I look about my kitchen one last time and dally in the immediate destruction that lay within. The clock radio continues its hymn of *help* or *hope*. Voices of an unknown tribe of the living offer their services continually. And as my eyes catch another glimpse of the outside, the reflection in the glass reveals to me my sluggish wife.

She drools like the jowls on the sweatiest of canines. Her chin gleams a thousand tiny diamonds even in the blackout of the day.

Many grooves are cut into her face and have turned it into a theme park of scars. Patches of fresh bruising have blossomed over her mouth, cheeks and eyes.

From here my hand pushes against the glass, stains it like a branding iron with sweat and blood, mucus and ash. Helena moves first and my newly risen wife follows obsequiously. The door pushes open and we trail out into the gloom of grit and granules and smog; of war and impending doom. Helena shows us that the outside is okay, that the prison of the bricks and wood was meant to be evaded and the night's rapacious call is welcoming.

The air outside is as molten and slow as hot glue. Corpses walk beside me, next to me, adhere to the same gait that my family and I have taken on. A world of endless meat is what we seek, what we need. Dead bodies are rampant, sopped in the rainbows of vital juices. Stringy intestines sucked dry of miasma and of human nutrition lay open—smelling clearly of rot.

Faces are frozen in frightened positions, their bodies curled like tiny fetuses. Claw marks dig into the flesh of the newly dead and are rimmed a dark scarlet. The walking cadavers carry on as if the dead can feed on the dead; they are uncultured to the unwritten law of the deceased. Only true delight can be found in the living, to devour innocence is what makes a tongue seethe and a belly rumble with insatiability.

The dead rake innocuous eyes from babies as frantic mothers are shredded in the battle against their killer. They destroy love and challenge loyalty, feasting on the wretched hands of a society that was never meant to survive. They indulge on the sheer ignorance of a social catastrophe.

Fathers protect their families, but are no match for the hunger that reverberates within us. This is the day with no tomorrow, we have made it that way, and we will spread this disease until every last breathing individual is carved clean of the wet cells in their bodies. We have risen eternally and now take solace in this everlasting exploration.

I move to the left and lose my family in the web of constant gun fire. A heavy red sun sinking into its necropolis of a dead gray sky is the direction I move. A mushroom cloud splits the dying azure in the near distance. Tall buildings crumble and heap upon one another like a shoulder to cry on. Concrete, paper and bone rain down upon the bodies and simmer at my feet. A hot amber flame whirls into the fog and licks my cold skin, sizzles it into an even more ghastly pallor.

The innocent souls running amuck sense the careless slack of my body, of my still heart. There is no other way or them to survive this unholy holocaust. The constant cannibal urchin within all of us can not resist the palpability of living limbs. The masses can not thwart our lust for the ruby velvet of tissue, or the silt texture of venison in our mouths. New York City is bloated with people like larva in garbage dumps.

Something nuclear or chemical has just occurred. News reports are stentorian through the blocks of this squalid Queens neighborhood. They claim the enemy has found a way to force the population to collapse into themselves. "The dead rise!" I hear from a screeching radio. I don't believe what they say as my consciousness doesn't make sense of fairy tales. Does it not take into consideration that a weapon of mass destruction can't initiate the mind of creatures like me?

Then more flaming mushrooms light up the withered sky. They continue to crack it open like a coconut bleeding coral light. The near pang is something I have never heard in my life. The recoil from the bomb pushes me to my knees with muscular force and more apartment buildings collapse into piles of pitiful rock and concrete. Train stations that can not withstand the sonic boom blow over to the side and break down more blocks of a once vibrant city.

But do I seek shelter? No. My body only prays that it can find some steady source of liquid life, the need that awoke me with desire as red as a virginal body.

I continue my uneven gait, a sorry excuse for a walk, but I forgive my legs for they don't sense the commands of my head. They walk like two aimless sticks, their direction only geared for food; for satiety. Boisterous cries emulsify my senses and crucify the fine membrane of control. Most of the bodies have their limbs, although the burning cloud of nuclear death has begun to deteriorate the elasticity of their skin.

And as they crowd around me and beg to breathe through the opaque cloud of bone and rock, their soft, spongy lungs seared with radiation, I find solace in a woman whose cry is that of despondency about a death she can't control. This beautiful thing stands before me in a judgmental position. Her arms are black as if bathed with charcoal, glossed in sweat, and slick with splashes of blood poisoned by radiation. Crackles of despair are etched on her young skin and tear lines have cleaned two measly tracks in her face caked in chemical dust. Her eyes are webbed bright red, the lids cleanly singed off from the blast. My only thoughts are to relieve her of this cataclysm and be benign to her suffering.

She grips burnt grass for food, stuffs a clump of it into her parched mouth and grimaces at the flavor of brick, scorched flesh, and synthetic residue. Downpours of tears commence again, her mouth sagging, as if the bomb forced the onset of a stroke. Uncontrollably loathsome, the woman screams as more mindless dead souls pass her and the bulbous staccato of her rapidly-beating heart. I find it my goal to put her out of her misery.

My arms reach for the haggard woman, to which she swats at me with agonized and feeble hands. I begin to rage with pleasure as my fingers roll up and down her weakened frame, traversing her half-scarred flesh for a soft spot to gnaw.

I can't stop myself from sticking two fingers down her throat, toying with her vocal cords like a guitar out of tune, digging deeper to bring up a damaged lung; the radiation's effect executed.

Chunks of clotted ash and grime fall from it like a leaking faucet. Her feeble grip gives up its place; flaccidly her arms snake their way back to her sides and I offer my gift to her. A life of no pain and a cessation of sentiments; she believes me to be the enemy but this catacomb of mass destruction around us is the true enemy.

I grasp her throbbing neck with my hands, press my mouth to her throat, then suck out her effervescent life. The pulse of her jugular is succulent. All I want to do is baste myself in warm her blood, her essence. My jagged teeth grate her throat again and sink deeper. They flay the skin, my tongue parting the meat, to expose her pulsing carotid. I caress the beating blood vessel with my dried lips, scraping it. I slurp it out as she releases control of her muscles completely, collapsing to dead weight in my arms.

I drain her of vitality, of the things she needs most to survive. But what she doesn't know is that she will wake with the gift of everlasting life—in death! To never feel the maladies that life has to offer and infringe upon ignorant souls. She will never have to suffer the end of the world or the end of time like the living. She will walk into the ever long shadows of power, hunger and resilience with her new mind and a singular goal.

The skin on her body may change and the hairs upon her head may fall off and rot into a swab of dust as the chemical combustions light up the sky and implode like a supernova. There may be a time when she may feel useless, albeit we don't feel, we only eat. What she doesn't know, as I am leaking my gift into her tissues, is that she has been saved from the devastation that has slaughtered the greatest city the world has ever known.

We shall walk the lines of these new ruins, not knowing why the bomb was dropped or why the ravenous caverns of our soul orders us to seek out the living. After all, the living has done the best job of obliterating one another, so what is the harm in tagging along? The dead are a brotherhood and will stick together as one, always against the living until there are none left.

The immolated path of the city is where the new addition of the dead shall rise. This is where we are destined to sanctify the flavor of fear as life crumbles. We will face the bombs that are fabricated to alter us forever as we walk the fine line of sanity and democracy.

And as the newest explosions of human deceit and narcissism raise high in the sky like a slithering, temperamental enemy, we shall follow the streaking, scarlet ribbons of its residue down the pathway in the labyrinth of no tomorrow; as I have somehow been born into a dead world.

LAND OF ZOMBIES

ANTHONY GIANGREGORIO

The Ford Bronco with a white number 8 painted on both front doors slowed to a stop outside the small town of Steubenville, Arkansas.

The engine idled softly as the four passengers inside the vehicle stared through the front windshield at what looked like a small town, devoid of life.

"It looks quiet," Idaho said from the passenger seat. He was just shy of his nineteenth birthday, with an innocent face and curly brown hair. He had the look of a scared cat, his eyes constantly darting back and forth, as if he expected the world to explode at any moment.

"Looks can be deceiving," Tennessee said from the driver's seat. He was in his forties with a bald pate and hard eyes. His jaw was square, giving him an angry scowl even if he was happy, but the eyes, where you would expect them to be cold, to match the rest of his gruff exterior, were two dark pools of compassion. Though his exterior was rough, he had a heart of gold.

"Are you two ladies gonna talk about it all day or are we going in?" Georgia asked from the back seat. She was just over twenty with dark black hair and eyes that any man would fall for. She was trim and in shape and the t-shirt she now wore accented her thin waist and ample bust. Since Idaho and Tennessee had saved her and her sister two weeks previous, the two had become an item, though things had cooled in the past week.

The sister in question sat quietly next to Georgia. She was twelve going on twenty, with long brown hair and eyes that were wise beyond her years. Like the others, she had picked up a nick-name, and now even her sister called her Atlanta.

The four survivors of the zombie apocalypse had become a tight-knit family since meeting so long ago in Texas, and now traveled together across a zombie blasted landscape that was once America.

Atlanta wasn't paying attention to the conversation; instead, she was concentrating on the PSP in her hands. She had found it in a store outside of California, and after raiding the store for whatever they could use, she had taken the hand-held game console as well as the five game discs found with it.

"Hell, yeah, we're goin' in," Tennessee said. "I'm out of Twinkies and I bet you dollars to donuts there's a general store in that town with a shelf full of 'em."

Idaho reached over the seat and picked up his double barrel shotgun. "Then lets go, daylight's wasting."

"That's want I wanna hear! Ye-haaaa, let's ride, boys and girls!" He floored the gas pedal and the Bronco surged forward, leaving a trail of rubber on the deserted highway.

The Bronco came to a screeching halt in the middle of town, the setting sun reflecting off the polished chrome like a giant mirror. Only the dried blood spots on the bumper and grille marred its perfect finish. The Bronco had been acquired just outside of California after three tires had been blown on the Cadillac they were using, when Tennessee accidentally drove over a spike strip left by some dead policeman.

With nothing else to do, the quartet had walked for three miles until coming to a car dealership. Tennessee had picked the Bronco, hotwired it, and off they went, no worse for wear with the exception of sore feet.

"You always have to make an entrance, don't you," Idaho said to Tennessee as he scanned the street for zombies.

Tennessee shrugged. "It's my nature, come at 'em hard and fast. You should know that about me by now. Now quit bitchin' like a woman and get ready to fight."

"Looks quiet enough," Georgia said as she looked through the rear window. The rifle in her hands was loaded and ready if needed.

Tennessee cocked the Uzi in his hands and opened the driver's door. "Quiet or not, that store has a Twinkie with my name on it and I'm gonna go get it."

His alligator boots slapped the warm pavement as he exited the vehicle, his white, wide-brimmed cowboy hat shading his eyes from the sun.

Across the street from where he stopped the Bronco was a general store, one that sold everything from milk, to smokes, to Keno every hour. The name on the sign read, **DEGREGIO'S PRODUCE** and below the name was the picture of a dancing tomato and potato.

"Atlanta, you stay here, Georgia come with me, Idaho, you watch our backs," Tennessee said as he crossed the street without waiting for an answer.

Idaho was stepping out of the Bronco as was Georgia. They made eye contact for a brief instant and it spoke volumes. She smiled wanly and he did the same, then they moved across the street behind Tennessee. Just because the town seemed deserted, didn't mean it was, and at any second a horde of zombies could come screaming around a building, hungry for human flesh. It had happened before and would so again, that was a fact of the new world order.

"You okay back there?" Georgia asked her sister who waved a hand in a *leave me alone* gesture. She was concentrating on her game and wasn't interested in their escapades at the moment. "Fine, but lock the doors, will you please?"

"Ugh, fine," Atlanta said as she reached forward, locked the doors, to then fall back into her seat. Like her three traveling companions, she had adapted to her new world quite easily, accepting a world ruled by the ravenous zombies as a matter of fact.

Georgia looked up to see Idaho and Tennessee walking to the front entrance to the store and she jogged after them, her eyes looking all around, waiting to see the first sign of a zombie. But so far, it was quiet.

Tennessee reached the door and opened it casually, as if he was a regular customer on a regular day that needed to do some shopping.

Stepping inside, the cool air wafted over his face. The power was still on, as it was in many cities across the U.S. He assumed it would go out eventually but for now the power plants across the

ANTHONY GIANGREGORIO

states were still on autopilot, chugging along and kicking out electricity.

His eyes took in the aisles of assorted items. Food of course, but also a section for hardware and magazines. To this left were a few items for those who succumbed to impulse buys and he grinned widely when he spotted an interesting item to use as a weapon.

"Looks clear," Idaho said from his side as he stood still, his shotgun in his hands, his eyes darting back and forth like a thief about to get caught. Georgia came up behind Idaho and stopped.

"Okay, boys and girls, I got a system how I clear these places out, just stand back and watch," Tennessee said with a grin. He picked up a glass jar of mustard and one of ketchup, and with a wink at the others, tossed them into the aisle so they scraped the ceiling.

As the two condiments arced through the air, they quickly soared downward. Upon striking the floor, they shattered, the loud crash filling the store and becoming a dinner bell to any zombies inside.

Idaho was looking sideways at Tennessee, taking the bigger man's lead and waiting, and Georgia was leaning against a rack of magazines. She was confident whatever happened would be taken down easily.

And then the first sounds of footsteps slapping the tiles came to their ears.

"Here we go, I knew there was some in here," Tennessee said as he picked up his improvised weapons, his grin growing wider in anticipation.

A second later, a skinny zombie rounded the end of the aisle, woofed twice like a dog, then charged at the three survivors. Idaho raised his shotgun but Tennessee placed a hand on the barrel and pushed it back down.

"I said I got this, just like before," he said calmly.

He took a step in front of Idaho, the wide smile on his lips never faltering, a gleam in his eye. He loved killing zombies and if he was seeing a psychiatrist, the doctor would have told him it was therapeutic.

The zombie powered forward, an apron on its torso, tan chinos on its legs and a pair of sneakers. It had been a cashier or a bag boy but it was obvious by the name tag—which read Brad—that the zombie had worked in the store.

As the zombie powered forward, Tennessee swung his improvised weapon under his arm, and with an underarm heave, like he was bowling, he let loose with the lawn dart in his hand.

The dart soared across the few feet separating him from the zombie, and true to his aim, the dart struck the head in the right eye. The metal tip—the darts taken off the shelves because of the danger—slid into the eye like a hot knife through butter—and the zombie's head snapped back to spin it in the air and fall onto the floor, flopping like a fish.

"Piece of cake," Tennessee said as he took a step forward, another dart in his hand. "What do you think, zombie kill of the week?"

Actually, the *zombie kill of the week* went to Mrs. Virginia Fulsome of Brentwood, New Jersey.

With the help of her neighbors, Mrs. Fulsome dug an open pit in which she then filled with Pungi spikes. She covered the pit with a large tarp and dusted it with light dirt and leaves.

Whenever a zombie would chase her home after she went out for supplies, she would make sure to avoid the pit by jumping over it to land on her front porch.

On this particular day, a large brute of a zombie with pus dripping from every orifice and teeth as red as a Crayola crayon, was chasing her.

Mrs. Fulsome hurdled the pit, almost slipping at the edge, and as she opened her front door and fell inside, the zombie, unaware of its doom, placed its foot onto the tarp. Plunging head first into the pit, the first Pungi stick entered its left eye, then continued straight into its neck until exiting out the zombie's rectum. Like a roasted chicken on a spit, the zombie flailed about until succumbing to death, more than a half dozen sticks now penetrating its body.

It should be mentioned that second place went to Mr. Jeremy Higgins of Johnstown, New York, who jury-rigged a leather couch over his front door, and when he was being chased, pulled the lever and dropped the couch onto the zombie just as it began to pound on his door after he'd entered.

Flattened, the zombie's insides were sprayed across the door and ground. Later, Mr. Higgins dragged the corpse away, hosed off the area, reset the couch, and awaited his next target.

No sooner did Tennessee step three feet down the aisle, then another zombie rounded the bend. It was female and she was covered in blood, her mouth a gaping maw of red and black, her once blonde hair painted brown with dried blood. She wore a yellow dress, now torn in the front, and her perfectly curved breasts—implants obviously—swung back and forth like two erotic pendulums.

"Next!" Tennessee said jokingly as the zombie powered forward, a screech on her bloody lips. Tennessee prepared another dart, and as the zombie came for him, he chucked it overhand like he was throwing a spear.

The dart went straight for the right breast, punctured it easily and then into the zombie's heart. Silicon squirted from the breast and oozed down the flat stomach but other than that the zombie kept coming.

He was out of darts but not out of ideas, and Tennessee reached out to both sides of the shelves and grabbed a can of chili and a can of beef stew. As the zombie ran at him, he threw each can like it was a baseball, the metal projectiles soaring at head level until they connected with the zombie's head. The first one hit hard and put a dent in her head and she slowed for a second, but no sooner did the can fall away then the second one was connecting. This one struck her head on the corner and sliced a jagged wound in her head. She fell to the floor, her brains exposed, but still not out of the fight.

Tennessee walked over to her as she tried to get to her feet and he took a restaurant-sized can of chocolate pudding from off a shelf next to him. Raising it over his head, he brought it down like a bludgeon, the can smashing the head to pulp and breaking open. Chocolate pudding and brains mixed into a gooey sludge as bits of blood spouted out to course through the mess like imitation lava running off a mountain.

Tennessee turned to look at Idaho and Georgia, his smile so wide it looked as if it would crack his face.

"I'd stay away from the pudding if I were you," he said, and was about to turn and search for his Twinkies when he halted in his tracks.

Normally, when he entered small grocery stores, there would be one or two zombies within, the few that were too stupid to figure out how to escape, but this time there was something different, something he couldn't quite put his finger on.

As he waited in the aisle, he began to hear the sound of dozens of slapping feet.

He looked at Idaho who only shrugged, not understanding what was happening. Georgia had dropped the magazine and was now standing with her rifle leveled at her waist, her beautiful face now covered with a mask of concern.

And then the first figure rounded the bend at the end of the far aisle. Directly behind it, more came around, a few taking the turn so fast they slid on the polished floor, their bodies crashing into the aisle and knocking canned goods to the floor. Others stepped on the canned goods and found it was like stepping on large marbles, these bodies then falling to the floor in a heap of arms and legs. But there were still more than a dozen who climbed over their fallen brethren as they charged down the aisle in pursuit of the three survivors.

"Oh, shit, this never happened before," Tennessee said and took a step backwards. It looked like a large crowd of people had seeked shelter inside the store only to all succumb to become zombies themselves. And now they wanted Tennessee and the others for a snack.

All fooling around aside, Tennessee pulled his gun and shot the first zombie as it charged down the aisle. The bullet hit it in the chest and the body flipped over backward, striking others who pushed it aside and continued onward. Three zombies stepped in the pudding gore on the floor and their feet went out from under them. They fell to the floor in a mock Three Stooges parody.

That gave him an idea and he grabbed more glass jars off the shelves, then began smashing them on the floor as he walked back to Georgia and Idaho who had begun shooting.

Tennessee tossed more than two dozen jars onto the floor, each one smashed and spewing its contents.

As the first zombie reached the slick floor, its legs went out from under it like it had stepped on ice. Horizontal for a moment, gravity took over and the body crashed to the floor, the head striking so hard the skull cracked. Seconds later, there was a massive pile-up of bodies as each zombie fell over the other and slid on the floor.

"I changed my mind, I don't like this place, let's go shopping at another one," Tennessee said casually, though his voice cracked slightly. He was fearless but not stupid and there were way too many to fight off for no reason. Retreat was the best option.

"No argument here," Idaho said as he popped open his shotgun, slid two more shells into the breach, snapped it closed, and fired at a zombie who was only a few feet away.

Spinning about, the three kicked open the door to leave, and before even one foot could be placed outside, the horn on the Bronco began to sound, the blaring an indication of two things. The first was the situation outside was so bad that Atlanta wasn't worried about calling attention to herself, and the second was that she was blaring the horn *and* calling attention to herself.

Georgia was in the lead as they exited the store and slammed the door closed behind them. A sign about free magazines was to the right and Tennessee grabbed it and shoved it into the handle of the door. No sooner did he do this then the first body slammed against it. The door shook on its frame but he could see they had more than enough time to get to their vehicle and vamoose.

Tennessee was grinning once more, proud of his escape, when he turned around to see what was going on out front in the street.

The horn was still blaring and the passenger window was open as a panicked Atlanta hung out of it, shooting her rifle. That, plus what was behind the Bronco, appearing like locusts, told him all he needed to know.

From down the street, swarming between alleyways and from out of buildings, more than a hundred zombies had appeared, and they were all hungry for human flesh.

"Oh, hell no," Tennessee said as he brought up his Uzi.

Idaho swallowed hard as he stared at the approaching horde. "I think we need to go, right now."

"Ya think?" Georgia yelled and jumped off the porch as she ran to the Bronco.

"Hurry up, they're almost here!" Atlanta yelled and shot a zombie in the chest. It was wearing a pair of grease and blood-soaked coveralls, the name **William** stitched in red thread over its chest pocket. The zombie fell back and sprawled on the ground to be crushed by two dozen feet. When it was clear to stand, its arms were broken, the ulna on both limbs jutting through the flesh.

Tennessee could see if they were going to escape alive, the herd would need to be trimmed, so he jumped onto the hood of the Bronco, then onto the roof, and sprayed the horde from left to right. His bullets peppered bodies, taking out fist-sized chunks of meat and flesh, the gore-splattered bodies falling to the pavement to twitch and spasm.

Idaho followed Tennessee's lead and shot two zombies in the face, one after the other. As the heads exploded into crimson gouts of bone and brain matter, he reloaded, trying to keep his shaking hands from dropping the shells.

"Come on!" Georgia yelled as she climbed into the driver's seat and put the Bronco into gear. "Forget them, let's just go!"

"Ye-haaa, look at 'em twitch!" Tennessee shouted and sent an entire clip into the mass of zombies. Bodies were piling up and so far none had managed to reach them.

From the far side of the street, independent of the horde, two zombies came at Idaho. He didn't know they were there until he heard their feet slapping the street and he was still loading his shotgun. Turning, trying to snap the weapon closed, he saw two puss-covered faces charging at him.

Then one, followed by the other, were shot down and he turned to see Atlanta smiling at him, her rifle aimed at where the zombies had been moments ago. He touched his index finger to his forehead and gave her a salute for a thank you. She smiled, her elfin face belaying the hardness she now held inside her. If she wanted to survive, she had no choice and her sister had already taught her how to be strong long before the apocalypse began.

"Whoo-haaa. Come and get it, kids!" Tennessee yelled as he popped in another clip and sprayed the horde. More than three dozen bodies now lay twitching on the ground as he fired relentlessly into the attacking horde. Then he lost his balance as the Bronco shifted into drive, Georgia rolling forward.

"Hey! Cut the shit, I'm up here!" he yelled.

"Well get the hell down, there's too many of 'em!" Georgia yelled back and revved the engine. She pointed to Idaho and waved for him to get inside the Bronco. Turning, Idaho shot a zombie that was too close, only clipping the sprinter as it came at him, then he spun and ran for the Bronco.

"Get in the back!" Georgia yelled, the front seat was full with her and Atlanta. Idaho did as he was told and climbed in while Tennessee continued to shoot and yell in abject glee.

"What the hell is he doing up there?" Georgia yelled and moved the Bronco again, then hit the brakes. Tennessee lost his footing and fell, landing on his back on the hood, hard. He was a big man and the hood had cushioned his fall but his eyes glared at Georgia, the two equals in spirit and will power.

"Hold on!" she yelled out the window at Tennessee who did as he was told, grabbing the edge of the hood right where it touched the windshield. She floored it, sending Tennessee's face into the windshield, his cheek pressing so hard it flattened. She ignored it, only worrying about the zombies coming up behind her. The Bronco's tires spun and it took off just as the first three zombies grabbed the rear bumper. As the vehicle drove away, the three zombies fell, only their tenuous grip on the bumper keeping them attached.

As the Bronco shot down the street, the three bodies bounced and swung back and forth at the rear, boots and sneakers grinding away or falling off completely until bare feet began to grind against the pavement. The Bronco swerved around a corner and Tennessee almost fell off, but he managed to hold on. Behind the Bronco, the three bodies left long, red streaks as feet were ground down and legs became nubs.

Finally, the zombies couldn't hold on any longer and one at a time they let go, their bodies rolling across the ground to remain still. One let go at a bad time and when it fell away, it immediately came up against a Postal mailbox. The blue box turned red as the body exploded on impact, internal organs and intestines shooting out in all directions like a water balloon.

The Bronco continued onward, leaving the zombie-infested town behind.

Outside of town, with nothing around but a few abandoned cars and open fields, Georgia pulled to a stop and an exhausted Tennessee slid off the hood to fall onto the road. The inside of his fingers were cut where he was holding onto the hood and he picked himself up slowly, leaning against the vehicle to steady himself.

Georgia sat behind the wheel, a sly smile on her lips as Tennessee walked around the Bronco and climbed into the back with Idaho.

"That looks like it hurts," Idaho said as he looked at Tennessee's fingers. He handed Tennessee a Kleenex to wipe off the blood.

"*That* is the stupidest statement I ever heard," Tennessee said in a low voice.

Idaho said nothing, knowing Tennessee had mood swings. One second he was amenable, the next he was angry, but deep down Idaho knew they had become friends and that was enough for him.

Georgia and Tennessee made eye contact in the rearview mirror and he opened his mouth to say something but Georgia's gaze was firm. Her eyes seemed to say, *go 'head, say something.*

Tennessee closed his mouth, waved his index finger at her in a threatening gesture, and began wiping the blood from his fingers. He looked at Idaho and said, "Give me another damn tissue."

Georgia looked at Atlanta, took her smaller hand in hers, and gave her sister a loving squeeze, then stepped on the gas pedal, the Bronco surging forward.

She looked in the rearview mirror to see Tennessee mumbling to himself. Idaho made eye contact with her and he gave her a salute. She winked at him and then turned her attention to the road ahead.

The highway was filled with the detritus of a fallen society. Abandoned cars, a burnt out hulk of a small, crashed Cessna, a school bus with bloody windows and flat tires, were just a few of the assortment of dead relics.

Accepting this as her new reality, and knowing her fellow survivors did the same, she drove around a stalled car with its hood up and headed for the horizon.

"Maybe the next town will have some Twinkies, Tennessee," she said and he looked up, his eyes alight with happiness, like a puppy glad to see its owner return home.

"I sure do hope so, I surely do."

"Maybe they have snowballs, too," Idaho said as an afterthought. "I could go for some."

Tennessee turned to Idaho, his jaw set tight, and said, "That'll get you one at half strength." He punched Idaho on the shoulder, making the skinny man wince.

Georgia laughed and so did Atlanta, and as Tennessee flashed each of them a wide grin, Idaho frowned while rubbing his sore shoulder.

He should be used to it by now; after all, it was just another day in a land of zombies.

TOMBS OF THE UNDEAD

DAVID H. DONAGHE

People ask me about what happened down in Haiti and wonder why I have such a hard time in tunnels and places underground. I got tired of always having to answer so I decided to put everything down on paper.

My name is Mike Monroe and I own Monroe's Paranormal Investigations. I served in the Persian Gulf War and I did some special OPS work. I've seen things and done things that people wouldn't believe.

Fresh out of the military, I needed some hard cash, so I put my skills to use and I opened up the agency.

Roxy was standing at the copy machine the day I got the call from General Kincaid. She wore a short black leather skirt that almost wasn't there and a black tank top. Of course, she wasn't wearing a bra, and her nipples pushed up the cotton, straining the fabric of her shirt. Roxy's the kind of woman that drive men crazy, with her long blonde hair that billows down the sides of her large breasts, her perfect skin, her pretty face, and long, sexy legs.

Turning away from the copy machine, Roxy accidentally dropped the papers she'd just copied all over the floor. "Damn it!" she cursed, bending over to pick up the papers. Her skirt hiked up in the back, revealing a pair of silky black panties that looked like nothing more than a piece of butt floss running up the crack of her shapely ass.

"You got eye problems, pal?" Roxy asked when she caught me looking.

"No, my eyes work fine. I think I can almost see what you had for breakfast this morning," I laughed. My mind danced back to that day six months prior when she strutted into my office, looking for a job. She came in wearing a short white skirt, a thin button up white top, and a pair of black 'come fuck me' boots. The top three buttons of her top were undone, revealing a deep valley of cleavage and a sexy black bra that barely contained her massive mammary glands.

"Can I help you, miss?" I asked, a shit-eating grin crossing my face.

"I'm here about your ad in the paper for a secretary."

"Sit your fine self down and we'll talk," I said, motioning to a chair. Her eyes shot daggers, but she sat down and crossed her sexy legs. "First things first," I continued pulling out an employment application. Handing her the application, I held it halfway across the desk. She leaned forward, giving me a perfect view of that deep valley between her breasts. She gave me another one of those looks and then rummaged around inside her purse for a minute.

"Do you have a pen I can use?" she asked, heaving a sigh.

My eyes darted back up from her chest; I took a pen from the drawer and handed it to her. She let out a huff and started in on the application. While she filled it out, I ravished her with my eyes. She kept looking up at me, glaring annoyingly. Finished with the application, she slid it halfway across the desk, making me reach for it.

"You've never worked as a secretary before? Do you even know how to type?" I asked while scanning the application.

"Yes, I can type just fine. And I'm a fast learner."

"And your last job was at Jack-in-the-box? I bet the customers loved you there."

"Look, pal. Just forget it! All you've done since I came in here is stare at my tits! Take your job and shove it!" she said and jumped to her feet, her breasts bouncing playfully. I let her get halfway to the door.

"That's it? You're just going to give up? You don't want the job?" I asked. She turned around, crossing her arms underneath her breasts. "Pretty much, yes."

"You've got nice tits. I wasn't just staring at your chest. I was also staring at your ass and your sexy legs. So, do you want the job or not?"

"You mean you still want to hire me?" she asked, a trace of a smile crossing her face.

"Sit down, please," I said, motioning to the chair. "I can hire any bimbo for a secretary. What I need is a partner. I like you. You're feisty. I don't care if you don't have experience. I can train you. Have you ever used a firearm?"

"Guns? No, guns scare me."

"You'll get over that. What about paintball guns?"

"I used to play with squirt guns when I was a kid."

"Squirt guns. Squirt guns are fine, too. You look like you're in good shape. Do you like to hike, go camping, anything like that?"

"I used to be a Girl Scout."

"A Girl Scout. That's something I can use. You're hired."

"Just like that?"

"Yes, just like that," I said.

"When do I start?"

"Right now," I said, rummaging around in the bottom drawer of my desk. I handed her a stack of video cassettes.

"What's this? 'Vampires are real.' 'How to kill a werewolf.' 'Zombie World'. What is this stuff?"

"Time to get educated, sweetheart. Go in that back room and slip those things into the VCR. When you come out, we'll talk."

"You don't actually believe this crap, do you?"

"Didn't you see the sign out front? It said 'Paranormal Investigations'. Remember those old movies you saw when you were a little girl? The ones that scared the shit out of you. The ones Mommy said weren't true."

"Yeah, but I thought you were like a ghost hunter or something."

"Well, Mommy lied. And I do ghost stuff, too," I replied.

Four hours later, after watching the tapes, she came out of the back room with a grave look on her face.

"Don't make any plans for the weekend, sweetheart. We're going to Las Vegas," I said.

"Why?"

"I'm taking you up to the Front Sight. It's a gated resort community on the outskirts of Vegas. Instead of golf courses, they have shooting ranges. We're taking a combat shooting course. It's part of your training. Pack enough clothes for four days."

We rolled into Vegas in my black 1984 Ford Mustang with its four-on-the floor and its 5.0-liter V8. Roxy wore a white tank top and a pair of Daisy Duke shorts that showed off her long, sexy legs. Her nipples pushed up the cotton on her tank top, reminding me of two mini ICBM missiles. I could barely concentrate on my driving and my hand wanted to slip off the steering wheel and rest on her thigh, but when I tried it once, she gave me an elbow to the ribs for my trouble.

"Knock it off, pervert," she'd said.

Heaving a sigh, I let my hand rest on the gearshift knob in between us. We pulled into the Front Sight that afternoon and started training the next morning. I signed us up for the combat shooting courses using handguns, fully automatic M-16s and pump action shotguns. Roxy was nervous at first and closed her eyes when she shot the handgun.

"Come on, darlin'. You're not gonna kill the bad guys by shooting with your eyes closed," I told her.

A serious look of concentration crossed her face, and the next time she fired, she hit the target. Once she got over the fear, she loosened up and started having fun. By the end of the first day, she could shoot almost as well as me. I enjoyed watching her shoot the M-16 on full auto. Every time she let go with a burst, her breasts would jiggle back and forth. She wasn't wearing a bra and believe me, she put on a good show.

After taking the combat shooting course at the Front Sight, I booked us into a short, basic training course at Camp Pendleton that the marines put on for some local reserve units. We did a lot of push-ups, ran obstacle courses, did some more work at the shooting ranges, and learned military style discipline. I'd been through it all before, but I wanted Roxy in good physical shape. Once done with that, I reserved some time at a local paintball course and we played war games. I even signed us up to go sky diving.

Roxy was terrified when it came time to jump out of the airplane, but we jumped tandem with her strapped to my back. She clung to me like a leech, but I didn't mind a bit. There I was, free falling with a raging hard on because of those massive breasts pressed up against my back. Back at the office, I gave her some hands on training on how to kill a vampire. I had a CPR dummy that I used to show her where to place the stake over the heart.

I invited Roxy to the KOA camp for a barbeque to celebrate the completion of her training. After we wolfed down a couple burgers, I handed her a Super-Soaker and grabbed one for myself.

"What's this for?"

"One last bit of training," I said and then squirted her in the chest with the Super-Soaker. She was wearing a white wife beater t-shirt and of course, she wasn't wearing a bra. Once the shirt got wet, it became transparent, revealing those lovely breasts through the wet cotton. Roxy jumped up and blasted me. We ran around the camp, spraying each other with the Super-Soakers.

"How is you squirting me in the chest with a squirt gun part of my training?" Roxy asked after the water fight. We were sitting underneath the awning of my motor home.

"Remember all that stuff I gave you to read about the occult? Didn't you retain anything?" I asked.

"Yeah, so?"

"I fill the Supper-Soakers with holy water and use them against vampires. Here, I've got something for you." Taking a gold chain from around my neck, I put it over her head. She held up the small gold cross at the end of the chain and looked at it.

"What's this for?"

"It's for protection. I wear one just like it. I had that cross blessed by every priest, minister and holy man in town. I work under the protection of the cross."

"Do you really believe all this religious baloney?"

I paused for a moment then said, "Belief is the key word. Belief is a powerful thing. Yeah, I believe in the power of the cross."

* * *

The telephone on my desk rang, bringing my mind back to the present.

"Monroe's investigations. This is Mike speaking," I said after I picked up the phone.

"Mr. Monroe, I'm General Kincaid's secretary at Camp Livingston. I have an urgent call from the general."

"Put the old buzzard on the line," I said, a smile crossing my face.

"One moment please."

"Mike, how are you, you crazy son-of-a-bitch?" the general asked.

"I'm fine, you crusty old bastard. What can I do for you?"

The general's voice turned serious.

"I need your help. My son Robert is down in Haiti with the occupation force. He's gone missing."

"How can I help?"

"He went AWOL. Someone saw him in the presence of a voodoo priest. My INTEL boys said that there's a woman involved somehow."

"Huh, isn't' there always? Say no more. I'll leave tonight."

"Mike, you know what kind of shit those bastards are into. Bring my boy home safe, if you can, but if you can't, you know what to do. I'd like to hope that he's still okay."

"Either way, General, I'll bring him home."

"Mike, he's my only son. I'll pay you twice your normal fee."

"That's not necessary. For you, I'd go for free. I owe you a lot, sir," I replied.

"Cut the 'sir' crap. I said I'll pay you twice the regular fee, and that's what I intend to do. You're not gonna go down there alone, are you?"

"No, I've got a partner now."

"I'll pay double for your partner as well."

"Fax me your boy's picture and everything pertaining to his disappearance."

"I'll have my secretary get on it, and I'll contact the base commander down in Haiti and let him know you're coming. I'll make sure you have everything you need," the general said.

"That would be great. Thank you, sir."

"Remember what I said, Mike. Bring my boy home alive if you can, or bring him home dead. I couldn't bear the thought of him turning into one of those undead things," Kincaid said and hung up the phone.

I looked up at Roxy wondering if she was up for this.

"What?" Roxy asked. She had seen my face change slightly while I was on the phone but hadn't heard the general's side of the conversation.

"Pack your bags, sweetheart. It's time to get your cherry popped. We're going to Haiti."

We caught a military flight out of March Air Force Base in Riverside, California that evening and Roxy sat beside me on the cargo plane, shaking like a leaf.

Putting my arm around her shoulders, I tried to comfort her. "It's gonna be all right. These old cargo planes receive regular maintenance and these flyboys are topnotch pilots. The ground crews are some of the best in the world," I said.

"It's not that. I'm scared of what's going to happen on the ground. I don't want to mess up."

I shrugged. "Is that all? You'll do fine. All you have to do is watch my back. We're partners. You watch my back, and I'll keep my eye on that pretty little ass of yours."

"I know I don't have to worry about that," Roxy said, elbowing me in the ribs. "I'm just afraid I'll freeze up when you need me."

"It's not gonna happen. I've been training you since I hired you and I can tell you're not the kind of girl that freezes up. You react. I'd trust you with my life." The flight chief came aboard and told us to strap on our safety belts. The pilot got the okay from the tower to take off, Roxy took my hand, and the old cargo plane lumbered down the runway. Once airborne, I pulled a cigar out of my pocket and fired it up. Fanning the foul smelling smoke from her face, Roxy leaned back and went to sleep.

Opening a manila envelope, I studied the pictures that General Kincaid faxed to me. One was a picture of his son; it showed a smiling, blonde-headed young man in a military uniform. The next picture showed a young Haitian woman, who looked pretty even if a bit malnourished. The last picture showed the whiskered old face of an evil looking voodoo priest. Stuffing the pictures in the envelope, I listened to the hum of the engines, wondering what awaited me in Haiti.

I draped my coat over Roxy's sleeping form, leaned back against the bulkhead and closed my eyes.

* * *

After a thirty-six hour flight, Roxy and I stumbled down the ramp of the cargo bay and onto the airfield at a U.S. military base outside Port-au-Prince. The humid weather hit me like a blowtorch, making me sweat. A stocky lieutenant colonel with short dark hair and a fleshy face met us at the foot of the loading ramp. He stood next to a Humvee with a big cigar clinched between his teeth.

"Mister, I don't know who you are, but you've got connections. I got a call from General Kincaid this morning and he said to give you carte blanche, whatever you need. I'm Colonel David Spencer."

"Is that our Humvee?" I asked.

"You bet, and she's all gassed up." He handed me a manila envelope. "Here's your hotel reservations, your government credit card and five-thousand-dollars in cash. The general said to assign you a squad of MPs to assist you," he said, glancing at Roxy.

"Where are my manners? I'm Mike Monroe and this is my partner Roxanne Delaney. We're here to find the general's son," I said.

"Hi," Roxy said.

"Yes. He went AWOL about a week ago."

"We'll need some U.S. issue BDUs with a U.S. contractor's patch on the shirts," I replied.

"There are five pairs for each of you in the back of the Humvee. I also took the liberty of supplying you with hand held radios and there's a radio in your vehicle also. If you get into trouble, get on the COM-Net. I'll have a Ranger company standing by."

"You can keep the MP squad. We work alone, but if we need to call in the cavalry, it's good to know that we have Rangers sitting on go. Those boys are some hard chargers," I said.

"Is there somewhere we can shower and get something to eat?" Roxy asked.

A bead of sweat dripped down her chin and disappeared between the deep valley of cleavage between her breasts. Roxy had the first three buttons of her shirt top unbuttoned."

"The mess tent is open and I'll direct you to the showers," Spencer said.

Visions of Roxy lathering up her nude body passed through my head.

"Why don't we head into Port-au-Prince?" I said. "We can get room service."

"Don't flash that cash around. There are people here who'll kill you for the change in your pockets. I put a map of the city and the surrounding areas in the envelope with your hotel reservations and the cash," Spencer replied.

"Thank you, Colonel," I said, sticking out my hand. We shook.

"Good luck. I don't know much about your mission but I heard a few things. If the general's son is missing, then I hope you bring him back alive."

We stashed our gear in the back of the Humvee, changed our clothes quickly into BDUs, grabbed a quick bite to eat, and then climbed into the vehicle and headed across the base.

Passing several Quonset huts, we fell in behind a military convoy heading to the perimeter gate. The guard at the gate checked out our ID and then called in to HQ. He stepped up to the driver's side of the Humvee and handed me back our identification.

"I don't know who you are, mister," the guard said. "But the base commander about chewed my head off for stopping you. He said that the mission you're on is above Top Secret and that I wasn't to impede it in anyway."

"Sorry about the ass chewing. You were just doing your job," I replied. Following behind the military convoy, we headed down a long dirt road leading into Port-au-Prince. The dirt road had a red tinge to it and a red dust cloud formed in our wake. Grassy slopes rolled down toward the sea to our left and people dressed in rags, some carrying heavy burdens on their head and shoulders, stood along the side of the road begging for food.

On the outskirts of the city, we passed through a shantytown; lean-to structures made from scrap wood and other debris lined the road. Naked, malnourished children played in the water at a communal fountain.

"You can tell we're in a third world country," I said.

"It's so sad. Look at those children, they're starving."

In the city, I noticed U.S. soldiers on patrol and groups of young black men standing on the street corners watching the soldiers. Several of them carried baseball bats and others held machetes. Parking the Humvee on the street in front of our hotel, I motioned to a policeman standing on the sidewalk. He wore a blue uniform with a wide brimmed matching blue hat.

"Good day, man," he said.

"Hello, sir. I'd appreciate it if you would keep an eye on my vehicle. We'll be here all night," I said, handing the man a hundred dollar bill. His eyes lit up and he grinned, exposing two gold teeth.

"Thank you, sir. No harm will come to your motorcar. I guarantee it, man."

"Good. When you go off duty please pass the word."

The policeman nodded and offered to carry our bags, but I declined. Roxy and I carried our bags and all of our equipment into the hotel lobby.

"I have reservations under the name Monroe," I said to a beautiful Haitian woman standing behind the registration desk. She wore a red satin dress that was form fitted to her figure.

"It's right here, Mr. Monroe. You are in room thirty-seven on the third floor. Your government has already paid for the room. The bellhop will take your bags," she said in perfect English when she handed me the room key. The bellhop met us at the elevator and helped us with our gear. Inside the elevator, Roxy stood close to me, making me acutely aware of the pressure of her right breast against my arm. A quiver passed through her body when the elevator jerked a few times before it came to a stop on the third floor. Inside the room, I tipped the bellhop and then sat down on the bed.

"Thank you, sir," the bellhop said and left.

Roxy stood with her hands on her hips, gazing about the room. Flies buzzed overhead and an overhead fan osculated above us, barely stirring the stuffy air. Noise from the street filtered in through an open window.

"There's only one bed."

"I guess that means we'll have to bunk down together," I said and then grinned.

"Oh, isn't that's convenient," Roxy replied.

"Don't get all worked up, I'll sleep on the floor."

"No," she said and then heaved a sigh. I watched the rise and fall of her breasts. "You just better keep your hands to yourself."

"I'll be a good boy. Scout's honor," I said, holding up two fingers.

"I'm taking another shower," Roxy said and then headed for the bathroom.

Leaning over, I took off my boots and then leaned back on the headboard of the bed to relax. The water in the bathroom turned on and a second later Roxy let out a shriek.

"What's the problem?"

"There's no hot water!" she yelled from the shower.

"Give it a minute. Things like that take a bit longer down here," I said and then laughed.

She came out of the shower a few minutes later with a worn white cotton towel wrapped around her that barely concealed her copious breasts. Beads of water glistened off her sensual bare shoulders and of course, she caught me looking.

"You got eye problems? It's your turn in the shower," Roxy said.

On my way to the shower, I swaggered by her nearly nude form with a cocky grin on my face. Breathing in her fresh womanly scent, I grabbed the bottom of her towel and jerked it down. "Hey, what the hell!" Roxy yelled, and then threw the towel at me. Dodging the towel, I let out a low chuckle, and then retreated into the bathroom.

Roxy was right; the water was cold, but it warmed up after a few seconds. After lathering up, I quickly rinsed off, and then strutted out into the hotel room wearing nothing but a smile. Roxy sat on the bed, wearing a fresh set of BDUs. Looking up at me, a red tinge crossed her face and she looked away. I bent over and took a fresh set of BDUs from my duffle bag. Roxy averted her eyes, but I saw her reflection in the mirror and she did take a little peek at my ass while I pulled up my pants.

"Do you want me to order room service?" I asked and then sat down on the bed.

"I'd love it. I'm starving. I didn't eat much at the base."

I picked up the phone, ordered burgers and fries plus a six-pack of beer for both of us, then put it on Uncle Sam's tab. Twenty minutes later, there was a knock on our door. I told the waiter to add a generous tip to the cost of our meal and to bill everything to our room.

"Do you always have such an expense account?" she asked.

"Only when Uncle Sam's paying the bill; they can afford it. If you look at the things I've done over the years, they owe me. If it's a private client, let say someone has a poltergeist in their house or something, I try to keep my expenses down," I said and then dove into my juicy burger.

After we finished eating, Roxy leaned back on the headboard of the bed and rubbed her belly.

"That was wonderful. When do we go to work?" she asked.

"We'll wait for a couple of hours until things start hopping inside the bars. Let's start with the girl. We'll show her picture around. Maybe someone knows her."

* * *

A few hours later, Roxy and I entered the hotel bar. Gazing about, I took in the patrons. Most were foreign nationals of English or French descent, but a few Haitian businessmen sat at a table near the doorway leading to the outside of the building. Off duty U.S. service personnel gathered at the bar. The buzz of conversation wafted through in the air and the smell of tobacco smoke filled the room. An overhead fan osculating above us barely swirled the stagnant air.

"You work the tables and I'll talk with the people at the bar," I said to Roxy, handing her one of the photographs of the young Haitian woman. Roxy nodded and then moved to the nearest table while I headed to the bar.

"Hey, guys. How you doing?" Then, motioning to the bartender, I said, "Set these boys up with another drink. I'm buying."

"Thanks, man. What're you doing in this shithole of a country? You might have on a set of BDUs but you're not military," a rugged looking sergeant said.

"I'm doing some contract work for the brass. Have you seen this woman?" I asked, setting the picture down on the bar. The sergeant studied it and passed it down the bar.

"Do any of you dog faces recognize that woman?" the sergeant asked.

"I've seen her. She used to be one of the local prostitutes hanging out near the main gate, but I haven't seen her lately," a private sitting at the end of the bar said. Glancing across the room, I noticed Roxy talking to a group of local businessmen.

"Enjoy the brews, guys, and keep up the good work," I said and then swaggered over to where Roxy was talking to a skinny black man in a plaid suit. He rubbed the gray stubble on his black chin, studied the picture and then glanced up at me.

"She is Adele Laurent. I knew her mother before she went to be with her ancestors. Now she raises her brothers and sisters alone," the man said, using a French accent.

"Where might we find her?" I asked, setting a hundred dollar bill on the table. He made the money disappear.

"She lives in the shantytown to the west of Port-au-Prince."

"How do we get there?" I asked.

"Follow the road outside until you come to the edge of the city and the road turns to dust. What has the girl done now? She's not still selling herself to the soldiers again, is she?"

"I don't know anything about that. We just need to speak to her. Thanks for your help," I said. Roxy took my arm and we headed for the bar.

"When do we go after the girl?" Roxy asked.

"First thing in the morning." I bought Roxy a few drinks and tossed down a couple of beers. Stumbling up to our room, I opened the door and we went inside.

"Turn around, so I can get undressed," Roxy said and I complied. A few seconds later, she said, "You can turn around now."

She had changed into a wife beater t-shirt and a pair of red boxer shorts. I enjoyed the way her breasts hung underneath the thin cotton fabric and I loved the way her nipples pushed on the cotton. She pulled back the covers, and shoved some pillows in between us. I took off my clothes and put on a pair of sweat pants.

"What are those for?" I asked, glancing at the pillows.

"So you don't get any ideas."

"I forgot to mention that I'm not into dumb blondes," I said and then climbed into bed.

"Hey! I'm not dumb!"

"A might touchy, aren't we?" I said as I turned out the lamp. But luckily for me, sometime during the night, the pillows disappeared, our nightclothes came off, and Roxy unleashed her passion.

To me, it felt like I was trying to ride a hurricane.

* * *

We left the hotel room at eight the next morning. After tipping the policeman for watching our Humvee, I took the canvas top off the vehicle and pulled out onto the road, heading west. The blazing sun caused a bead of sweat to track down my forehead.

"Did you see that?" I asked Roxy.

"You mean that skinny black guy watching us? The one talking on the cell phone?"

"That's the one. I knew I hired you for a reason, other than your looks, that is. Notice anything odd about that guy?"

"Other than that his clothes were dirty and shabby, no."

"He's loitering on the corner, watching us. He doesn't fit in. This part of Port-au-Prince is the business district. Most people on the street dress a little better. I checked my mirror as we pulled out. As we left, he called someone on his cell phone and then split. Are you armed?"

"Yes, I'm armed."

"Good. Be ready."

We passed through the business district and approached the outskirts of town.

"Where do you think they'll hit us at?" Roxy asked.

74

I paused for a moment, thinking. "I don't know. I don't think they'll try anything in the town. There would be too many witnesses."

Twenty minutes later, we left the city behind and entered the shantytown west of Port-au-Prince. Plywood shacks, tin sheds and other makeshift structures lined the road. People moved up and down the road carrying goods to their shelters while others sat by the side of the road offering trinkets for sale. Pulling up next to a stone fountain, I parked the Humvee.

"Why are we stopping?" Roxy asked.

"This is their only water supply. If we're going to find our girl, this is the place."

In a clearing across the street, a group of people danced around a tree. An old man with a scruffy-white beard knelt down and drew something in the sand. The dancing continued. The old man took a chicken from a cage, cut its throat and sprinkled blood on the ground. One of the women fell to the sand in a fit of convulsions.

"What are they doing?" Roxy asked.

"It's a voodoo ceremony. That guy that just killed the chicken is a voodoo priest. He looks a lot like the old man in one of the photos I have. It's hard to tell, I didn't get a good look at his face."

"What happened to that woman?"

"The ceremony is to conjure up spirits. A spirit from the other side possessed the woman. They believe that by sacrificing animals like that chicken, they give the spirits the power to possess the people. It's supposed to be a great honor when you're possessed."

"Do they ever do human sacrifices?"

I nodded. "They keep it on the down low, but I've heard rumors that they do."

"Why don't we go after the priest?" she asked.

"We'll deal with him later, when he's away from his flock." A grubby looking Haitian, wearing tattered jeans and a dirty white shirt, came up to my side of the Humvee and started begging for money.

"There's our girl!" Roxy yelled pushing open the door of the Humvee. I climbed out of my side of the vehicle, making the beggar jump back.

"Adele!" I yelled. For an instant the woman stood still, giving me the look of a deer caught in a set of headlights, then she bolted.

"I got this!" Roxy yelled and went sprinting after her. I followed, watching Roxy's breasts bounce up and down when she ran. She made a lunging tackle and brought the woman to the ground fifty yards from the vehicle. Tears streamed down the young woman's face and she began to babble in French.

"Adele. Stop crying and talk English. We're not going to hurt you. Let her up, Roxy," I said as I reached them and went to one knee. Roxy climbed off her back and Adele sat up. She was wearing a worn blue dress with flowered print.

"How you know my name?" she asked. I showed her a picture of General Kincaid's son.

"Do you know this man?"

Her eyes widened and a look of terror mixed with sadness crossed her face. "He is dead, but not."

"What do you mean, 'but not'?" Roxy asked.

"He is zombie man now. My heart is sad for him. He treat me kind."

"Where is he now?" I asked.

"He is in the tombs," Adele said, pointing toward the west.

"What tombs?" I asked.

"The Tombs of the Undead."

Roxy's eyes widened.

"Where are these tombs?" I asked.

She pointed west again. Taking the picture of the voodoo priest from the envelope, I showed it to Adele. "Who is this man?"

"He named Deville. He Bokor. Voodoo priest."

"What's a Bokor?" Roxy asked.

"It's a voodoo priest that practices black magic. The Hougans practice white magic," I replied. "Where can I find Deville?"

Adele looked around taking in her surroundings.

"Him gone now. He live in plantation house near Tombs of the Undead. Beware. Him bad man. Turn you into zombie man. He catch me, he make me into zombie, too," she said and started to cry.

"No, he won't," I said, standing up. "I'll take care of Mr. Deville. You can go now." I looked through the crowd gathered around us, but I saw no sign of the voodoo priest or his flock.

"Zombies? Do you really believe this shit?" Roxy asked. We elbowed our way through the crowd on our way back to the Humvee.

"Down here it's mostly hocus-pocus. The Bokor injects the victim with a neurotoxin that causes death-like symptoms. They bury him and the Bokor digs him up later and gives the victim the antidote, but he also makes him ingest hallucinogens that keep him in a trance-like state. He makes him his zombie slave."

"It sounds creepy," Roxy said.

"It is, but that's not the worst of it. There are rumors that a voodoo priest can conjure up spirits that possess the dead. The dead rise and have a craving for human flesh. That's where the zombies get their power. That's also where the rumors of human sacrifice come in."

"But do you really believe it?"

"What do you think?" I asked, glancing at Roxy as we climbed into the Humvee.

"I think it's crazy."

"I think that by the time we're done here in Haiti, you're gonna think differently about a lot of things." Firing up the Humvee, I pulled out onto the dirt road, heading west.

* * *

The plywood and tin shanty's gave way to wide-open spaces and green, rolling hills. Scattered brush and trees lined the road. We reached a small rise and descended the crest of the hill when an old army Jeep pulled out from behind a clump of trees. I slammed on the brakes, creating a dust cloud. Four Haitians, dressed in rags, jumped out of the Jeep. Two stood in front of the Humvee and fired AK-47s into the air as one ran up to my side with a machete. A forth pulled a handgun and approached Roxy's side of the vehicle.

"Don't hesitate! Shoot the two with the AKs first!" I yelled as I pulled my .45. The one with the machete raised it in a killing blow and I shot him in the face. His head exploded and he flew backwards as the sound of the gunfire wafted across the surrounding hills. Roxy jumped up and fired over the top of the Humvee's windshield, taking out the two men with the AKs, and then dropped back into her seat. One of the men with an AK managed to get off a few rounds that shattered the windshield. The glass exploded, showering us with pieces of broken glass.

The fourth man pointed a.357 Magnum at Roxy's head. Grabbing her by the back of the neck, I pulled her down, her face landing in my crotch, as I fired over the top of her, hitting the man at her door in the chest. The .45 caliber bullet punched a hole through his heart and stopped his clock.

"You can let me up now," Roxy said.

"I don't know. I kind of like you down there," I said as I laughed. She put an elbow into my stomach and I let her up.

"I guess, I owe you my life," Roxy sighed.

"Forget about it. That's what partners are for. Let's drag these bodies out of the way and get out of here."

It took less than five minutes to drag the bodies off the road so the Humvee wouldn't drive over them. Once finished with the bodies, Roxy climbed in and drove the Jeep off the road, then jumped back in beside me. I noticed her hands shaking.

"You did good. I knew you wouldn't freeze up," I said as I drove away.

"That scared the hell out of me."

"Fear is good. Fear gives you an edge. You just have to control it. The first time is always hard," I said.

"Is it always like this?"

"Not always. It comes in spurts. Boredom, inactivity, then intense action, fear, and an adrenaline rush."

Down the road, we passed another U.S. military convoy and left them in our dust. The road snaked its way up a large hill and then descended into a small valley. A large grove of oak trees was on the left and a narrow dirt trail branched off leading into the oak grove. A flash of white caught my attention, so I brought the Humvee to a stop.

"I think this is the plantation house Adele spoke of," I said. "Those look like the pillars of an old Victorian mansion behind those trees. I think we'll have a word with Mr. Deville," I said while pulling off onto the dirt trail. Tree limbs slapped the side of the Humvee, making us pull are arms inside the vehicle. The old dilapidated mansion sat in the midst of a clearing in the oak grove. Mr. Deville, the voodoo priest, was sitting in an old rocker on the rickety front porch. When he saw us pull up, he jumped to his feet and an evil grin crossed his face. Roxy and I climbed out of the Humvee and walked toward the front porch.

"Sir, have you seen this man? He's a soldier in the occupation force," I said, holding up the picture of Robert Kincaid. Deville stepped to the ground, grabbed a handful of dirt, threw it into the air, and began chanting in French. He moved about, waving his arms in the air.

"Sir, the picture? This is Robert Kincaid. Would you please look at the picture?" I demanded.

"He is my zombie slave. You shall join him soon," Deville said and continued chanting. In one fluid motion, I forced Deville to the ground, grabbed him by the throat, pulled my .45, and jammed the barrel against his forehead.

"I curse you, white man! I give the curse of the zombie!"

"Yeah, and I'll curse you with a bullet through your brain if you don't start talking," I said.

"You'd better talk. He means it," Roxy said, squatting down next to us.

"I curse you, too, woman. I make you my zombie bitch."

"Bring it on," I said, pulling the gold cross from under my shirt. "I'm protected by a higher power. Now where is he?"

"He lies in the Tombs of the Undead," Deville hissed.

"Show me," I said, jerking him to his feet. Roxy took his arm, and I took his other arm as we started moving him toward the Humvee.

Deville stomped his foot down on Roxy's instep, jammed an elbow into my ribs, and ran towards the house.

"Damn it!" Roxy snapped.

Spinning around, we ran after him, pushing our way through the front door of the mansion. I slid to a stop in a dusty ballroom and gazed about. Antique furniture covered with white sheets filled the large room, but I saw no sign of Deville.

"Where'd he go?" Roxy asked.

"I don't know. How could he have disappeared so fast?" A noise came from the hallway. "He's in there!" I yelled and ran through a doorway to our left. Bursting though the door, I saw a trapdoor in the middle of the floor just closing. Bending over, I tried to pry it open. Roxy ran into the hallway and knelt down next to me.

"I think he locked it from the inside. I need a crowbar," I told her.

Roxy ran outside, found a tire iron in the back of the Humvee, and ran back inside. Taking the tire iron, I attacked the trapdoor, but after a full ten minutes of trying, I gave up in frustration.

"Shit! Shit!" I yelled, throwing down the tire iron. It chipped the polished hardwood floor as it bounced.

"That girl back at the shantytown pointed to the west when she talked about the Tombs. Maybe it's further down the road. Maybe there's a graveyard," Roxy suggested.

"Let's go then," I said, heaving a sigh. Outside, we jumped into the Humvee and took off through the oak grove. At the main road, we headed west at a high rate of speed.

* * *

The land opened up as we passed through an open area and then headed up another hill. Dropping down the other side, I saw an abandoned graveyard against a bluff to our left.

"I think this is it," I said, stopping near the graveyard.

"This place creeps me out," Roxy said.

Taking a pair of binoculars from underneath the seat, I studied our surroundings. Most of the gravestones were askew. Peat moss covered the gravestones, scattered oak trees filled the graveyard, and old tree limbs lay on the ground. Training the binoculars on the bluff behind the graveyard, I noticed several caves leading into the bluff.

"This is the place. Look at those caves behind the graveyard. See that larger entrance in the middle? I say we head in there first."

"Okay," Roxy said, trying to hide the quiver in her voice.

"I know, it sucks, but we've got to do it," I said and then climbed out of the Humvee. Rummaging around in the back of the vehicle, I took out our equipment and helped Roxy into her pack. Swinging my pack over my shoulder, I carried my AR-15 and handed Roxy a miner's hardhat, placing one on my head as well. She slung her Ruger Mini-14 on her shoulder, put on her hardhat, and snapped on her utility belt.

"Okay, let's do this," I said and we entered the graveyard.

The ancient looking tombstones looked weather-beaten by time. Some of the inscriptions dated back to the eighteen hundreds. I led Roxy around patches of weeds, over fallen limbs and avoided boggy sections of ground. The earth felt spongy, and had a rotten smell to it. Pausing at the freshly dug grave of a child, I read the faded inscription on the tombstone. A cold breeze blew through the trees, sounding like a doleful spirit.

"Let's go," I said, continuing across the graveyard. Halfway to the caves, I noticed a smell that reminded me of rancid meat.

"God! What is that? It smells like three day old road kill," Roxy said.

"That, my dear, must be the Tombs of the Undead."

Stepping over a rickety fence on the backside of the graveyard, I headed for the main entrance leading into the tombs. Pausing at the entrance, I took a military flashlight from my web belt and peered inside. Bones, bits and pieces of decaying flesh, and a few skulls littered the mucky floor of the tunnel. Rats scurried around and maggots wiggled back and forth; a putrid smell emanated from the tombs.

"Do we really have to go down there? I see rats. I hate rats," Roxy said.

"The rats are the least of our worries," I said.

Switching on our miner's lanterns, we descended into the abyss. Taking point, I cradled my AR-15 in my hands and stepped into the gooey muck on the floor.

"God what is this stuff?" Roxy asked, trying to pull her boot from the muck and mire.

"Looks like decayed flesh, mixed with mud and pieces of bone."

Moving further into the darkness, I saw crypts built into the sidewalls of the underground passageway. Some were empty, while others had their stone covers broken, but the skeletal remains lay in place and a few remained sealed tight. Noticing Roxy's heavy breathing, I moved forward, descending into the earth as we became one with the darkness. The deeper we progressed, the more pronounced the smell became.

"I don't know if I can handle this! I need to get out of here!" Roxy gasped.

"Get a grip! Watch my back and keep that Mini-14 handy. We don't want anyone coming up behind us. Here," I said, handing her two small cotton balls coated with Petroleum Jelly. "Put these in your nose. It'll help with the smell." Further in, we came to a large junction. Several smaller passageways branched off from the main tunnel leading in different directions. Shining my light, I tried to get a sense of direction.

"Which way do we go?" Roxy asked in a quivering voice.

"Let's stay with the main tunnel." Taking her arm, I felt a shudder run through her body. A dull rumble came from one of the tunnels branching off to the side that sounded like the hounds from Hell had awakened. I couldn't tell which tunnel the sound came from; it almost seemed to come from all of them. "Run!" I yelled and charged backward just as a horde of flesh-eating zombies lurched out of the side tunnels and lumbered along behind us. Tripping over a body laying on the ground, I went sprawling and the lights went out. I heard the tinkling sound of breaking glass when my miner's light hit the ground.

Roxy tripped, letting out a blood-curdling scream, and landed on top of me. It felt like the entire weight of the earth pressed down upon me, a sharp pain shot through my chest, and I couldn't breathe. Fumbling with the straps on my pack, I dug into it and rummaged around frantically. Then found a pair of night vision goggles, and slipped them on my head. A flesh-eating zombie with rotting lesions on its face and wiggling under its skin hovered over Roxy. Pulling out my .45, I splattered what was left of the undead thing's brain against the wall. The muzzle flash lit up the darkness, revealing the zombie crowd behind us.

"Put these on!" I yelled. Pulling Roxy to her feet, I handed her another pair of night vision goggles. Shoulder to shoulder, we opened up with the AR-15 and the Mini-14 on the zombie horde. The sound of gunfire echoed throughout the tombs. Bits and pieces of dirt and rock fell from above as the zombies fell to the ground, stacking up like cordwood.

"Let's go!" I yelled and then ran, descending deeper into the earth with Roxy right behind me.

This time the attack came from in front. Coming around a curve, we ran into a wall of flesh-eaters. Through the night vision goggles, I saw a worm crawling in and out of what was left of one of the undead thing's left eye, its smell causing me to taste bile. It had its arms raised, letting out a howl, and then moved forward with the pack. Leaning against the wall, I froze. Hyperventilating, a sharp pain shot across my chest and moved down my arm.

"I...think I'm having a heart attack. I can't go on," I stammered.

"Man up, Mike!" Roxy yelled, backhanding me across the face. "You don't have time for a heart attack! There's another pack coming up on us from behind!"

"Right," I said getting my breathing under control. "Take out the ones coming at us from behind, and I'll deal with the ones at our front."

Stepping away from the wall, we stood back to back and opened up on the advancing horde. Even in the middle of the attack, I didn't fail to notice the firm pressure of Roxy's shapely bottom pressed up against mine. Her body jiggled back and forth as she fired. The loud crack of gunfire almost made my ears bleed and by the sporadic muzzle flashes, I saw what was left of the zombies retreat into the tombs. The acidic smell of gun smoke masked the putrid smell of undead flesh. Once the attack broke off, we moved deeper into the earth.

Roxy screamed.

"What?"

"A snake! I felt it try to crawl up my leg! There's rats every-where! I've got to get out of here!" she yelled and began to cry.

"We've come too far for that," I said, taking her arm.

"I thought you said these voodoo zombies were just a bunch of hocus pocus? That the voodoo priest just drugged people to make them seem to come back from the dead. Those zombies looked like they've been sitting in the grave for years."

"Yeah, Deville's more powerful than I thought he would be. Those zombie sons-of-bitches are the real deal. I could smell the stench pouring off them and I'd lay money that Deville is into human sacrifices."

Further into the darkness, we passed another series of passageways branching off from the main drag. The moan of flesh-eating zombies wafted on the cold damp air. Taking a grenade from my web belt, I pulled the pin and tossed it into a cave branching off to the side. There was a loud thump followed by the sound of falling earth.

"I know we don't have enough grenades, but let's try to block off as many of these side tunnels as we can," I said. We tossed grenades into the side passageways and caverns branching off the main one, sealing them off until we ran out of grenades. The place seemed honeycombed with underground channels and warrens leading everywhere. Dust filled the air and we covered our noses with our sleeves until it began to settle.

"What's that? I saw a light. It looked like a hot spot in my night vision," Roxy said.

Peering through the darkness, I saw a flickering red spot, followed by the unmistakable scream of a woman. The zombies showed up green on the goggles because of their lack of heat. Taking the night vision goggles off my head, I peered into the darkness with my naked eye. In the distance, I saw a flickering light. After traveling for another fifty yards or so, we stepped into a large rectangular cavern. It looked like a cathedral in Hell. Candles, mounted in crevices in the walls, provided enough pale light for us to see without the night vision gear. Ancient looking wooden pews were in rows facing forward. Two stone altars were located at the front of the hellish cathedral, and behind the altars, was a wooden platform. Human heads hung from the walls and body parts lay at the foot of the altars. A foul odor emanated from the cavern as flies buzzed overhead.

Adele Laurent lay bound on the stone altar to my right and a young man in a military uniform lay on the altar to my left; he wasn't moving.

Deville, dressed in a black robe with chicken bones sewn into its hem, struggled with the Haitian woman. He had her head pulled back and was attempting to pour some type of liquid into her mouth.

84

"How did they get here so fast?" Roxy asked.

Jerking Adele's mouth open, Deville looked up, gave me an evil hiss, and tried to pour the liquid down her throat, but Adele turned away at the last second, the liquid missing her mouth and pouring down her cheek. Deville pulled a dagger from underneath his robe, brought it up over his head, and was about to stab the Haitian girl in the heart. I pulled my .45 and put a hole in the center of his forehead, spattering his brains upon the platform behind him. Deville flew backward, landing behind the altar. Jumping over a pile of body parts, I ran down the center aisle to the front of the cavern, Roxy by my side.

Pulling my K-Bar knife, I cut the ropes binding Adele. "Take care of her," I said to Roxy and moved to the man. Now that I was closer, I recognized the features of Robert Kincaid. "He's still alive," I said, checking his neck for a pulse.

"What's wrong with him?" Roxy asked, rushing forward to restrain Adele.

"Deville gave him a neurotoxin. It's a poison extracted from the Puffer Fish. It causes near death-like symptoms," I said, dropping my pack on the floor. Bending over, I rummaged around again and took out a needle and a syringe.

"What're you giving him?" Roxy asked as I put the needle to Kincaid's neck.

"It's a saline solution mixed with a vitamin cocktail. He needs salt. The poison prevents his body from producing salt and causes the death-like symptoms. Deville wanted him docile so he could offer him up in sacrifice. Once his body has enough salt, he'll come out of it," I said and depressed the plunger.

Adele fell into Roxy's arms, crying and blubbering incoherently.

"It's okay. We're gonna get you out of here," Roxy said.

After cutting the ropes binding Robert Kincaid to the stone altar, I heaved him over my shoulder using a fireman's carry.

"Time to go," I said.

Roxy gave Adele a gentle push and got her moving in the right direction. Hearing a noise behind me, I whirled around to see a mob of undead flesh-eaters pouring out from behind a curtain to storm the platform.

"Run!" I yelled and then fired a short burst with my AR-15, strafing the platform. We ran through the cavern with Roxy pushing Adele along in front of her and me carrying Robert Kincaid over my shoulder. The sound of the undead fiends emanated from the cavern behind me. My heart did drum rolls inside my chest and my breath threatened to run away like an out-of-control freight train.

Oh God, oh God, if you just let us get to the surface, I'll never go under ground again, I swear, I silently prayed.

Roxy opened up with her Mini-14 on a group of zombies to our front. Every now and then, I would spin around and fire a burst with my AR-15, fighting a running battle on our way to the surface. I charged out of the tomb's main entrance and into the pale moonlight.

"To the graveyard! We're not safe yet!" I yelled, charging across the open ground. Roxy pushed Adele along in front of her. The zombie horde came spewing out from the mouth of the tomb, moving in their slow, lumbering gait. Their moans and snarls floated on the night air. Setting Robert Kincaid behind a gravestone, I fired at the horde again.

Roxy opened up with her Mini-14 on the approaching zombies. Adele fell to the ground, hiding behind a nearby gravestone. Pulling the two-way radio that Colonel Spencer had given me when we first arrived, I called in the cavalry.

"May day! May day! This is Mike Monroe! We need a MEDEVAC ASAP!" I yelled into the radio.

"Who is this?" someone answered.

"We're on a top secret mission and we need help now! Contact Colonel Spencer if you don't believe me!"

The young radio operator came back on the line a few seconds later and I gave him our grid coordinates. Putting the radio back in its pouch, I grabbed my AR-15 and fired off another burst.

"If they make it to this edge of the graveyard, we'll retreat back to the road!" I yelled. Ten minutes later, I heard choppers. It seemed Spencer worked fast.

A gunship strafed the area between the graveyard and the tombs, mowing down the zombies. The MEDEVAC chopper set down at the edge of the graveyard while several more hovered just above the ground, off-loading Rangers. Grabbing the now semi-comatose Kincaid, I carried him to the MEDEVAC chopper. Roxy grabbed Adele by the arm and followed me. The MEDICS took Kincaid and began working on him as I helped Roxy into the helicopter, to then climb in behind them.

"Is this who I think it is?" a young medic asked.

"This is General Kincaid's son. A voodoo priest gave him a neurotoxin extracted from the Puffer Fish. He needs salt!" I yelled, trying to communicate above the roar of the chopper's engines. When the chopper lifted off, I watched the Rangers approaching the entrance to the tombs. They were in the process of setting up explosive charges.

Seconds later, an explosion lit up the night, sealing the tombs for good.

* * *

Six days later, Roxy and I walked down the cargo ramp and onto the airfield at March Air Force Base. Robert Kincaid and Adele, arm in arm, followed along behind us. After a three day stay in the hospital, the doctors released Kincaid and sent him home to his father. His time in Haiti was over. Robert refused to go home without Adele, so I made some calls to some people I know in immigration. On the flight home, Robert and I spent most of the time in deep conversation. He seemed fascinated by my work. Much of what I do for the government is classified, but I told him what I could.

Roxy and Adele hit it off, right away. Before we left Haiti, I gave the general a call to give him the heads up. He didn't say much; he was just glad to know Robert was alive and safe. I wondered what he would think about his new daughter-in-law. When our feet touched the ground on the airfield, the general stepped past me and grabbed his son in a huge bear hug.

"Robert. I'm so glad you're safe. When I heard what happened, it almost killed me," the general said.

"I know, Dad. I'm sorry." He pulled away and wrapped an arm around Adele. "And this is Adele."

The general pulled away from his son and took the Haitian woman by the shoulders. "Little lady, I need your help. Someone's got to keep this son of mine out of trouble. I can't keep my eye on him all the time," he said and then smiled.

Adele laughed, relieved she was welcomed into the family. "I will watch over him. He risked everything for me."

The general hugged her and then stepped up next to his son and whispered into his ear. "I hope she's worth it, son. She almost got you killed."

"She is, Dad. You'll like her, trust me."

The general turned to me. "Mike, I don't know what to say. It goes beyond words. I owe you big time." He handed me a manila envelope and then glanced at Roxy. "Introduce me to your partner."

"This is Roxanne Delaney.

"Call me Roxy, sir," she said with a smile.

The general gave her a hug. "My dear, I'm glad to meet you. You got your hands full working with this old boy. He gets into some weird stuff, that's for sure."

General Kincaid stuck out his hand and we shook.

"Thank you again, Mike. You saved my family," he said.

"My pleasure, sir." I looked at Robert and said, "So where to now?"

"Oh, I'll go where ever the army sends me next but I have thirty days leave first."

"When you get out of the army, come see me. I could always use someone like you."

Robert laughed. "I might just do that, Mike."

Finished with our goodbyes, Roxy and I headed to my Mustang, which had been stored in a nearby hangar for my return; one of the perks of working for a general.

Before we left the base, Roxy did a quick change, putting on her Daisy Dukes and a black tank top. When I drove through the gate and left the base behind, I reached over and laid my hand on her thigh.

"Watch it, pervert," she said and gave me an elbow to the ribs.

Later, after we arrived back at the office, I sauntered up to Roxy's desk and handed her an envelope. It held a check for her part of the work we'd just finished. Roxy's eyes widened and her mouth dropped open when she saw the amount written in the Pay to the Order line.

"Hot damn! I love my job!" she yelled and let out a happy squeal.

A big grin crossed my face. "Me too, darlin'. Me too."

Want to find out what happens next?
There's more adventures of Roxy and Mike in
Dead Worlds: Undead Stories Volume 5 and
Eternal Night: A Vampire Anthology.

THE SCENT OF ROT

KEVIN MILLIKIN

Prologue

Olivia Prescott was all but the age of twenty-two when the first wave of destruction hit American shores. For twenty-two years of her life she had called the Pacific Northwest her home, and as she attended Portland State, she knew her life couldn't get any better.

When the first cases of the outbreak occurred, it was strictly an east coast phenomenon, restricted to areas that represented a vast and diverse population.

Early reports were sketchy at best, but then again, the virus was still in its early stages. Those infected would simply drop dead, with no warning, no symptoms, a far cry from what the virus would later become. However, these reports were few and far between.

The virus' second stage hit quick and in far greater numbers than its precursor, the new strand of the virus entered the body through means unknown. Eventually, it began to grow at an alarming rate, swelling any and all of the vital organs that it adhered itself to until the organ reached its breaking point, causing the victim to drown in their own fluids as they ruptured.

At first, many of the major news outlets ran stories of bioterrorism and swine flu mutations; some regarded it as mere hoaxes and cults as the CDC rushed to research all claims, often lost amidst a sea of red tape.

Needless to say, something was going horribly wrong within the United States.

Olivia, however, was none the wiser; with finals less then a month away, she found herself shying away from the outside world to focus on her studies.

As July came around, new reports arose; this time centered on claims that those who died as a result of their infection would later rise. Nobody wanted to face the possibility that the truth *could* be stranger than fiction.

Regardless of its absurdity, the CDC took notice. The following week, they released a report on what they referred to as the victims' 'trance like state.'

Originally, reports of the dead rising were isolated incidents, all of which was quickly swept under the rug, no thanks to the local governments.

* * *

The first official outbreak of the new strain occurred in Evans City, Pennsylvania on October 1st.

Reports of the events raged across the news as nearly half of the towns two-thousand residents became infected by the virus. Following infection, the victim fell into a deep state of dementia, accompanied by homicidal tendencies.

In just under a night, local and state authorities regained temporary control of the situation.

In the following days, it seemed that everywhere you looked, you couldn't escape the word: *zombie*. It raged across the television stations, newspaper, and the internet, sending the talking heads into a frenzy.

By now, Olivia had taken notice, but it wasn't until the outbreak spread beyond Evans City and into the outlining communities, but by then it was too late.

The dead were already knocking at her door.

* * *

The undead plague spread like a wild fire, engulfing most of the nation before jumping shores into Europe and Asia.

Overnight, the city of Portland was thrust into a whirlwind of panic and violence. Thousands upon thousands attempted to flee, but many stood their ground, fighting for what was theirs.

Rioters and looters took to the streets, entire city blocks disappeared behind a dense wall of flames. Buildings burned and crumbled as the dead shambled through the remaining smoke, like a grim reminder of the Hell that dwells below.

Olivia tried to flee when the local government set up rescue stations at public places, most importantly the train station, Union Station, just blocks from her apartment.

Initially, she was to embark to Canada, where the infection was still at a minimum. However, crowding and violence from those who refused to wait prevented her from leaving on the set day, delaying her salvation a couple days.

Problems were quick to rise as everyone who attempted to relocate via train attracted the attention of the living dead. Soon, they had congregated around the surrounding streets and train yard, all of which made the journey next to impossible.

Olivia sat by the window in her apartment, listening to the trains whistle as her only means of hope faded away.

Since the outbreak first occurred, that was the first day she cried.

* * *

In the following days, Olivia sat alone in her apartment, wallowing in misery. Outside on the street, the sounds of gunshots and screams sang her to sleep on a nightly basis, but even then, the shrill moan of the walking corpses penetrated her slumber, gnawing at her will.

Eventually, the news stopped broadcasting and the phone lines and internet failed. A few days after that, the power went out, plunging her world into darkness.

It was then and only then that she decided something had to be done. Rather than die alone, she lusted for human contact and cringed at the possibility that she could be the only living person left in the city.

The next morning, as the sun rose across the smoky skyline, she set out on her own.

1

As Olivia rounded the stairs, she wondered how long it had been since she had set out from her apartment and the zombie outbreak first began.

One year? Two? She wasn't sure, after the fall of the United States to the walking dead, people lost the need for calendars and clocks. It only seemed fair, because in a world where the dead walked, such devices became trivial.

Behind her, the voices of her comrades echoed throughout the lone walkway as they joked with one another, muttering immature nonsense to pass the time.

Most of it came from the 'horse's mouth', known only to her as Jack.

Jack was the newcomer to their little scavenger group and already she knew she didn't like him. Something about him got to her, like a junkie asking for change on the street corner, so he could 'make a phone call.'

Maybe it was Jack's way of holding onto the last of his humanity; regardless it offended her, she didn't care who screwed who or why the preacher was in the bar.

She only wanted to survive and live for a day when all of this would be behind her...behind them.

As they rounded the bend at the top of the stairs, the small group came to a quick stop next to the door that led towards the outside world. Olivia stepped forward, shoving the door open with a mighty heave that slammed it back at them.

"Whoa there, darlin'," Jack chuckled, pushing the door aside with a shit-eating grin. "Anger issues?"

With a roll of her eyes, she pushed forward, sidestepping everyone as she walked outside. "What the hell's her problem?" Jack muttered as Olivia disappeared into the smoky haze.

In a past life, Portland had been known as the City of Roses, but now, so much had changed. The scent of rot and decaying flesh hung heavily in the air, aided by the fires that were slow to die.

Welcome to Hell, she smiled to herself, looking across the city as Steven took the lead, walking across the steel and wire walkway towards the building's ledge.

All around them, the hellish cacophony of moans filtered up and over the Portland skyline like a dense fog. Though, it was sunny and warm, thick patches of clouds dotted the sky, signaling the darkness slowly rolling in.

This isn't right, she thought, looking at the surrounding apartment buildings, as she tried to imagine the horrors that shambled through the hallways and down the streets.

The thought of it hit Olivia at the core of her being, sending a shiver down her spine. Zombies had all but become a way of life and many of the survivors had grown accustom to it, not her. Olivia dreaded the day when she would grow to accept this reality as normal, because she knew when that day came, her will to survive would be gone.

She gazed off across at the dead that wandered aimlessly across the rooftop of the adjoining building, when a little voice echoed in her mind.

This isn't right, it warned as she walked across the access way to the ledge, where Steven waited, turning around to address the group.

She smiled at the sounds her boots made as they clanked across the steel walkway, screaming out in a discordant echo. Even though she was positive such things meant next to nothing to her comrades, she knew that the simple sounds of her lively footfalls was in itself a luxury that was lost against dead ears.

As they reached the ledge, she still couldn't shake the ill conceived feelings that touched her shoulders and whispered in her ears. *Today is the day.* Olivia knew better than to take it at its face value. *Maybe you shouldn't go, just tell them you're not up to it. They'll understand.*

After all this time, she still couldn't shake the fear that consumed her every time she came face to face with one of the living dead.

Olivia glanced over the ledge as she allowed her inner voice to fade into the background. Below, the streets were fairly free of debris; a few cars stood alone, long forgotten. Their doors left askew were the only reminder of the panic that once gripped the city. Newspapers and trash danced in the wind and then there were the dead; Olivia counted six in all. They posed no immediate threat, and by the time the scouting party left the building, the zombies would have most likely wandered off into parts unknown.

"Should be fairly simple," Steven said, pulling his gaze up from the streets below to make eye contact with everyone gathered around him.

Allen stepped forward, glancing down at the dead below. "Are they gonna be a problem?" he asked, squinting to make out their pale features. Clearly, Allen was the runt of the litter, green from his lack of conflict.

He wasn't their first choice for duty but rather the result of a lottery system installed followed by a failed coup that hit them hard the previous April. Twenty lives in all were lost, and since then the survivors in Oasis Towers teetered at one hundred and eighty-two.

"If we're lucky, there won't be a lot of confrontation. Actually, most of 'em will probably have wandered off by the time we make it down there," Steven replied, his voice strong and confident, just how a leader's should be.

His eyes, however, told a different story. Bloodshot and weary, they reflected the grim reality that lacked in his voice.

"And if everyone inside manages to keep it down while we're gone, it should be smooth sailing." He smiled, and Olivia had to turn away. She was growing more and more depressed by the insecurities reflected in his eyes.

Even though he showed a great weakness, he also represented a greatness that made him a natural leader. Steven was still a young man, in his early thirties.

He was the reason why they had all survived thus far. He had selflessly defended the building when the dead stormed the doors in the early days of the undead uprising, eventually turning it and all of the outlaying buildings into a makeshift quarantine zone for those that survived the early attacks. Each building adopted the moniker 'Oasis Towers' along with the numeral tag of 1-4.

All of the apartments managed to withstand numerous waves of advances until the barricades crumbled and the dead swarmed into the foyers.

In less than two years, building after building fell, infecting those who sought refuge within, all the while transforming them into the disease ridden corpses they all feared.

Olivia and the others did what they could to keep the buildings from falling, but as hundreds of walking corpses took to the surrounding streets, their masses grew and grew until it resembled a tidal wave of rot that writhed and stumbled about as they smashed into the buildings with such violence and fury it made a ground fight next to impossible. Instead, they took to the roofs, waging a senseless fight against the ever growing number of zombies below.

It was that night Olivia first witnessed the sickening symptoms that now plagued human nature. Up until that point it had been people working together in order to stay alive.

In attempts to flee, many of the remaining survivors of Oasis Two took to the rooftop, adjacent to Olivia's.

However, seven stories up, many of them soon found they had nowhere to go. Many of the people she saw there took their last stand against the dead.

One man charged a group of zombies as they swarmed a huddled group of frightened youths, taking many of the zombies over the ledge with him as they disappeared into the rotting sea of bodies.

Sadly though, it seemed that for every good deed, many more horrible acts were committed. A mother with her child, who could have been no less than three, flung her baby at her undead attackers in an attempt to selfishly protect herself.

The zombies removed the limbs from the screaming infant as eight more corpses justly took down the mother, ripping her apart from her intestines to her breasts. She was torn asunder, her body eaten.

Olivia knew their time was limited, as did everyone else. Unless they didn't act fast, they too, would be the next to fall.

2

It was still early in the afternoon when they crossed through the apartment's underground parking structure. Their boots echoed through the vast chamber, falling short of the cars that rested in their respected parking spots, forgotten and dusty.

It was supposed to be a quick raid. They weren't supposed to be gone for more than a couple of hours but she still couldn't shake the feeling that something was wrong.

When they reached the gate, Steven turned to address the group. "All right, just like I said: scrounge for what you can, weapons, antibiotics and canned goods. If you find anything you think might be of use, grab it if you can, but remember; priority items first."

As he spoke, Olivia realized how much he fidgeted with his rifle, tapping his fingers against it with a nervousness that echoed in his eyes.

It was understandable, nobody liked venturing outside anymore no matter how noble a cause, and nobody really liked doing much of anything anymore, but who could blame them?

Everyone had a different reason, but for most it was the knowledge they could rightly be the last survivors on Earth. Many of them had seen their friends, family, children and lovers ripped from them into the snapping jaws of the undead, only to join their ranks soon after.

Many of the people spent their time alone in their rooms, no longer socializing. Instead, they sat in the dark and stared at the walls. At the moment, Olivia counted thirty-two people in the apartments that suffered from this condition and the number continued to rise.

These people were placed under a special 'watch' to ensure they didn't kill themselves or others.

Other's who didn't suffer from being shell shocked worked in the kitchens, washed clothes and kept watch. They were lucky enough to have a working generator.

There was still the threat from those who believed that they were somehow owed something after all they had gone through. In their minds, they were kings and queens. Many of these people refused to do anything much less help, rather they preferred to order others around. But they were quickly taken care of, if by containment or their own hand.

Everyone got what they rightly deserved sooner or later.

"We're going to do this like before," Steven said, his voice bouncing off the stone walls of the parking structure. "Jack and I are on Team One. Olivia and Allen are Team Two. All right?"

They all nodded in agreement.

Thank God, she thought. The thought of being alone with Jack was surely enough for her to eat a bullet.

Steven turned away from the group as he fished the gate keys out of his pocket. From their angle, it was impossible to believe the world had fallen apart. The sun was shining and somewhere nearby, birds were chirping.

"If we have to break, let's try to keep in contact, no more than three minutes silence, tops," he said, sliding the key into the padlock.

"And you two," he added, turning back to Allen and Jack. "Don't try to be heroes."

"Wasn't planning on it, boss," Jack laughed. "And I doubt this kid can take a piss without getting scared!" He beamed proudly, patting Allen on the back with more force than was probably necessary.

"Sure," Steven replied bluntly, slipping the chains off the gate. "All right, lock and load," he said while swinging the gate open with a soft squeak. As they stepped out onto the street, they were instantly greeted by the scent of decay and rot as it assaulted their senses.

They waited on the street while Steven locked the gate behind them.

"Uh, boss," Jack muttered. "Let's say you die. How are we gonna get back in?"

"I got a key," Olivia said, speaking up.

"Oh, joy," Jack replied, rolling his eyes.

She stepped forward, and in a moment of frustration she muttered, "Well, I'm sorry I ain't in the kitchen cooking you your dinner," she said as she pushed past him.

"What was that?" he asked angrily.

"Calm down, both of you," Steven demanded, pushing forward. "Let's go."

Every step they took away from the safety of Oasis One, the little voice in the back of Olivia's mind seemed to grow louder and louder. *Oh, shit, shit, shit.*

3

They went slow, careful not to make too many sounds. Lucky for them, the dead seemed to veer away from direct sunlight, though not for long if they knew food was present.

There was something about direct sunlight that forced them into the shadows. There had been some speculation amongst the survivors as to why the dead behaved in this manner.

The general consensus was that direct sunlight on dead flesh increased the rate of decomposition at an unimaginable pace, which explained why some of the street walkers blistered and popped and the shadow lurkers appeared to look freshly dead.

Though it could simply be a coincidence, one thing was sure, the dead always came out at night and anyone caught out on the streets would be doomed.

* * *

Everywhere Olivia looked was a constant reminder of how life once was. Even now, she longed for the beach, though she found the urge quite out of character, even for her.

The thought of warm sandy beaches and cool ocean water made her think of her childhood. It wasn't that she didn't like the beach or that she wasn't fit, there was just a time when she found such things to be trivial when compared to her education.

Now, she thought, *what I wouldn't do for a chance to lounge on the sand and have not a care in the world.*

She glanced at the others in the group. The only one that she knew from prior excursions was Steven, as they had been together since the beginning. Allen and Jack were the new blood; replacements to be more precise.

It had happened a few months ago. Steven and Olivia were together with Skip and Ruth. They were the core scavengers. There was nothing they couldn't find.

Steven and her were busy one day, emptying the remaining goods from the Safeway on 13th Ave, while Skip and Ruth went to the pharmacy in back to gather up the remaining medication for the cold and allergy season that was fast approaching.

None of them had ever had a problem in the store before. When the dead invaded, this Safeway in particular had been closed.

They worked quickly, shoving can after can into large duffle bags set up between them when suddenly, the silence was smashed by a scream, followed abruptly by a burst of semi-automatic fire.

Before the two of them could register what was happening, a single gunshot ripped them from their confusion and into a mad dash down the aisle.

Together, their hearts raced as they rounded the corner. Olivia came around too fast, colliding headlong into one of the undead. She fell back just as the zombie reared forward, it's arms outstretched before it, broken fingers reaching for her.

The creature loomed before her, it's bulky build resembling that of a football player, it's Portland Blazers jersey hanging in tatters on it's feeble frame.

"Kill it!" she cried and reached for her fallen rifle. The zombie moaned loudly as spittle fell from its dry, cracked lips.

The ghoul lunged forward a second time, but the thundering round from Steven's rifle making it topple backwards and take out a display of cartoon endorsed band-aids as it fell. With Steven's help, she quickly pulled herself back to her feet.

"You all right?" he asked.

"Yes, I think I sprained my ankle," Olivia replied, flexing her foot against the linoleum before remembering the previous gunshots.

"Shit!" she cried, limping forward.

Moments later, she and Steven found Ruth and Skip, both dead near a killed zombie.

A large chunk of flesh was peeled away from Ruth's skinny neck, causing her to bleed out quickly. Skip was the lucky one; following the attack, he quickly ended his life with a single shot that had entered under his chin to then exit from the side of his skull. Their attackers lay dead on the floor.

The door beside them led to the pharmacist's office. It appeared the dead had been slowly beating against the door for some time, judging by the filth left behind by their putrid hands.

"Oh, Christ..." Steven moaned, slowing his pace. Sadness quickly overshadowed his emotions as he looked down at his fallen friends.

Olivia stood motionless, stunned.

"How?" she asked, but quickly trailed off, it took her a couple of seconds to find the words. "How did we miss them? We should have found them," she said and gestured to the destroyed zombie.

Steven walked over to the corpse that clearly did the deed, judging by the fresh blood still dripping off its chin.

"You son-of-a-bitch!" he spat and he swung his foot out quickly, kicking the corpse across the face with such force that it sent its neck aside with a snap.

She didn't say anything.

A low moan pulled there attention back to Ruth. Her eyes opened lazily as she spotted them. Olivia's first instinct was to stare in shock, but survival quickly took over as she brought her rifle up to her shoulder. She took aim, placing a single bullet between her eyes.

The remaining seconds crept by as she and Steve stood in silence, honoring their dead.

"We should go," Steven said. "I'm sure half the area of undead within earshot will be coming through the front doors any second if we don't move."

She said nothing, only nodding in agreement. They returned to gather the supplies and leave out the back door.

* * *

Olivia walked in silence, her memory of that day playing and rewinding over and over again in her mind as broken glass and bullet casings crunched below her feet.

It was weird going out on a supply run without Ruth or Skip. Since nearly the beginning, it had always been the four of them. Olivia wondered if the new recruits would be able to hold their own if the dead were to attack in droves.

She wasn't sure about Allen...and Jack, well, she hoped he didn't last. She couldn't stand doing this forever with him, let alone being by herself with just him. Something was definitely wrong with that man.

A moan echoed through the empty street. It sounded close in proximity. They stopped and listened.

In the distance, they could hear the hellish moan of many, if not hundreds, of the dead, but none were as close as the one they now heard.

"Where...?" Allen muttered before being cut off by Steven with a less than welcoming shush.

With guns at the ready, the group of four scanned the surrounding windows and storefronts, waiting for an onslaught they knew was coming, as the dead stumbled out of the shadows.

Seconds passed at a crawl as they waited. Finally, Steven held up his hand, signaling their advancement onward. It was then that Olivia noticed the numbing pain that radiated throughout her hand. She looked down to see her knuckles had turned white from the death grip she held on her rifle.

As the group passed by an old street car, they slowed their pace, studying the wreck along the way. The street car's shell had been badly burnt when a police car had crashed into its side, causing it to jump from the tracks and wrap around itself in the shape of a U.

Inside, were the skeletal remains of nearly a dozen people, their bones long since picked clean from the elements. Skeletal arms and legs protruded from beneath the tattered remains clothing.

Olivia envied the skeletons in the street car, their deaths were clearly the result of the crash, since they had not reanimated. Even though it was probably a slow, painful demise, surely it was a hell of a lot better than becoming one of *them*.

4

The first zombie exited the gutted remains of a Starbucks, snapping the group to attention.

The corpse had once been a girl, somewhere around fifteen, if not older. She was once attractive, dressed in what would be considered a hipster fashion.

The skin across her forehead was peeled back, revealing the glint of her white skull. She limped towards them, and Olivia saw that the girl's right thigh was torn away, revealing rotted muscle and flesh that seemed to pulsate with insects that had burrowed into her body.

She moaned, reaching her arms forward.

A single shot rang out, jerking her head back in a shower of skull and brain matter; she fell to the ground.

It was then Jack said, "We got more." Nearly a dozen more undead made their way from the abandoned businesses on the street. They moaned in unison, aroused by the sound of gun fire.

Olivia spun around to see three more coming up from behind her.

Had they been following us this whole time? she thought, bringing her rifle up to her shoulder and taking aim.

The closest zombie to her was an older man, dressed in casual attire; shorts and a button up shirt. His cheek was torn away, allowing his tongue to rest limply outside his jaw. His dead eyes flickered with what looked like excitement as he struggled to quicken his pace. Olivia fired, and the shot ripped through his face, snapping his head back as he fell.

All around her, the street came alive with the constant chatter of gun fire.

"Got one!" Allen screamed behind her as he dropped a body.

Olivia took aim, this time it was on old Chinese lady dressed in a running suit. Her belly was torn open, leaving an empty hollow as she dragged her dry intestines behind her.

Olivia fired, dropping the old lady in a spray of viscera and blood.

The next zombie was badly decomposed, possibly from the first wave of risings. Its three-piece suit was badly stained with its own filth. It limped forward, its jaws snapping hungrily.

She was about to end the creature's misery when a pain singed through her body, causing her to lose her footing and fall.

Oh shit, oh shit! The little voice in her head returned as her rifle slipped from her hands.

Her eyes burned with tears as she hit the pavement, but out of the corner of her right eye she was able to see the remaining members of her group scatter and break formation as the dead closed in. It was then that the zombie crawled on top of her; a horrid thing, with milky eyes and a snapping jaw. Like the others, it too, was badly decomposed.

She struggled to hold it back, but her hands broke through the parched skin like it was old paper, leaking its putrid fluids down her arms. She tried to scream for help, but stopped herself, knowing it would surely fall on deaf ears.

Suddenly, the corpse went limp, falling onto her. She could smell the burnt flesh as the bullet destroyed its brain.

Quickly, she shoved it aside, getting to her feet as another shot rang out and whizzed past her ear, hitting the zombie she had originally tried to kill.

"You all right?" Steven called, running to her side.

"Yes, thanks to you," she replied, dusting herself off. She looked around to see what damage had been done to the approaching dead.

All of the advancing zombies had been disposed of, and were now sprawled across the road where they would be left to rot in the sun.

Olivia muttered, "I didn't see it coming."

"Neither of us did," Jack smiled, walking towards the group. Allen was close behind. Judging by the smug smiles of their faces, she guessed they were proud of their victory.

"We better get a move on," Steven said loudly as he yelled over the ringing in his ears. "There'll be more here soon."

His words reminded Olivia of that night in the Safeway, but alas she agreed, as she gazed down on the animated corpse that had attacked her. She then realized why she hadn't seen it coming.

The corpse's legs had been chewed off to stumps. Leaving behind a bloody trail as it crawled along the pavement.

Allen stuttered, "Let's go!" as a cacophony of moans echoed through the street, the cries growing closer with every second.

As they ran, Steven chuckled. "You know, you're gonna have to stop falling all the time, it's starting to look bad for the team."

Even as they ran, Olivia could feel herself blush.

5

Minutes later, the group of four was on a new street and for the moment, safe.

"I've never been in anything like that before," Allen muttered. His face had grown pale and long as the adrenaline worked its way out of his system, allowing reality to rear its fangs once more. "They just came out of nowhere, didn't they?"

"You better get used to it," Olivia said. She didn't mean to sound like a bitch, even though she knew her words lacked the effort.

"Really?" Allen echoed, his voice trailing off. For both Allen and Jack, this was their first foray out into the world since taking shelter at the Oasis.

Olivia hadn't seen Jack around before, but she heard that he was on the janitorial staff. Allen, she knew from working in the kitchen and though both men were a few years older than her, she realized they had grown to live somewhat sheltered lives since the outbreak.

"Yes," she added, hoping her words would become more hopeful. "But it's not always that bad. Actually, we've become pretty good at dropping them before it gets *too* bad, and their moans are pretty good at giving their location away."

"Yeah, looked like it, especially when that one pulled you down," Jack sneered.

Olivia walked in silence, not knowing his intent. Malicious or not, she had no given response.

"But they took all of us by surprise," Allen said, coming to her aid. "And you weren't the greatest of shots either, Jack."

Olivia didn't look at Jack's response to the statement, but she figured Allen was going to get shit from Jack for it later. Jack was by no means someone you wanted to mess with on an individual basis. He was tall and slender, and what might have been years of drug abuse plagued facial features that he concealed beneath his long, brown hair and trucker's cap.

Steven remained silent to the conversation. Taking the lead, he pushed forward, his eyes scanning their surroundings constantly.

"And what about you, Steven?" Jack spat. "You ain't really said shit since we left."

"I didn't know I had to," Steven replied, a hint of sarcasm underlying his voice. "I thought you had that taken care of."

Jack didn't answer; instead, he sulked to the back of the group. Olivia couldn't see it, but she was sure Steven was smiling at his remark. He always did.

* * *

With the exception of the zombie attack, the walk had been more or less uneventful. Occasionally, a lone zombie would stroll into their path, only to be dropped quickly.

Jack had made it a point to do all the shooting, beaming at his own marksmanship, all the while cursing and throwing excuses for when he missed.

Jack missed most of the time, but only because the sun got in his eyes, or so he said.

They stopped for a breather on the corner of 10th and Adler. There, they were greeted by a block of booths that sat abandoned in an empty parking lot, the venders long since fled or worse, been pulled from the shanty kitchens and devoured for all to see, as was the case with the Thai booth.

Blood was smeared down its front facade as if its occupant had been ripped apart before hitting the ground.

The scent of rotting food hung heavy in the air and still, after all this time, birthed swarms of flies that buzzed and hovered about in thick, gray clouds.

"Anyone hungry?" Allen joked.

Olivia chuckled, she was starting to like Allen. However, her chuckle was short-lived as the nearest booth, proclaiming, **The best burgers in Portland**, sprouted movement. A zombie was trapped inside, having reanimated while the shutter was down, and it had nowhere to go.

The zombie moaned and thrashed about, beating its rotting fists against the walls

"Hold up," Jack said as his wide grin creased his face. He stopped next to the makeshift burger joint.

"Hey!" he shouted as he put his ear against the wood of the booth and kicked it with the side of his boot. "Come on out, ya dead fuck. Got four main courses here for ya!"

"Jack, will you knock it off! You're gonna attract more of them here!" Olivia pleaded.

"Hey, asshole! What's the matter, can't get out?" Jack sneered, paying no attention to Olivia's request as he began hitting the burger booth with the butt of his rifle.

"I said stop it, dammit!" Olivia screamed.

"Listen, bitch, I..." he shouted as he turned to confront her when he was suddenly slammed backwards with Steven's fist clenched tightly around his windpipe.

"Listen here, you piece-of-shit," Steven growled, his face inches from Jack's. "I'm in charge here, and that *bitch* over there," he motioned towards Olivia with his free hand, "has been with me since the beginning, which technically makes her second-in-command. You obey her, you obey me. Got it?"

Jack didn't respond though fire and hatred burned in his eyes.

"And one more thing. Any more acts of disobedience will get you a bullet in the fucking head and no one, I mean *no one*, will ask questions. You hear me?"

Trapped in Steven's grip, Jack struggled to nod in agreement, fear showing across his face as it gently turned baby blue.

"Yeah," he moaned over the zombie's wails, the corpse growing aware of the activity just beyond its confines.

"Uh, guys," Allen muttered; his voice was distant as he stared off down the street. "Guys, they're coming!" he said louder as he raised his left hand, pointing down Adler Street.

Jack fell to his knees when Steven let go of his throat, Jack choking and wheezing for breath. Everyone else turned their attention down the street, towards the direction Allen was pointing.

They were greeted by a hellish sight as hundreds of zombies, comprised of varying stages of decomposition and a melting pot of all races, shapes, and sizes, poured into the street from the surrounding stores, banks and boutiques.

The zombies joined one another, creating a wave of rot that stumbled its way towards the shocked four.

The sight of so many undead made their previous scuffle with the undead small in the grand scheme of things. Together, the zombies moaned as one, their hoarse voices echoing into air as if it was created in part by one discordant choir.

"Oh, shit!" Steven yelled. The color drained from his face as he brought his rifle up to his shoulder. "Everyone, get ready to fall ba..."

His voice was lost as a loud crash startled them from behind, and the Thai booth exploded from within, sending the trapped zombie forward in a hail of wood splinters.

Olivia spun around to greet the closest attacker as it dug its yellow teeth into Jack's face.

"You fucker!" Jack screamed, flipping the zombie over his shoulder. The body hit the pavement with such force it caused it to spit up the chunk of Jack's cheek.

"Goddammit!" Jack screamed as tears filled his eyes, his own mortality underlining the anger in his voice.

Jack brought his foot down hard on the corpse's face as it struggled to get back to its feet; the dead recovered quick.

The zombie reached forward, and Jack kicked it again. As he exacted revenge, Steven, Olivia and Allen engaged the enemy in their own fight for mortality, shooting the zombies that quickly fell within their scopes.

They were surrounded from every angle, as the numbers of the dead continued to grow, drawn from the shadows by the moans of brethren and the never ending chatter of gunfire.

"I'm almost out of bullets!" Allen shouted, his words barely audible over the gun fire. "What do we do?"

That's a damn good question! screamed the little voice in Olivia's head. *What the hell are we going to do?*

Movement behind her pulled her attention back to see Jack as he continued his abuse against the fallen zombie. His hand was held tightly against his bloody cheek, as he yelled, "You son-of-a-bitch!" He fell to his knees and a fury of punching ensued. It all seemed next to useless but Olivia understood. Jack was a goner, as dead as the zombie before him.

"Olivia! Olivia!" the voice screamed.

She turned her attention towards its direction only to realize that the rifle shots had ceased, giving way to sounds of more moaning.

She turned in time to Steven and Allen dash into an antique store to the left of her position. Allen turned and waved for her to join them.

"Run!" he screamed, waving her onward.

She looked down the street towards the advancing horde to see she had seconds before they made their way to the store. She looked around in all directions to see that every connecting street was choked off by the hungry dead, all of which eyed her with vicious intent.

The hell with it, she thought, breaking into a full run. Behind her, Jack's remaining screams filled the air as he continued to pummel the corpse.

There were only a few zombies blocking her access to the antique store, but those were quickly dispatched as Steven and Allen laid down cover fire for her.

"Get inside!" they screamed as she ran past them, through the open door, and into the waiting darkness.

6

"Fuck you!" Jack screamed, repeating it over and over again as he brought his bare fists down upon the corpse's face.

The zombie had long since expired due to blunt force trauma to its brain, whether or not Jack was aware of this was another story. The only thing Jack knew was that *he* was already dead.

He was barely aware that his former comrades had abandoned him or that the gun fire had ceased. As he continued to reign down blow after blow, the corpse's face caved in and the skull cracked, falling inward on itself.

Suddenly, from out of nowhere, a blinding white pain ran through Jack's body as the first of the advancing dead reached him and sank their teeth into his exposed neck and arms.

He was pulled away from the destroyed zombie and into the gnashing jaws of dozens more. A dozen hands came forth to rip and tear at him as he kicked and screamed.

"Fuck you!" he screamed as blood dribbled from his mouth. "Fuck you all!"

At first, the zombies were content with the flesh around his throat and arms, but as it wore thin, they moved on to his legs and torso.

Those in the second and third row pushed forward, anxious for their turn at the human meat, and reaching out, they grabbed what they could, pulling bloody bits of Jack to their mouths.

When Jack finally died, the last thing he saw from beyond the ever growing darkness engulfing him was his arm as it was pulled from his shoulder.

His blood painted the ground red as one of the zombies reached their long nails underneath his shirt and into the cool wetness that lied within, tearing out his intestines, organs, and finally, his heart.

7

The others didn't see Jack die, but to say they didn't hear it happen was an understatement. His screams were that of a rabid dog being torn apart, violent and loud, ending as quickly as they started.

Olivia flinched at the dying man's cries, as she took shelter behind the front counter next to the cash register with Allen. Steven was somewhere in the front of the store, checking it for zombies, lost between the scuffed furniture and racks of dusty old clothes. They were lucky the building was empty. Steven had told them to get to the back, away from the windows, as he pushed some of the old desks to barricade the glass door, hoping to keep them safe.

Most of the zombies had been attracted to Jack, but many others had followed them to the store. They gathered outside the windows, watching Steven as he worked to keep them out, and many began to beat against the thick glass while others stood behind, watching with a childish wonder. All in all, hunger glowed in their dead eyes.

Steven knew the glass wouldn't last for long. Seconds or minutes, sooner or later it would break. He only hoped it would last long enough to buy them some valuable time to formulate an escape plan.

The building seemed to shake with every fist that beat against it. He only hoped that the store had a rear exit they could use.

* * *

"What are we going to do?" Olivia called as Steven hurried around the counter; he came to a stop, squatting next to her and Allen.

"Is there another way out?" he asked.

"Through there, I think," Allen replied, pointing towards a small, dusty purple curtain hanging from the ceiling a few feet behind them.

"All right," he said, "the glass in the windows won't hold for long, we gotta get out of here."

As if on cue, a thunderous crash snapped them to their feet as the first of the zombies crashed through one of the windows in a shower of glass to tumble to the floor. The first row of bodies was quickly trampled by the second row of advancing dead as they poured through the breach.

The three survivors jumped to their feet from behind the counter, as behind them, the zombies moaned with joy at the sight of their food magically appearing.

Olivia, Allen and Steven were running as the first of the ghouls reached the front counter. From outside, more of the zombies pushed their way through the broken window, knocking over priceless lamps and classic knickknacks as they stumbled through racks of dusty old clothes.

After crashing through the rear exit of the store, Steven struck the trash can hard, knocking it over with a metallic *clang* that echoed through the small alley.

"Keep going," he said, stepping over the trash can. The alleyway was a tight squeeze, allowing only one person to pass at a time. It had once been a connecting point for the rest of the stores on the block, but luckily, the other doors were closed, leaving it free of the walking dead.

They reached the gate at the end of the alleyway as the first of the dead filed into the opening behind them.

"You first," Steven said, pushing Olivia in front of him. Reluctantly, she agreed, clenching the iron bars tightly as she pulled herself up and over the gate to land hard on the other side.

They were in luck. There were no zombies in the immediate area. All of the noise and excitement had drawn them around the corner, towards the front entrance of the antique store.

The zombies were growing frustrated. In their attempts to reach their meal, they clogged the alley, making it impassible for the others behind them. Many of them were trampled as their undead brethren stepped over them, creating a wall that slowly crumbled as others joined the heap.

Allen was next. He pulled himself over the gate with little to no effort and Olivia helped him up as he fell forward. "Thanks," he said, dusting himself off.

As Steven climbed over, one of the zombies reached forward and grabbed his left pant leg. He kicked back, sending the zombie backwards into one another. He made it over the gate in once piece as the zombies trapped behind the gate continued to grow, smashing into it again and again. As they did, the constant pressure from so many bodies nearly ripped the gate off its hinges and in time it would collapse.

"Where are we gonna go?" Allen asked, his voice growing hoarse.

"We gotta get back to Oasis, there's no point in finishing the mission anyway, Steven said. "It's too risky with too little fire power." Getting to his feet as he spoke, he popped a fresh clip into his gun. Allen and Olivia nodded quickly as the dead bashed against the iron gate, seeing their meal escaping. Olivia looked at them, their pale, drawn faces pulled tightly between the bars, peeling back layers of skin and grime as teeth snapped at her.

It was then she realized that little voice in her head hadn't spoken to her. Perhaps it had grown weary of her failure to comply to it commands, or simply Olivia Prescott was already dead and just didn't know it yet.

8

It had been a busy day for both living and the dead. The zombies kept to the streets, possibly because they knew that a meal was to be had.

Allen, Steven and Olivia were left with the task of evasion as, they too, found themselves creeping in and out of the shadows that hid the undead.

"I didn't think it was going to be like this," Allen whispered as they crouched behind a small grouping of trash cans lining the corner of Pine Street and Oak. "Maybe shoot a couple of them, run in, grab the shit, and leave."

"It usually is," Steven said. "But then you got people like Jack that fuck the whole thing up. We could've been done by now."

Jack, Jack, Jack. Olivia thought to herself. He'd unleashed Hell on them all and for nothing more than his petty actions. For that she was glad he'd gotten what he deserved.

"We're gonna have to go back and regroup, 'cause we got a lot of people depending on us out here," Steven said, shaking his head in disgust. "Give it a day or so once we get back, rest up, then we'll head back. Follow through with it this time."

"At least you don't have to hear those racist jokes anymore," Allen said, hoping to break the gloom that had fallen over them. Steven eyed him with pity even though Allen was only attempting to find hope in a sea of hopelessness.

Olivia nodded in agreement before asking, "How are we gonna get back?"

"What do you mean?" Allen asked.

"If we go back the way we came, then we're going to be treading through undead territory," she said, shuddering at the thought of returning to the nightmare that they'd escaped from.

"She's right," Steven said, turning to Allen. "I don't know about you, but I ain't got shit for bullets. We might as well let them eat us now."

Silence fell over them as they contemplated their actions.

"How about this," Allen whispered. "We make our way down 1st and cut up through Chinatown?"

"That's a lot of ground to cover," Olivia said, horrified over the distance that the dead controlled.

"No, maybe he has a point," Steven said, pulling a small map out of his pocket. "Look," he said and pointed to their current position. "We can make it here," he said, tracing his finger down Pine Street, "through Skidmore and over onto 1st. I wouldn't count on the waterfront being too active; most of them seemed to migrate towards City Center when all the shit went down."

As they discussed their options, their hushed voices drifted through the air in all directions, falling upon dead ears lurking just beyond their location.

"Yes, but if we can make it to the waterfront, it'll bring us up by the train station," Olivia said. "And that place could still be crawling with them."

"Maybe, but we need to go somewhere. We can't stay here." When Steven replied, his words guided the zombies to them and as the three corpses pulled themselves to their feet, and they knew exactly where to go. Their throats had long since been torn out, preventing them from moaning and alarming the three survivors.

"So it's settled," Allen added. From behind, out of the shadows, the closest of the approaching zombies lunged forward, tightening their grip upon him.

He screamed in agony as the zombie dug its diseased teeth into his neck, pulling back skin and muscle tissue.

"Shit!" he screamed, sending his assailant backwards with a hard shove, flesh sticking out of the ghoul's mouth.

Olivia and Steven were taken by surprise. It happened so quickly neither of them had time to register Allen's attack until it was too late.

"Allen!" Olivia screamed.

Steven quickly dropped the zombie that attacked Allen, dropping it with a head shot that sent a shower of brain chunks across the pavement. Olivia fired twice at the approaching zombies, but each of her bullets failed to hit their target as her hand shook uncontrollably.

The little voice had returned, screaming bloody murder. *Run, you idiot, run!*

This time she listened.

She ran for her life while behind her, in between bursts of gunfire, Steven screamed after her, "Olivia, wait!"

She didn't pay any attention to him, and as her legs took over, she let her fears get the best of her. Her vision blurred with burning tears as the realization sank in—she was going to die.

All around her, the dead took to the street once again as they crawled from within buildings, behind the cars, and from the darkest recesses of her mind.

This is it, she thought, as the first of the dead managed to grab her foot, tripping her to the ground with such force that the air left her lungs. She cried out as the ghoul crawled its way towards her. Its jaws snapping as the scent of rot filled her nostrils, the urge to vomit rising.

The creature had once been a little girl, no more than seven. Her long blonde hair now hung in clumps of gore, long since dried. Blood and dirt coated her once pretty face, which now lacked emotion, her jaws snapping with rapid intent.

Olivia struggled for control. In a matter of seconds, her life flashed before her eyes, reminding her of her struggle to live.

How long was it since all of this happened?

She couldn't remember what life was like before the outbreak; had she come so far only for it to end like this?

Through her tears, Olivia yanked the girl's head back and away from her. Beneath the dry skin, the neck snapped as bone stabbed through decayed flesh, ripping the girl's throat, the wound torn open from ear to ear. The girl moaned loudly, loosening her grip around Olivia's throat, giving her enough leeway to throw the small corpse aside.

The girl's head hung grotesquely sideways as she crawled along the sidewalk towards Olivia.

"You're lucky," Olivia muttered. "You're already dead."

The zombies closed in, surrounding her from all sides. As they reached forward with mangled limbs and bloody stumps, she pushed forward, shoving and dodging all the bodies that stood in her way.

Not today, she told herself. *You don't die today.*

"Damn it!" she screamed, shoving a dead old lady aside, realizing she'd dropped her gun when the little girl had tripped her. *No use in crying about it now,* she thought as she moved forward.

The pale hands left putrid blood and dirt smeared across her face as their fingers brushed past, grabbing at the air she left in her wake.

The group of zombies slowly grew as the seconds progressed. Tightly bound, they formed a wall she found tough to break as she plowed through their ranks. Their moans built as she rounded the corner onto 4th Street, it was then that she spotted salvation, temporary looming ahead of bobbing heads in the shape of a telephone booth.

Her heart fluttered as she reached the phone booth. Flinging the doors open, she ran forward, slamming against the far side like a bullet against a brick wall.

The scent of untainted air hit her like a ghost from long ago, as she spun quickly around and slammed the door shut. She sighed, catching her breath with rapid gasps, to slide backwards against the wall, just as the tears broke forth.

The voice cheered her on. *You did it! You're safe!*

"But I left them behind!" she screamed as the first of the zombies reached the phone booth, slamming its undead hands against the glass door in protest.

But you survived, it replied, justifying her actions.

Outside the phone booth, the dead quickly multiplied, blocking out the surrounding buildings, and replacing them with nothing but more and more rotting bodies.

"At what cost?" she screamed, jumping to her feet. "I'm going to fucking die in here!" She slammed her fist against the glass of the booth, sending a shock of pain down her forearm.

She couldn't tell what she had become. Losing an argument with her own conscience, she knew deep down that living in a world of the walking dead had finally taken a toll on her sanity. Olivia looked through the glass of the phone booth. She gazed upon their pale faces, past their rotting exteriors, and saw them for what they really were, a release from the horrid reality that had befallen mankind before the uprising.

It was then something caught her eye. It was a word, no, a sentence, written on the brick facade of the building near the phone booth.

The words stared back at her as she studied the sloppy black lettering, running her hands across its surface.

The dead have come to cleanse the living.

As she read it, a burst of laughter erupted from deep within her as she fell back against the booth.

"It's true," she muttered as her tears burned her eyes. "It's true! They have..." she said before falling into a deep silence.

As she looked into their dead eyes, they looked back.

Somewhere overhead a gentle rain began to fall across the Portland sprawl, temporarily wiping the slate clean.

It'll get better, I promise, the voice said.

"I hope so," she whispered as she slowly drifted off into sleep, too exhausted to care about the banging of pale hands on the glass of the phone booth. "I truly hope so."

GONER

GERALD RICE

Terence had caught one in his trap. He supposed it was pointless to destroy it only to set the trap again to capture another zombie and destroy that one, too, but that kind of thinking was deadly. That kind of thinking got you bit.

You had to keep a routine to survive. Nothing crazy. Zombies were creatures of habit and if you could mirror that, then this place was survivable. He'd been here for the last three years, since they had overrun the city.

But the traps were a vice of his. He didn't need to capture them before destroying them. But he was just...curious. Who had they been? What had they done? How did they die? Only the last question was easiest to answer—a bite on the hand or arm, or a ripped out throat. The death wound was in most cases, obvious. Some had been mailmen, police, EMTs or delivery people, but most were indistinguishable by their clothes.

Terence picked up a box of something and dropped it into his sack.

A woman in a power suit could have been a lawyer or a single mother on her way to an interview. A man in jeans and work boots could have been in construction or an urban youth dressed how young men once dressed in his neighborhood. Terence watched the thing strung up in his net and coughed into his arm. He knew what she'd done for a living even before he saw the bite mark, the circumference of a fifty-cent piece on her wrist—she was a teacher.

He knew who she was, too—his ex-girlfriend.

The last time he'd seen Alice, she was dumping him. Terence might have wished her dead at the time. Now the thought seemed as ridiculous as the guilt he felt for having wished it.

There wasn't a hint of recognition in her eyes as she wasted her time clawing at the net. He'd made a habit of cutting them down after he'd finished watching them and bashing in their skulls with his hammer. He left it tucked into his pants and untied the rig, gently setting her down to the alley floor.

It was bad to stay in any one place, out in the open, for a lengthy period of time. But there had been a lot fewer of them lately, like they were heading south for the winter or something.

He spotted one at the end of the alley, shuffling *his* way toward them. No, not *his, its*. Alice wasn't an Alice anymore. She was just another corpse, reanimated by unknown means with the sole agenda of killing any living she could find.

She was moaning and he had to find a way to shut her up. It took some maneuvering and she still managed to nip the finger of his thick rubber glove, but he got a loop of the net around her neck and cinched it until she couldn't utter so much as a squeak anymore. He tied her arms to her sides, put a sack over her head, and moving her became much easier.

Well, not that easy. She thrashed and kicked, her foot caught him just above the eyebrow, and he saw stars for a moment. And either he'd gotten weaker over the years since he'd last been with her or she'd gotten heavier, because by the time he reached the end of the alley behind his house, his arms were shaking.

Terence put her down and just in time, too.

Two of them shambled out from behind a tree. They were both ripe, like they'd walked into a body of water and festered there for a while before getting out. The one on the left had no flesh on the right side of its body, and the one on the right had skin that looked all but ready to slide off.

"Were you guys at the pool party?" Terence asked, taking out the hammer and putting his sack down. He always wished he'd had something cool to say in times like these, but his comments always came out lame. He shouldn't be talking to them anyway; a living voice would only attract others within earshot.

He backed up, hoping the two would separate and give him a little more room to work, and almost tripped over Alice's legs. That should have been reason enough not to bring her home. The two zombies stayed shoulder to shoulder and Terence had to circle out into the street to put one before the other.

The loose-fleshed one pushed the other out of its way. Zombies didn't really work well with each other. If there were two arms for two zombies to chew on, half the time they would go for the same arm.

The one with half its skeleton showing stumbled and Terence leapt at it, delivering a kick high up on its chest. Its feet got tangled up and it fell. Terence landed in a crouch and circled away from the other one as it lunged at him. The zombie that had fallen was just getting to its knees when he swung the hammer, clipping it on the side of the head.

He'd found that head shots weren't as easy as he once thought. Zombies didn't just hold still. If they did then more than likely it would be easy to destroy them. The human skull is pretty thick and damaging the brain, most importantly the cerebral cortex and cerebellum was more difficult for Terence then he ever would have believed.

The zombie Terence hit fell over on its side, but immediately began to crawl back up. The loose one lunged at him again and grabbed his arm. Its finger bones pushed through its flesh, daggering into his arm through double layers of sleeve. Terence gave it a left hook, but it snapped at his hand after the blow as it tried to grab onto him with its other hand.

Terence brought his arm up and around its arm, breaking the grip and locking its elbow. This kept the zombie at arm's length while he transferred the hammer to his free hand. Terence brought it down over and over again until he realized he was now holding the corpse upright. He let it slump to the ground and gave the head a final kick for good measure.

The one with half its flesh missing was five feet away and attempting to shamble toward him, but it could only walk diagonally. Terence walked around to its skeleton side and it was unable to turn to face him. It kept walking farther away across the broken street, groaning as it tried and failed to correct its path.

There was an open sewer a few feet away. Terence grabbed its fleshless arm and pulled it back until its 'good' leg fell in the sewer and its knee snapped. It howled and thrashed in vain at the air until he smashed the side of its head with the hammer, thus severing it from the neck.

Terence tucked the hammer back into his pants, crouched low, and crossed back to the alley. Alice hadn't stopped thrashing, but at least she couldn't make any noise. A zombie from another alley emerged, but it shuffled south. Terence watched it from behind an overgrown weed sticking out between the cracks of two concrete slabs of sidewalk. Had Alice still been moaning, she would have led it right here.

Terence knew he was lucky. Even two weeks ago he would have had to fight four zombies with several more on the way. He looked up. The sky was nothing but white. Eventually those clouds were going to burst.

He scooped Alice up, slid his sack over his shoulder, and trotted down the alley leading to his house. The alleys were narrow and a zombie could easily be back there, waiting, but they provided cover as well. It was easier for him to hide from zombies, and when there were other survivors, they tended to look out front windows and so never saw him as he skulked about in the alleys and through backyards.

He was glad the city had gotten rid of the dumpsters years ago. Any number of zombies could be in there or worse yet, people who would spring out of a hidden area and kill you, or worse, wound and rob you and leave you stranded. He hadn't been caught yet, but he knew there were people who did that sort of thing.

Gladys, his scarecrow, was standing guard outside behind his next door neighbor's garage. He would have to replace her robe soon; it had gotten tattered and sun-bleached in the weather. Terence grunted at her and hefted Alice over his shoulder to open his gate. He'd found that by not locking the gate, other survivors wouldn't wonder if there was someone inside. Because that meant they had something to hide. Besides, he had traps all through the backyard that would catch anything that didn't belong.

He weaved through the yard and onto the back porch. All the yards were overgrown with weeds, reducing visibility. He knew the houses next to his were empty as he had set traps in both of them, but he still checked the windows. Arnold was there, waving blindly towards the alley, his bells tinkling. Terence pushed open the back door and looked to see there were no footprints in the sand he'd left on the floor. He didn't bother with cloths or strings wedged in the doorway; that would only fan the flame of anyone already intent on breaking in.

Terence crossed the threshold and laid Alice and his sack on the floor. He closed the door and peeked out the peephole a moment to make sure no one had snuck up behind him before brushing away his boot print. Alice was thrashing as much as ever and she had managed to get an arm free. He walked to the front of the house to see if anything had been disturbed. Nothing had.

He went back to Alice, and picked up the net by the end where her head was. Her hand fumbled and scratched at his sleeve and glove, but she wasn't getting through. He dragged her down to the basement to a rig he'd set up just in case he ever got interested in keeping a zombie for a while. He grabbed her arm and picked up one pair of handcuffs lying on an old wooden speaker doubling as a stand. He cuffed her wrist to a clip connected to two ends of a chain looped over a support beam of the low naked ceiling. He stood behind her and undid her other arm after cuffing it, placing his forearm beneath her chin to pin her body against him.

Once her other arm was secure, he went about putting the chains over her ankles. It was a lot harder as she only doubled her kicking once her arms were shackled above her head. She'd kicked him twice in the head–luckily she'd always worn soft-heeled, sensible shoes–before he had her feet secured to a concrete block.

He took off the hood and she snapped at his hand. Terence stared at her. He didn't know how well zombies could see but her eyes hadn't gotten that film yet, perhaps only dead for a few days.

"What happened to you?" he asked.

Her mouth was working, but no sound came out. He must have crushed her vocal cords. She had no business being in this area after they'd broken up. She didn't live here and didn't know any-body here.

Wait.

She still taught in the city. Kindergarteners, wasn't it?

Terence checked the single bite mark on her arm; about the size of a fifty-cent piece.

"Oh, no." He'd honestly never thought about it, probably because they were the first to die. But there had to be zombie children out there somewhere. But if she died a few days ago, that meant she had to have been in or around her school. Had she snuck in there recently or had she been there the whole time?

Terence took off his gloves as he went back upstairs. She had to have been there the whole time, but it didn't make sense for her to have gone back. There was nothing there. Maybe a few zombie children that were trapped in the school, but that was even more reason not to return.

Alice shouldn't be dead.

He checked between the cracks of the boards covering the windows. There was a single zombie ambling down the middle of the street. He went over to his chair and eased into it. His arm was sore, like he'd pulled something fighting the two by the alley. He promised himself he'd get some ice in a moment, but had slipped off to sleep within seconds.

The shaking chains woke him. It was dark again. He couldn't remember the last time he'd slept this long. He vaguely remembered a dream where there was an endless alley filled with zombies and he was armed with only an over-inflated basketball to fend them off, the entire time a woman just behind him whispering, "The children," over and over in his ear. He couldn't recall getting bit, but he had the growing feeling of them pressing ever closer as he could only hit them with that basketball to fight them off.

He hadn't slept for more than an hour in a long time, and as he stretched and checked his watch, he saw it was after nine.

"Time to do some work," he said, lifting himself off the chair with a low groan.

He went into the kitchen, took out a plastic freezer bag from the counter drawer, and pulled the freezer door open. He didn't question why electricity and water still ran, but he thanked whatever gods responsible for them, knowing sooner or later he knew it would finally stop.

Something scratched at the back door.

He turned and listened as another one was heard. He wondered about the dead's cognitive function at times. He'd seen a few stand at a door, as if waiting, but that didn't necessarily mean anything; he'd never seen one stand in front of a wall and try to push it open like it was a door. It stood to reason that on some distant level they understood what doors did.

The zombie began to groan.

Great, he thought. Once they had it in their heads they'd found food, they got persistent, and once they began making noise, they eventually brought company.

Terence peered through the peephole and saw the top of the zombie's head. In the creamy moonlight, he could just make out its face. It was a petite one that looked like it was about twenty or so before it died. He ran around to the living room to get a look at the porch. Just because only one was making noise on the porch didn't mean there weren't several others waiting just beyond it.

On the porch was a circular picnic table, two lawn chairs, and a sun umbrella.

He picked up a screwdriver and a claw hammer off the table and went to the back door. Pressing his ear against it, he listened.

The zombie groaned again. It was doing just enough to attract more attention to itself, but Terence needed it a little more excited.

"Who is it?" he asked as if a friend had just dropped by for a cup of coffee and a pastry. The zombie responded with a high octave grunt and he watched through the peephole as it lunged again at the door.

He yanked the door open and the body all but tripped its way inside. He stuck his foot out to help it along and the corpse went sprawling across the kitchen floor as he closed the door. Its head bounced off the linoleum, and before it could rise, he planted a shoe on its back, placed the screwdriver on the back of its neck, and hit it with the hammer like it was a giant nail.

The screwdriver went into its neck at an angle, the zombie turning its head sharply as it tried to snap at him. In his annoyance, Terence whacked it with the hammer, tearing open its cheek. The zombie's head bounced off the floor again and he yanked the screwdriver out and forced it back into the base of its skull, severing the spinal cord.

Finally it lay still, but Terence didn't breathe a sigh of relief. He stood and looked at his hands. They were bare. He'd completely forgotten to put his gloves on.

"Stupid-stupid-stupid," he muttered as he went to the sink. He put his tools in the sink and turned on the hot water. He cupped his hand and dumped a glob of liquid soap into his palm, then scrubbed. His heart raced. If he'd gotten a cut from hitting that thing...

Terence put his hands beneath the hot stream. It burned, but it was good. Let this be his lesson learned, not an infection. He made another vow not to be so careless in the future.

He flicked on the light and quickly checked his hands–nothing, no wounds. He turned the light back off. A few seconds was risky enough. He'd have to do something about Alice's chains. It was the most noise he'd ever had in the house since the outbreak. The noise might have attracted his friend on the floor and if so, more would be coming.

He put his gloves on and looked out the peephole again–it looked clear. He cracked the door open and stuck his head out–empty. Then he stepped out and looked out on the yard–all clear. He kept the door open and stepped back in, grabbed the corpse by its pants and shirt collar, hefted it, and took it out to the edge of the porch. His lower back screamed but he had to get it out of the house. He pitched it over the waist-high fence into the neighbor's yard and went back inside.

Once he was inside the house, he went back downstairs to check on Alice. She had rubbed a great deal of her pale skin off her wrists trying to get free of the handcuffs. He'd have to come up with something better otherwise she would eventually break her thumbs and have her hands free. Zombies were tenacious, relentless in their actions.

He found a thick towel and cut it in half. He dug out two large clamps out of his toolbox and went back to Alice. He had to put a sack over her head, but after wrapping her forearms in the towel and fastening them to the support beam overhead with some clamps, she was secure. He took off one of the handcuffs and tugged hard on her arm. No way would she be able to get out of that.

He took the hood off her and stared at her slack face. She was the most beautiful woman in the world, it was a wonder he'd recognized her like this. Her skin was a purple-gray and a good deal of her hair had fallen out. But the hazel, almond-shaped eyes were unmistakable.

Terence looked her up and down. She must have died recently as there was very little decay to her body. There were no broken bones, no giant gaping wounds, but her stomach was pretty big. He knew that was what happened when you died. He couldn't think of the reason why, but it was fluid that pooled in the stomach or something like that. Maybe he could poke a hole in her and let it out.

He ran upstairs and grabbed a knife and a big metal bowl out of the kitchen cabinet. He then returned and set the bowl down at her feet. He undid the first few buttons of her shirt from the bottom up and immediately saw new, black stitches coming from her belt line up to her breast bone. They were crude, hurried. And there was something hard inside her stomach.

He prodded it with his fingers. It was beginning to look more and more suspicious. Was someone using her as a mule? Were there others? He went back to his toolbox and pulled out the fishing line. Surprisingly, a needle was in there too. He wondered why he'd put that in there as he went back.

Before he started, he made another trip upstairs for his thick gloves. He wished he had a face mask for this as the smell no doubt was going to be terrible. He folded his turtleneck sweater over his lower face and began sawing at the stitches.

The smell hit him first before he saw the grayish dew seep out of her belly. It was slow going with the gloves on and he was half tempted to take them off to hurry up and get this done, but it would be too easy to nick himself and get the fluid in the wound.

He'd just crossed her navel when the fluid began leaking out of her stomach more freely. It soaked the front of her pants down to the knees of her inner thighs. He stopped to gag twice before all the stitches were out, and when he was through, most of the dark brown fluid was in the bowl.

He reached in and felt around. There was something in there that wasn't an organ and he grabbed it. To his surprise, he pulled out a jewelry box about the size of a baseball. He turned it over, wiping the top clean with his thumb. It was ivory white with the initials 'S.R.' engraved on it.

"Who gave this to you, Alice? And where were you taking it?"

Alice shook her head back and forth as an answer. A loop of intestine poked out of the wound so he pushed it back in.

He placed the jewelry box in the bowl and took it and the knife upstairs. He put everything in the sink and turned on the water with his forearm. After washing the gloves several times, he washed out the bowl and everything else. There was a tinge of death in the air, but it would fade in time.

Once back downstairs, he threaded the fishing line through the needle and put his gloves back on. It would be difficult to sew her back up, especially since she was constantly moving, but he wasn't about to risk sticking himself. He took off a glove and used that hand to thread the wound closed.

Between his trembling hand and Alice's thrashing, he was surprised when he managed not to stick himself. He pricked the glove several times, but it was thick enough to protect him. He'd almost caught his finger twice when her writhing body yanked the needle out of his hand, and when he was finally done, his sutures were impressive. The light blue fishing line barely showed and he'd managed to sew up the two ends of the wound to look like there was barely a scar.

There was a mirror on the shelf behind him and he used it to show her the stitches.

"See?" he said. "Just like new again."

Alice lunged, her teeth clapping together a few inches in front of the mirror.

Odd, zombies never attacked each other directly, he thought. Did she know this was her reflection on some level? Did she hate being dead?

Another topic to be tossed on the ever growing pile since the dead had risen. Still, it might be good to let her get some of the aggression out. Terence found a wire hanger on the floor, unraveled it, and tied it through the loophole in the handle of the mirror, then around one of the exposed copper pipes in the low ceiling. He let the mirror hang in front of her as she continued drawing back and lunging for it over and over again. It was as if she had forgotten he was there.

He watched a few minutes then went back upstairs. He was tired again and thought he would try to get some sleep.

* * *

He still didn't sleep well over the next few days, but it was still considerably better than in the past two weeks. He attributed that to Alice being in the house. He kept checking on her and studied her watching the mirror. He found she had developed an alternating habit of deep curiosity where she would pull as close to the mirror as she could, to then fall back into mindless thrashing as she tried to attack her reflection again.

On the third day, he awoke with a fever.

"Oh, no," he groaned at the mirror, the portent of doom filling him to his very core. He put his fist into it and shards of regret penetrated his knuckles. Terence spent the next hour and a half plucking small, razor bits of glass out of his fist and then dressed the wound.

How could he have been infected? Maybe from one of those two in the alley when he was bringing Alice home. He could have gotten some of their blood in his eye. Maybe even the one trying to break in the back door.

No, it wasn't from them. He was careful with the first one, and the second time he checked himself for cuts or scrapes but had found none.

Surprisingly, other than his initial outburst, he wasn't scared. He'd been here a long time and survived several situations unscathed. He didn't actually *hate* zombies, and in a way, they were the closest things he had to friends. There was no malice in his actions against them; he was simply surviving.

But no way was he going to become one of them. He had the .22 for that.

His mother had kept the handgun in the utensil drawer when he was a teenager. She had bought it for safety and had then promptly forgotten it in the back of a drawer. Terence had snuck it into his room and hidden it behind a panel in the wall.

When he had finally made his way back home after the outbreak had begun, he'd taken it out and placed it back in the drawer. No need to hide it anymore. It was one of the first things he thought of when he got to the house after he found a fistful of bullets in the cup holder of an abandoned car.

So no, he wasn't worried about himself but his mind went back to Alice.

"What were you doing out there?" he asked her again after an extensive coughing fit. He wiped the grayish phlegm on a dirty rag and tossed it on the floor. She was paying only her reflection attention, calm this time.

Terence stared at her a few moments, pondering his future. His mind kept creeping back to what her last few days must have been like, and where she'd been. She didn't know anybody from the city; her family was from Ohio. She was either going to her old school to seek companionship from fellow humans or she'd been there all along. He supposed there were other possibilities, but these two were the ones that made any sense. He looked at the small bite mark on her arm; just above the bend on her bicep. It was about the size of a quarter.

She'd been bitten by a child. She was unharmed, well, other than the fact that her belly had been sliced open and stuffed with valuables for some reason. No gunshot, stab wound, torn throat or broken bones. A child had infected her.

But there were never any children about; at least he never saw any. Maybe she'd found one in a building; at her school.

But as slow as zombies were, how could a child-sized one get her?

Perhaps that child had snuck up on her and the child was infected but hadn't turned.

Maybe there were other children.

He could imagine her taking care of them; venturing outside to forage for supplies. Then one of them slips outside for some reason and gets attacked by a zombie. She would have let the child back in, treated him, and cared for him in the hopes he wouldn't turn. She wouldn't know how the infection worked and that child turning and biting her on the arm would have come as quite a shock.

Maybe she understood after that and she wanted to be as far from the children as possible. She would have gone as far away from them as she could have before the infection turned her, too.

She wasn't too far from his mother's house when she'd gotten caught in his trap. Had she been heading to his house?

Alice was caring enough for him to believe that any of it was possible, and even if he was completely wrong, he needed to find out. His life didn't matter anymore. He would turn, too, eventually.

If he found the children he would make sure they were safe, that nothing could get inside and reach them. If they had turned, hard as it would be, he would destroy them. If it were too unsafe for them to stay at the school, then he would find someplace else if there was time. If there he ran out of time, then he would make sure nothing would get them—including him.

Terence wasted no time. He took a shower and checked himself over as best he could for cuts—none were visible. The shower also helped lessen his scent. He believed zombies maintained a sense of smell and not having oily, smelly skin in combination to the cool air would make him invisible to most of the zombies he would come across. Terence would deal with the ones who saw him like he always did.

He'd come across some antibiotics a few months ago, but they were on the verge of expiration. He took them out of the refrigerator and shot up a dose of both bottles from a bag of syringes found in his mother's closet. She'd been a diabetic and thankfully his brother hadn't cleaned out her room. Terence wondered what happened to his brother, why the house seemed long abandoned when he had arrived, well before any of this had begun.

He prepared his backpack; various jerkies, a few corn muffins, stale but still sealed in plastic wrap, and a bottle of water. He grabbed a pack of M-80s, his mini toolkit and stuffed them in with an extra pair of sneakers. He put in the .22 with the bullets in a plastic bag. He didn't want to load yet. Then he checked his flashlight.

Flashlights brought unwanted attention, as someone using one was easy to spot in the darkness, but he knew it might come in handy. He put it in and zipped up the pack. He put a small knife in his back pocket along with a cigarette lighter and a half-used book of matches. He didn't know what he would need and what would be unnecessary, but he wanted to be as prepared as possible.

He strapped on a belt and hung his weapons on it; his hammer, and a machete. There was a short baseball bat on the kitchen table that would go with him, too.

He peeked outside and saw nothing as he felt cool sweat trailing down his back. Even this much activity was taxing now that he was sick. He would have to walk swiftly instead of running and hope for the best about being spotted by the dead.

He opened the door and stepped outside. It was cooler than the last time as winter was raring to go. He cinched the pack on his shoulders and walked down the stairs. He walked his zigzag pattern through the yard until he reached the back alley.

Wait—someone was coming.

He heard the motorcycle moments before it passed and ducked low behind an old tree stump cut off at knee height. If the person driving by had looked over in his direction, he would have seen the back of Terence's head and upper back, but the rider never slowed.

Terence poked his head up, checking both ways to see if it was now clear. The alley was so overgrown with weeds that he was surprised the biker was brave enough to drive down it. Zombies could be fast in close quarters.

He crossed the alley into an abandoned lot between two houses. One of the homes had been burned extensively. It was a shame the neighborhood had come into this state of disrepair *before* the dead began to walk. He was halfway through the lot when he heard the whining engine of the motorcycle from the street ahead. There was no place he could duck or hide.

Terence knelt like he was tying his shoe. The rider came into view and stopped directly in front of him. He turned his helmeted head, and for a moment, Terence wasn't sure where the rider was looking, then the motorcycle helmet came off.

Brown locks fell from the helmet and from where Terence was, he could see the man's dark green eyes. He had a sharp nose and a youthful-looking face.

"Hi, there, it's good to see another living soul," the man said as if they knew each other. Terence had never seen him before. He put a hand up and cranked a finger for Terence to come closer. "Relax, I won't hurt you...much anyway," he sneered.

Terence moved closer hoping he might be able to talk himself out of this situation.

"What are you doing out here, man? It's dangerous." He looked around, as if checking for approaching zombies.

"I'm just looking for supplies," Terence lied. "I've been on the move. I just came from downtown."

"Downtown? Man, that's crazy? Nobody comes from downtown anymore. Downtown's 'Meat Central'."

"I stick to the alleys." Terence wanted the subject off him.

"What you got in that pack?"

"Nothing, some old clothes," Terence lied, changing the subject. "So how'd you find a motorcycle that works?"

"'Cause I'm *me*," he said. "Now who are *you*?"

"Name's Terence. You?"

"I'm Griff, now don't move and you won't get hurt too bad," he said and pulled out a two-way radio from inside his jacket and spoke into it. "Finch, I'm at the old lot on Madison, I found someone; get the others and get over here, pronto."

He was rounding up the troops. Terence knew he had to get going before more people arrived. Griff smiled at him and Terence saw he had perfectly straight, white teeth. The man put the motorcycle up on its kickstand, leaning it to the side as he sat.

Terence looked up and down at the houses around him. Most of the houses were intact. If he could subdue Griff he could reach one and hide out till Griff and his friends left. They'd get bored and leave before dark if they were smart. He wouldn't be surprised to see them in the moonlight, that's when the zombies came out in greater numbers.

"Don't do it, man. We gotcha. We just gotcha." Griff said, seeing Terence looking around at the closer homes. He reached to his side to fish something out. Terence swatted the arm and Griff yelped, off balance. Terence whacked Griff's hand with his bat and felt the satisfying crunch of a knuckle being dislodged.

Griff howled in pain and Terence gave him a shove. Griff and the motorcycle fell over and Griff was pinned under it, his leg trapped.

Terence didn't wait around but ran across the street, between two houses and into a backyard. He heard more motorcycles come around the corner and crouched behind some trashcans to make himself smaller.

Terence heard two voices but couldn't make out what they were saying.

"He went over there somewhere!" Griff shouted. "Just search for him! I want him found!"

His heart raced. Not ten minutes out of the house and he was already being hunted. No wonder he hated people. It was fitting that he would be killed by the living as he would be a zombie soon enough if he didn't finish himself off first.

"Hey!" a voice whispered. "Over here!"

He turned and saw a teenage girl looking out the back door of the house of the yard he was in.

"Hurry!" she whispered. "Before they see you!"

Terence looked in all four directions. He could hear the rustle of boots in the dead vegetation, a benefit of winter. He turned around and ran up the back steps and through the door. The girl shut the door and locked it. He hoped they didn't try this house or else they'd be caught.

"You can stay here. My daddy won't mind..." she began.

"Shhh," he hissed. She was barely on the other side of womanhood. Not quite pretty, but not ugly either. She would blossom into a beautiful woman someday if she lived long enough. She wore a white t-shirt and a tan skirt with white fringe.

Terence moved her away from the door and into the center of the kitchen. The layout to the house was a mirror to his.

"Daddy will let you stay here." She shook her head. "He's sleeping now but he'll be up soon and you can meet him."

Terence didn't want to waste time now that he was sick. He kicked himself that he hadn't been able to set out in the morning as it would be dark soon. That would be the absolute worst time to travel. Hopefully, Griff and his gang would realize this and leave.

"Window?" he asked.

She guided him to the front room and the corner of the third window on the left. They were covered in cardboard and tape, but one corner had the tape peeled up. Terence got on his knees and peered out.

He got a good look at Griff and one of the other riders standing next to him, a burly dark-skinned man with no sleeves on his shirt and fingerless leather gloves. He wouldn't last long out there dressed like that, Terence thought. Looking tough didn't stop the infection when he became bit. Griff was dusting himself off and shaking his injured hand. Terence smiled—he'd given him a good crack.

The big one pointed between the two houses; maybe they'd seen him duck into the yard or the third one had gone that way after him. He gripped his bat, realizing he was hoping for the chance to hit someone with it. But he knew that now wasn't the time to be foolish. He put the bat back in the side pocket of his pack, where a water bottle could have gone. It was the perfect holder for it.

Terence watched and listened for what felt like ten minutes, but was only a few seconds, until the third one came back; a skinny white guy who towered over the other two. He had on the same fingerless leather gloves, but his heavy coat went down to his knees.

All three looked up, examining the darkening sky before climbing onto their motorcycles. They rode off, but Terence had a feeling he'd be seeing them again. At the end of the day, it was a small town.

"Lemonade?" the girl asked and Terence jumped; he wasn't used to being around people.

"Uh, yeah, thanks." He took the glass from her. A tinge of guilt spread through him, the glove still on his hand, like he was being rude somehow. It didn't bother her, though. She whirled about and headed back to the kitchen. He took a sip and then found himself tipping the glass back, drinking greedily.

The tail end of the drink was bitter-tasting and cloudy. She was in the kitchen, setting out plates while she hummed something and Terence began to feel dizzy. He'd been drugged. What did she put in it? He yanked off a glove and stuck his finger down his throat. The lemonade came back up, splashing onto the brown shag carpet. He did it a few more times, dry-heaving as his stomach emptied, before taking the pack off and getting the water bottle. He took a swig and swished his mouth out and then drank some down.

"I don't think that'll work," the girl said. She had a stack of plates in her hand.

"I'm sick—why would you poison me?"

"Not poison. Sleeping pills. I want you to stay. I don't want to be alone."

Sleep was the last thing he needed. He'd probably die if he slept as the infection would overtake him in that time.

She was standing next to the basement door and he heard something on the other side bump into it. The chain lock—similar to hotel doors—on the door held, but pale fingers reached out through the crack.

The girl turned her head and cried happily, "Daddy!"

Terence climbed to his feet. It was obvious from the state of his fingers that 'Daddy' was dead. Let the girl fall victim to her own devices. He headed for the back door, intending to push past her, when the basement door burst open and several 'Daddies' filed out, blocking his escape out the back door. He could only see a sliver of what was going on as the basement door blocked the majority of his view and more and more poured out of the doorway.

The girl dropped the plates.

"Daddy, I was good. I was good. I just don't want you to go outside. It's not safe out there. No, Daddy, no, *Daddy*!"

Terence's stomach lurched. He didn't know if it was the lemonade or the thought of what was happening to her. Maybe if he was quiet, they wouldn't know he was there.

Too late. One of them turned and looked right at him with milky eyes. The stairs were just ahead, next to the basement door. Terence dashed to them, almost eye-to-eye with the zombie as he passed the door. It reached out and barely missed him, yanking the bat out of his pack as it tried to grip his arm.

There was the sound of heavy footsteps behind him but he didn't turn to look. He had to find a way out of the house as quickly as possible. If there were only a few, he could probably take them— kick them downstairs until they were broken and unable to get back up again. But there might be a lot of them and if that was the case, it would only be a matter of time before they overwhelmed him.

She must have been keeping them down there, but why? he wondered.

No time to think about that. Upon reaching the top of the stairs, he found a small hallway with three closed doors. Before he grabbed the first knob, his vision began to spin. What was left of the drugged lemonade still in his system was getting to him. He shook it off. If he was going to faint, he needed to reach a secure place; maybe the roof.

He noticed there was an upstairs deck when he was outside. He tried the doorknob on his left but it was locked. Several footsteps were stomping their way up the stairs. He tried the door directly in front of him. It opened and he saw a bunk bed and scattered items covering the floor.

He raced to the windows and opened up the blinds; they were boarded up except for a hole smaller than his fist. There were two other doors in the bedroom, a closet and the attic access. He couldn't risk getting trapped, but if the third bedroom had its windows boarded up, too, he would be.

He dashed back into the little hall and hid by the banister as the first zombie was coming up. He waited until it was near the top, spun out and kicked it in the chest. The zombie lashed out at his foot but was already tumbling backwards.

He knew it would only buy him a little time, but hopefully that was all he'd need. He took out his hammer and went into the third bedroom. He leapt back from the still form on the bed, but realized it was a dead body—an actual dead one. It was desiccated and withered, the skin resembling dried leather. Terence opened the window shades and his heart skipped when he saw more wood.

But the far window wasn't boarded up completely. A television and stereo system on a dresser were in front of the window. Before pushing them over, he closed the bedroom door and pulled the bed away from the wall. He moved behind it and pushed it over to the door just as the first fist pounded on it.

Terence dumped the TV and stereo system on the floor like it was nothing but trash and pushed the dresser and stand out of the way. The wood over the window looked strong, but when he kicked it, his foot went through and knocked the slats to the ground below. He tried to kick out a higher section but sent a shock up his shin and into his thigh when his foot bounced off the heavy two-by-four.

The opening still wasn't big enough for him to squeeze through.

Whether by luck, intelligence, or a remembered instinct, the zombies on the other side of the door managed to turn the knob and were now trying to get in. Terence shoved his weight against the bed and it slammed the door closed again. He figured he could use his hammer to knock out the rest of the wood from the partially uncovered window; he just needed time to do it.

He took out his hammer, holding it in one hand and the hammer in the other, then prepared to go to the window.

He waited for the zombies to push at the door again. When they did he pushed it back closed and dived for the window. He beat furiously at it, knocking away pieces of wood as the zombies pushed the door open an inch at a time. Terence could hear them behind him, climbing onto the bed, and knocking the desiccated corpse to the floor.

Finally, the hole was big enough for him to fit. There was no time to look behind him to see how close they were, but it couldn't have been more than a few feet, their moans making him feel as if they were only inches away. He ducked through the window as one pale hand reached for his neck, but then he was gone and it missed. Terence slid a few inches down the sloped roof, losing the hammer over the edge as he grabbed onto the shingles to keep from falling. It wouldn't do to survive the zombies only to drop off the roof and have a leg broken in the fall.

A single zombie peered out the window at him, its face only three feet away. Then the first one placed its hands on the window sill and began climbing out onto the roof. Terence got to his knees carefully and stood as the first one poked its head out and he whacked it twice with the hammer. The zombie fell, only to be replaced by another a second later. He'd never thought about it before, but this was a fantastic position to defend himself. It didn't matter how many came through, they were bottlenecked and could only emerge one at a time. He could destroy each as they started to come out or wait until they were on the roof and dispatch them just as easily. Zombies had terrible balance and he could either crack their skulls or just push them off the roof.

But he couldn't forget the promise he'd made to find out what happened to Alice. He needed to get moving but first he had to get off the roof without breaking his legs. In the cool air, he could feel his thin t-shirt clinging to him with sweat. He was in better shape than this; the virus must have been eating away at his immune system.

He looked around at the other houses. They were close enough and had roofs he could leap onto, but what was inside them? He figured his best bet would be to climb down the gutter.

A zombie had crawled out while he wasn't looking and was on all fours. He stepped over and put his shoe on its side and shoved. It scrambled helplessly at the shingles before pitching over the edge and landing with a crunching thud.

Another one looked at him from the window, its body half out. It had chunks of its face missing, the muscle black and seeping pus. Its tongue hung freely out from its jawless mouth, a choice few upper teeth still there. Terence turned away and climbed onto the upper tier of the roof.

He now had a better view. He looked out into the backyard of one of the adjacent houses and spotted a pool. It was close enough to the house to try and he smiled.

Another zombie began climbing up the roof. Terence stepped close enough to reach it and lifted his foot as it tried to grab at him. Other than the wind nipping at his ears, it was too easy. He brought his foot down on the top of its head and it disappeared off the roof. He heard it crashing onto the lower part and then a moment later came a ragged thud as it landed hard on the ground.

Terence walked to the side and gently slid off onto a narrow, lower tier of the roof. The tier on the other house was just as narrow. This was going to have to be as precise as he could make it. He took a deep breath and bent at the knees, preparing to jump, when a small hand grabbed his ankle.

Terence screamed in surprise and threw his arms in the air. The hammer landed on the roof and rolled away to be lost somewhere below.

"Please don't leave me," the girl pleaded.

He turned and looked at her. He should hate her, should break her arm, slit her wrist, but he only pitied her, so he took her hand. She was only a kid, with no one to look after her and now she was doomed. There were several fresh bite marks on her arms and a large chunk of flesh was missing from her right elbow. Her skin was pale; no doubt she was fading fast.

Maybe killing her would do her a favor.

He didn't know how she had survived this far or why they hadn't torn her apart.

"Barricade the door," he told her. "If you have any blankets, wrap yourself up. Keep warm. Sterilize those wounds. Use alcohol if you have it; fire if nothing else. I'll try to bring back help for you."

He realized the words flowed out of him with no intonation. He didn't like lying and he was sure he didn't do it well, but he couldn't tell her she was about to die. It would be very painful, and it wouldn't be quick.

She let go of his hand and withdrew her arm, then slid back down and into the window.

"Go on then, just leave me." Her voice was flat, like she was disappointed.

There was nothing more he could do, but he felt guilty just the same.

A zombie that had managed to climb out onto the roof before the girl did moaned at him from his side.

"Hey, over here!" Terence called. The creature bent its head, looked at him, and leaned over as it tried to grab him with outstretched hands. It lost its balance, tipped over, and fell, catching the back of its head on the roof on its way down. Terence peered over the edge and saw it was still, its legs broken, its neck snapped and now at an odd angle.

He looked for the girl, but she was gone. He didn't dare say anything as it would only come out hollow in his ears. There wasn't anything he could do to make it better, she was dead already, she just didn't know it.

He readied himself to jump again. There was only room for one big step and then he'd have to jump across. He counted to three, took the step, and threw himself across.

He clawed and kicked at the air until he landed with both feet on the other roof. He stumbled into the side of the other house, bounced, and for a terrifying second thought he'd fall off until he caught himself.

It was almost dusk as he climbed up to the upper tier of the roof to feel around under muted moonlight as the sky filled with clouds. He hoped it wouldn't rain.

By the time he found a window he could get into easily without breaking glass and alerting anything inside, there were three zombies on the other roof. They stared at him, mewling like lost animals. The one in the middle bumped one of the others and it threw its arms out to catch its balance but went tumbling down the shingles.

There were more on the ground now, attracted to all the noise. He could hear them scratching and moaning. They knew he was on the roof. It was a great position to defend himself, but also a death trap. He would need food and water eventually. He was like a cat chased into a tree by a dog.

He was going to have to move fast. He had the feeling Griff and his gang of two others were still in the area.

He slid down to the lower tier of the roof as quietly as possible. He peered over the edge and couldn't see anything but the pool. He could just about step off the roof and land in it. He tossed his backpack to the side so that it landed on the yellow grass, missing the pool and thus not getting wet.

He turned his back to the edge, standing up. Though his heart was in his throat, he let himself fall; the wind whooshed past him before he connected with the water.

Landing feet first, he went straight down, his feet touching the leaf-caked bottom of the pool. As soon as he felt the bottom, he kicked off, rushing up to the surface. He ignored the yellowish-green tinge to the water and the floating rodents and began to swim to the ladder.

Behind him, the zombies began to file into the yard as he struggled to swim to the edge of the pool.

Terence climbed onto the deck surrounding the pool and lost his footing, the side of his face striking the flagstones. He could feel the blood begin to stream down his cheek and was suddenly cold as the air touched his wet body. Even though the wound bled freely, he knew his chill wasn't from the blood loss. His body was beginning to shut down and the dunk in the foul water of the pool wasn't helping. At this rate, he'd never make it to the school.

He picked up his backpack, hobbled to the back gate, dripping water the entire time, and peered out into the alley. It looked empty so he hopped over. It was getting darker by the minute so he had even less time to waste.

"There he is!" a voice yelled and a light struck him in the face, temporarily blinding him.

He couldn't tell which one of Griff's men had spotted him, but he had to escape fast. The man was midway down the alley and coming closer. Terence ducked back over into the yard, keeping an eye on the zombies just as they were passing the pool. Two fell in and promptly sank to the bottom. They flailed about but seemed to be unharmed.

He crossed the yard, avoiding the first zombie and hopped the fence between the next two houses. He ran across the yard then climbed over another fence. He knew he couldn't keep this up. Even if he wasn't sick, it was just a matter of time before the man caught up to him.

There was an old garage in the new yard. He tried a side door for pedestrian traffic and it opened. Terence stood and listened a moment. Nothing moved inside, but that didn't mean the place was empty.

"Whoa!" he heard from two yards over. The man must have run into his other, undead pursuers. Terence stepped inside, the door creaking shut behind him. He went on one knee, his fists curled tightly, shaking a little.

"He had to go this way," the man said, jogging past the garage. He waited for a few minutes, then heard the same voice cry out in pain. But he didn't check, wondering if it was a trap of some kind. When he thought it was safe, he peeked outside and saw the zombies still milling around in the yard. They hadn't figured out how to get the gate open. There was a small worktable in the corner of the garage and he went to it. He found assorted tools and a hammer similar to the hammer he lost, so he picked it up, liking the way it felt. Then he exited the garage and looked around its far side. The big man was lying in the middle of the alley. He was either dead or unconscious.

Terence went through the gate, his head on a swivel as he looked for danger. There was a break in the clouds, and he could see the man in the pure moonlight, its pale light bathing the alley in its luminance.

The underside of the man's arm was torn up and bleeding. He lay unconscious on his stomach. Terence went to him slowly, ready to run if it was a trick, and when he reached him, he nudged him onto his back with his foot and saw the huge knot on his forehead

He suspected this man was one of the people who had sewn the jewelry box into Alice's stomach and they had probably done it to other zombies, too. And on top of that they were hunting him.

"Whip, we're almost there," the walkie on the man's hip squawked. "You got 'im yet?"

Terence leaned over and took it off him.

"Whip!" the voice yelled.

He wanted to say something, but decided to wait. Instead he dug a tiny vial out of his pack filled with a dark fluid, courtesy of Alice. Terence popped the cap and poured half the contents on the man's bleeding arm and half in his mouth. It was dirty pool, but if anyone deserved it, it was this guy and his buddies.

Satisfied he had gotten some justice for Alice, Terence hopped the fence into the next yard. It was filled with thick trees, overgrown bushes and weeds. He ducked down low; the man's friends were coming.

A moment later and he heard Griff and Finch climb off their motorcycles. They left them running. Terence wished he knew where Whip had left his. It would save a lot of energy and time if he could steal it. It was full dark now.

"Whip, what the hell are you doin', man?" Griff spat. "Get the hell up!"

Terence could hear light slapping as Griff whacked Whip's face and a moment later Whip groaned.

"What the hell happened? I thought you had him," Griff said.

"I did. I thought...ow, my head," Whip moaned.

"Yeah, *and*?" There was another slap, much harder and Whip groaned again.

"I was running down the alley and I... I tripped."

"You gotta helluva bump on your forehead." That must have been Finch, Terence thought. "Hey, look at your arm, man, it's bleedin'."

Terence couldn't make out what was said next, but it sounded like Griff was swearing. All three men were silent for a moment.

"What, am I cut?" Whip finally asked.

"Yeah, maybe, it might be a bite, but we can bandage it when we get back home."

Whip was helped to his feet and the men left, their motorcycles roaring off into the night.

Terence rose as quietly as he could from his hiding place and backed away. He bumped into something—a trash can—and a tiny yelp slid out of his mouth but the zombies couldn't hear it over all the noise they were making. He began to move, sticking to the darkest shadows of the night.

The next hour passed uneventfully. He saw lone, shuffling figures in the distance, but kept up a brisk pace the zombies couldn't match. He noticed there were fewer zombies around than he'd seen over the past two weeks ago. He'd felt like this was the calm before a storm. Occasionally, he heard something that sounded like a motorcycle, but he didn't see Griff and his gang.

Terence had reached Colorado Street before he ran into any real difficulty. Several school buses were blocking him from crossing Colorado. He didn't think too much of it; he'd just go between two houses. But that proved to be more difficult when the first few houses had razor wire strung up between them. The last one he checked still had a zombie stuck in the wire. When he moved closer to investigate, he saw that it had been killed by a bullet to the forehead.

Somebody in one of those houses wanted to keep the zombies away, so it was a good sign of living humans.

His feet hurt and he was sweating buckets. Plus, his cheek was killing him and the pain was throbbing into his eye. He figured he should go into one of the houses and use the bathroom, with the aid of a mirror, he could sew up his cheek and maybe find some aspirin for his splitting headache.

Besides, the short rest would do him some good.

The front door of the second house was unlocked but someone had pushed something heavy against it, or at least, something heavier than he was capable of moving right at the moment. The first floor windows still had the glass intact, but the second house over didn't, telling him it was probably vacant or crawling with zombies. Terence stuck his foot inside the door and pushed harder, the couch and end table sliding across the carpeted floor with infinite slowness. When he had just enough room to slide inside, he entered, closing the door behind him.

He didn't want to get trapped in another house so he moved the couch away from the door. By the time he was through, he was breathing heavily and sweating profusely.

It smelled like urine and old paper and Terence took out his flashlight and held it at waist level with the beam aimed at the floor. He didn't want to be seen walking around the first floor as he checked to see if it was clear. The bathroom was on the second floor and he went to the stairs and slowly climbed them.

He swept the two bedrooms first, and then knowing he was alone, he went to the bathroom, glad to see that the mirror was fully intact over the bathroom sink.

Placing the flashlight on the edge of the sink, he examined his cheek to see it was a good two inch gash. Searching the small bathroom, he found hydrogen peroxide under the vanity. With the corner of his shirt, now mostly dried from his jump into the pool, he began wiping at the cut until the crusted blood was off. Fresh jabs of pain made his eye water as foam bubbled in the wound.

He sterilized the needle with a cigarette lighter and commenced sewing up his face. When he was finished, he realized he hadn't checked behind the shower curtain and cursed his carelessness.

Terence spun around, the needle and thread dangling from his face. He reached out and pulled the shower curtain aside to find nothing but a filthy tub. There was about an inch of black water in it, but he didn't care to investigate further.

"Hey, who's been in here?" someone called from downstairs.

Terence cut the flashlight off and snipped the fishing line. He wasn't done with the stitching, but it would have to do. He held still, hoping whoever it was would just pass through.

"I dunno, but I gotta take a leak," another voice said. Someone was coming up the stairs in heavy boots. Terence grabbed his things, stepped into the tub, and slid the shower curtain closed as quietly as possible. He stood immobile as the man burst into the bathroom.

"How you doin', handsome?" the man said as he looked into the mirror. He didn't notice or didn't care about the blood in the sink from when Terence was cleaning his wound.

The hairs on the back of Terence's neck stood up. He slowly slid the .22 out of his pocket. His hand was shaking so much he thought he might miss even at this range. His nose began to tickle as his sinus leaked, but he didn't dare wipe it as the man might hear him moving.

He was burning up and freezing at the same time. Like his core temperature was rocketing, but he was wrapped in a thick blanket of ice. It was the fever, but if he could just get out of the house and back outside it would be tolerable. But he couldn't get a full breath of air as he stood in the confines of the bathtub.

Whatever Terence was standing in began to soak into his already damp shoes. His head swam and whatever the man was saying became a blur. This was it, he was either going to faint or have to shoot the man and then faint. It was over. At best Terence could kill one man, but the other one downstairs would then kill him.

Kill him; that's what you did to zombies. And Terence was about to join them. He shifted on unsteady feet, gripping the gun tighter in his sweating palm and trying to steady himself.

"Hey, Griff, how's Whip doin'?"

Oh, no, this was their home? he thought.

Terence paused, ice pouring onto the fiery pit inside him. For a moment, his vision cleared and his hand steadied. Then the man left the bathroom, humming a tune as he went. Seconds later, the sound of heavy footsteps going down the stairs came to him.

He grabbed onto the shower curtain, slowly falling over the lip of the tub to rest on the floor. A throbbing rose in the back of his brain and crested to just beneath the top of his skull. He pulled his knees up to his chest, unable to do anything but ache. This really was it for him.

He could hear the voices of the men downstairs as they talked and laughed, but Terence was so exhausted he couldn't keep his eyes open. Though he knew he needed to leave, he told himself he would rest for a few seconds, just close his eyes for a couple of heartbeats.

Before he realized it, he was in a deep, sickness induced sleep.

When Terence woke up, it took a moment for him to realize the grunting voice in the background was him. He peeled his face off the floor. His head felt like it had split open, the pain radiating into the back of his eyes.

The fever was gone.

As soon as he felt it coming on, he had automatically assumed he was infected. He'd come into contact with the dead often enough for it to have been the most logical conclusion. But the flu? He never would have guessed.

He stood up on unsure legs, using the sink as leverage. His entire body ached, especially his hip and arm as he must have slept the entire time on them. He stretched, everything cracking, before he checked himself over in the mirror. His eyes were bloodshot and he had blood in his nose. He turned on the sink and washed up.

After washing his face and relieving himself, he set about re-packing his stuff. Finch must have had to go really bad for not noticing Terence's little scissors and assorted items left on the sink. He retrieved his flashlight from the floor, but the needle and thread were lost. He began to panic when he didn't see his gun, but when he looked around a little more he found it behind the toilet.

He sat on the floor and had a bite to eat. He didn't want to eat and his stomach concurred, but he knew he needed some kind of energy before continuing his journey.

When he was as ready as he could be given the present circumstances, he proceeded downstairs. His joints still ached, but it was a good ache, like his body was telling him it was on the mend. The pain didn't go away as he moved, but he became more tolerant of it.

He wondered how long he'd been out as he crossed the kitchen to the back door. There was something going on out there and he knew the busses blocking off the street was for a reason. A line of floodlights lit the night and there was a patchwork of fencing surrounding the elementary school.

He saw a handful of guards, but they were so separated that he might be able to sneak past them if he was careful.

But what were they protecting?

Something told him he didn't want to know, but he had to keep his promise to Alice. Except he'd made that promise to her when he thought he was dying and she was already dead. And whatever had happened to her, well, these were *living* people. Was he going to kill several to avenge one and possibly lose his own life in the process? He didn't even know if these people had done anything; weren't they just protecting what they had scraped together the same way as him? He couldn't begrudge them for doing a better job of it.

But there wasn't something right about it. Griff and his troupe were here as he saw their motorcycles parked to the side of the building. They at least did business with the people in the school. Terence's mind kept going back to the jewelry box. He could accept that she had died, but she had no business being *dead* here. That school had something to do with her death and he was going to find out what.

Terence gripped his hammer as he set his jaw with determination.

Lord have mercy on anyone who got in his way.

He emerged into a thickly weeded backyard and immediately spotted what looked like a homemade bear trap. A zombie would walk right into it, and some poor living sap who thought he'd found utopia would find a harsh reality biting his leg in two. He spotted two more traps with leaves and other vegetation covering them and he stepped around them before peeking out of the yard.

The guard closest to him was standing and facing away from him with a large joint held in his hand like a cigarette. He took out a lighter and spent the next fifteen seconds lighting it. Terence could either stand and wait or try moving a little farther down to where the man wouldn't see him. He scanned around for the other guard and saw he was at least two hundred yards away from him, looking off in the opposite direction.

The air had turned from cool to cold since he was last outside. Terence pulled out his earmuffs, and put them on. He wished he could have found a pair of gloves construction workers wore in the winter, as they were tougher and helped protect his hands from the elements. But the ones he had would have to suffice.

Finally, the guard with the joint sauntered away on his rounds. Terence looked for the other guard and couldn't spot him. He came out, looked both ways and crossed the alley. It would have been ironic if Griff spotted him in an open lot like he had last time but his luck was coming around.

No one had spotted him by the time he was crossing the street.

Thompson Elementary had been his first school when his parents had moved into the city. He attended it from kindergarten through fourth grade. When he went to Barber Middle school in the fifth, they closed Thompson.

He was by the wall when two men dressed in biker garb came around the corner. Terence gripped his .22, but didn't raise it. One of the men looked over at him and lifted his chin in acknowledgement. Terence did the same, acting like he belonged.

After they were a good two dozen feet away his heart had slowed. He headed in the direction they came from. Hopefully that was the way in.

It led to the main entrance, he remembered it now. A tall, heavyset woman had just gone in before him and had handed her bag to a giant of a human being at the door. Terence didn't want to give up his pack, but he saw no choice if he was going inside. He tucked his gun into the rear waistband of his pants and headed for the entrance.

"Never saw you before." The man's voice was higher than Terence's.

He smiled, not expecting that. "I saw some guys headed this way," he said. "I wanted to tag along, but, y'know, I didn't want to bring any company with me." He lifted his pack off his shoulder with his thumb. "I brought some stuff."

"Put it in the box." The big man pointed to a huge cardboard box just behind him. It was filled with other bags. Terence took a deep breath, knowing he probably wasn't going to get it back.

"Wait a second, is that a bite?" the man was looking at his wounded cheek.

Terence's hand went up to his face. He laughed, hoping it was disarming. The man's expression didn't change.

"No, no. I tripped and busted my face on a rock."

"Homey, all the same, the medic needs to look at you." He pointed to a table with crude-looking equipment on it, about twenty feet behind the box. There was a man wearing a white lab coat with a bloody smock, a face mask, and gloves. A pile of something covered in carpeting was against the wall beside him. The 'doctor' was in the process of wrapping a forearm in a grocery bag and putting it atop the carpet and then covering it up. A guard was dragging a body through a door next to the cafeteria. If Terence's memory served, that was the kitchen area, too.

"Thanks," Terence smiled and began walking over. He thought if it was just the doctor he might be able to subdue him and make a run for it if necessary while the other guard was on corpse collection, but another guard stepped away from the wall where Terence hadn't seen him.

He stopped and waited for the doctor to turn and look at him. The doctor stripped off the gloves and put on a fresh pair. He had dark black hair, and looked like he was in his early sixties.

"Is that your only cut?" He pointed at Terence's face.

"Yeah."

"Who stitched it for you?"

"I did."

The doctor stopped a foot away and it was apparent that he didn't want to touch Terence. That was okay, he didn't want the man touching him, either.

"It looks good, but be careful of infection. Here, take a bottle of alcohol."

Beside the crude saws, picks, and other non-medical equipment, were mini-packs of cotton balls, band-aids and alcohol. He took one and nodded to the doctor.

"Thanks. Where do I...?"

"The cafeteria."

Terence went in, passing the guard on his way back out. There were at least a hundred people inside. People's low conversations had descended into a dull roar. It looked mostly the same as he remembered except most of the paint had peeled away from the walls and a large black curtain was on the stage the end of the room. The cafeteria did double duty as an auditorium when needed.

Whatever was about to happen was going to be up there. He began to weave his way through the crowd.

At any moment Terence expected to run into Griff and his men. He'd made it through three-fourths of the crowd when a man emerged from behind the curtain on the stage. He was short and thin, wearing all black with a shiny white cravat. His face was gaunt, his eyes and cheekbones jutting out of his head to almost cartoonish proportions.

Griff jumped on stage. His hand was bandaged, the same one Terence had struck with his bat. Griff stalked over to the thin man. The man was so short even Griff had to bend down to whisper into his ear. The man stood still as Griff gesticulated and whispered. Griff took out a wad of bills and began counting them off in front of him. The man put a hand to Griff's chest and pushed him away and the taller man tried handing the bills to him. He turned his head away and two guards walked toward them.

Griff slammed the money on the floor and turned away before they got to him.

"You can't do this!" he shouted, walking down the stairs.

"You know what this place is?" a man in front of Terence turned and said to him. "A tombstone. And they…" he poked a thumb over his shoulder, "are coming to etch all our names on it."

A conversation would actually be a good cover. If Finch and Whip were looking for a lone person they would be more likely to overlook him if he was with someone else. It was dark in the room and they hadn't gotten a good look at him before.

"So how long are you staying?" he asked.

"I'm not," the man said. "Just came for the show."

"What's the show?"

"Shhh," the man said, putting a finger to his lips.

"No! No, man, no!" It sounded like Griff somewhere ahead. The crowd parted and there was Finch and Whip dragging him like he was a prisoner; he was sobbing.

"Not like this, man," Finch said. "We need these guys."

"But she's just a little kid," Griff moaned. He sagged in their arms.

Whip was silent. Even in the low light his dark skin looked grayish.

Terence turned his head as they passed. They didn't notice him and a moment later they were gone.

The curtain opened. In a large cage, there was a three-year-old and an eight-year-old girl. The younger one was playing with a stuffed penguin on a key ring. The first thing to go through Terence's mind was how much she looked like Alice. Same hazel, almond-shaped eyes, same upturned nose...

Wait a minute. Could that be Alice's daughter?

It made sense if Alice had been living in the community, if you could call it that.

So then what were they about to do with her?

As if in response, two guards emerged from behind a rear curtain with a zombie in tow. They had poles attached to a metal collar around its neck. The zombie was in an agitated state, reaching in vain for either guard, but kept out of arm's reach.

"No," Terence said. "They couldn't."

"What was that?" the man next to him asked.

"They're not going to put that zombie in the cage with those little girls, are they?"

"If that's the show, that's the show."

"Why isn't anyone stopping this?"

The man shook his head at Terence. Either he hadn't heard over the rising roar of the crowd or he didn't have an answer. How could anyone think of this as entertainment? These were just *children*.

Terence pushed his way ahead, catching a couple punches and elbows through his thick clothing. He took his hand out of his glove and it was knocked away. No time to crawl around on the floor and find it. Someone would probably step on and break his hand. He found a little gap at the front of the stage and looked up.

The thin man had opened the cage and the two girls had backed into the rear of it. The guards maneuvered the zombie into the cage and released it. It turned and lunged at the kids, but they jabbed it in the chest until the little man closed the cage. It reached for him, temporarily ignoring the children.

Terence had to move now. A child wouldn't stand a chance against a zombie and two would fare no better. He drew his gun and pointed it at the zombie's head. Terence aimed, but before he could shoot, someone grabbed his arm.

"Gun!" someone shouted as the crowd exploded in panic. Terence tried wrenching his arm away, but the man had him in a two-handed grip. Terence fumbled for his hammer jammed in his pants under his shirt, but he still had his other glove on. He jammed his hand between him and the other man and yanked it free from the glove.

Another man grabbed him from behind, ripping his pocket open, the extra bullets and everything else spilling out. The three of them struggled as Terence began beating the man with the hammer.

After the third blow, the man's grip loosened and he grabbed his side in pain. Terence caught him in the jaw with the hammer, spinning him around to drop to the floor. There was rapid gunfire somewhere behind him and more people screamed.

The man holding Terence's arm slid away and he turned and saw the glassy-eyed dead stare, blood leaking onto the floor from a gunshot to the back of the head. Terence crouched and looked up at the stage. He saw the zombie hunched over someone and the thin man standing still, staring directly at him. The two guards were gone.

Terence aimed and shot the thin man in the neck; the man falling back as he grabbed his throat. Terence shot him again in the chest as he charged the stage.

He hopped onto the stage, grabbing the thin man before he fell. He pulled him over to the cage and threw it open. The zombie had the older girl's arm in its mouth as she screamed, holding onto one of the bars with her free hand. The younger girl was trying to push her body through the bars in desperation. Terence put a bullet in the back of the zombie's head and it slumped forward to remain still.

He climbed into the cage and scooped up the younger girl. She was definitely Alice's daughter, she had to be. And she was the right age to have been his daughter and he really wanted to believe that. She buried her face into his neck as she held a dirty, stuffed penguin in her arms.

"Please don't leave me," the other little girl said, crying. There wasn't anything he could do for her. He aimed and closed his eyes, wanting to save her the suffering to come.

Then he lowered the gun; he couldn't do it.

The thin man was still gurgling on the stage next to him. He wasn't wounded as badly as Terence originally hoped. Terence kicked him in the butt, then dragged him into the cage. He locked it and the thin man stared at him with wide eyes.

"Serves you right," Terence said and nodded to the girl, then turned and headed to the rear of the stage.

The curtain muffled a good deal of the noise from out front. It was dark in back, the walls made of gray cinderblocks. There were more gunshots and more screams from out front.

"I want my daddy," the little girl whined.

He found an exit door and went to it. As he was about to open it, a guard burst through the door and Terence shot him. The man fell face-first and lay still in a growing pool of blood.

Terence opened the door and saw a long hallway to his right; at the end the double doors leading to the gym, now chained. He remembered where he was now. At the end of the hall to his left were more double doors that would open onto another hallway where several classrooms were located and a set of stairs to the second floor. He couldn't remember where exactly, but there had to be an emergency exit over that way.

He began moving.

"Don't worry, baby. I'll find your father. I promise," he said to the small girl in his arms.

He turned in the direction of the stairs and found an emergency exit. But it was barricaded and there was too much for him to move with the amount of time he had before he was discovered. Besides, it looked like there was a chain on the door as well. Terence opened the door on his right leading to the stairs and saw a an exit.

It was chained, too. There was no way he was going upstairs. They might never make it back down. By his count he had two bullets left.

The little girl had no coat and it was getting colder by the hour. He could see through the foggy window it had begun to snow. He figured he could take the chill a little better than she could.

He pointed the gun at the center of the window and shot. A hole appeared with a semi-diagonal crack going through it, but it didn't shatter. Must have been some kind of plastic. He went to put the girl down but she clung to his neck.

"No!" she said.

"C'mon, baby. I gotta put you down. I have to get the door open so we can leave. You want to leave, don't you?"

She let him go after a minute. He set her down and began kicking at the window. The crack widened and the hole grew bigger until the entire pane fell out and crashed to the ground.

Cold air blasted him in the face.

"Okay, I want you to take this." Terence took off his coat and wrapped her in it. He had all kinds of junk in the pockets he'd never needed; maybe she would get some use from some of it.

"It's you," a voice said.

Terence looked up to see Griff standing at the end of the hall after coming through the same door Terence just used. Terence instinctively pulled the girl closer to him and saw Griff's eyes go wide when he saw her.

"Baby, you're okay?" The little girl pushed out of Terence's arms and went to Griff with her arms outstretched. Terence wanted to grab for her, but in Griff's face, he saw relief and gratitude. "You saved her," Griff said.

"I...I..." Terence stammered.

Griff's mouth worked up and down as he tried in vain to blink away tears. He kissed the little girl's cheeks over and over again. It took him three times before he was able to speak.

"They're coming," Griff said. "Look, things have changed here since I last saw you. You saved my baby, I owe you for that, but you need to go, they're coming."

"Okay," Terence said. "But I don't have any transportation."

"Whip's dead, you can have his bike," Griff said and tossed him a set of keys. "It's on the south side of the building." He turned away, then back again. "Thank you."

Terence nodded, turned, and climbed out the window as Griff disappeared through the door.

He saw a few guards running about as they searched for him and he waited until a count of fifty after they rounded the side of the building. He worked the key ring onto his belt loop so he wouldn't lose it. Without his jacket he was cold and his clothing was still damp from his dip in the pool, but he shrugged it off.

He found the motorcycle and it started on the first try, and he shifted it into gear and drove off, avoiding a few zombies that were far too slow to grab him. The roads were still clear but he knew he wouldn't get far before the snow became too heavy to drive. There would be no plows to clean the streets.

He glanced over his shoulder and saw the fence had been pushed over and the living dead were slowly beginning to swarm the school. He wondered if the people in the school would be able to stop fighting each other long enough to fight the dead off, but from what Terence saw, it wouldn't matter, there were just too many.

Humankind was living on borrowed time anyway, by his estimation. To be alive at this point meant to be lucky and Terence had been the luckiest of all. If he'd stayed at his home they would have eventually broken into the house and perhaps even right now he would have been knocking zombies off his roof until he finally died of starvation or exposure.

He suppressed a shiver. He would bear the cold like he had born the end of the world. Just like he had born his girlfriend dumping him and going on to have a child with another man. Besides, finding fresh clothing wouldn't be difficult as most of the local stores were empty of life.

Terence prepared himself for the long road ahead.

He didn't know where he would go next, but he knew wherever it might be, he would survive.

THE SHERIFF OF NOTTINGHAM

JONATHAN McKINNEY

Fin watched the woman on the monitor, screaming as the zombie tore into her neck. The death bite severed her jugular, a cloud of blood erupting from her mouth, escaping with her last breath. More zombies crowded around the newly defeated and took it upon themselves to clean the street. Welcome to the new reality TV.

The cameras belonged to the building's previous owners, and Fin powered them through the generator that ensured if an outage ever happened, the bank could operate. The bank took up the first floor. The second and third consisted of office space, and a worker's lounge, perfect for Fin's kitchen. The only thing he missed was a shower, but then, who was he trying to impress?

He washed...sometimes.

The zombies moved away from the heap of mangled flesh that once breathed, ate, and wiped after she urinated. Fin just stared. They never completely devoured the dead. The more he watched this ongoing cycle of crazy people just rushing out of their homes into the outstretched arms of the hungry dead, the more he got upset at these lifeless son-of-a-bitches.

Who the fuck did they think they were? he thought. Here he sat, with his rations depleting and the zombies were out there, not even cleaning their plate. Made him sick to his stomach.

The entire way society handled the beginning of the 'epidemic'– that was the favorite word used by the media to describe the mess– made Fin sick.

"Don't panic," they said. "Don't leave your house," they said. "Don't agitate the infected." Don't do this. Don't do that. That's America's problem.

Fin shook his head in rage. The media should have filled our heads with do's, not don'ts. *Do* grab a gun. *Do* shoot them in the head. *Do* whatever gets you by; regardless of any *don'ts* that happen along inside your head, as long as you survive. A *don't* will get you killed, a *do* might get you killed, but at least you *did* something.

Fin grabbed the empty Chef Boyardee can from off the desk and tossed it into the corner. All this talk about doing something, and he was trapped inside, just sitting until he went crazy like that woman earlier–or he ran out of food.

He climbed the stairs up to the roof, and walked across the small pebble rocks covering it until he reached the flagpole. Untying the rope, he pulled it down for the night.

Why he flew the flag every day, even he didn't know, but he did. He was still in America.

He wondered sometimes if other countries were having a good old time. Wondered if the zombies had infected the entire world, or just the United States.

He locked the roof door behind him, and carried the flag down the flight of stairs. Why lock the roof door? Why the hell not?

His protection this long amounted to the sheets of metal that slid on rails, covering every window and door on the first floor of the office building/bank. He surmised these existed for riot purposes to protect the bank.

With the day over, he went to bed and thought of his trip tomorrow.

He needed food, some booze–he deserved some–and maybe some piece of mind.

* * *

The crash stole Fin of his slumber. He knew a crash that loud, that sudden, that *felt*, had succeeded in penetrating his impenetrable fortress.

Something probably most unzombielike. The world's largest threat, only second to the zombies, was still man.

Fin jumped out of bed and grabbed his shotgun. On his way to the stairs, he hit the elevator down arrow. The elevator would arrive before him, and while the elevator attracted the visitors, he could get a first look at them. Maybe they broke into a new place every so often, used the resources, and then moved on. He doubted this was the case, but you get a hell of an imagination when you're holed up day after day.

He heard their voices first. A woman yelled, "You fucking idiot. You broke the damn wall."

"Shut up, Clair," a man said.

"Hold on, you two. Someone's here. The elevator," a third man said.

Fin crept down the remaining steps to the landing. He sized up the three in a matter of seconds after seeing them ogle the elevator doors when they opened. These were survivors. No matter what they did, however dangerous, they were running wild and taking crazy risks. The only reason these people lived as long as they had was through luck and determination; how else would they have made it this far.

"Hold it right there," Fin confronted them, shotgun aimed at chest level.

The three remained still.

The oldest answered Fin. "What are you, a cop?"

With a grin, Fin replied very slowly. "No."

The big guy seemed to relax and he moved once more, hauling out bags from the car. "Then why the fuck you getting all worked up? Shit, man." He stopped working and raised his right hand. "We come in peace."

Fin dropped the gun from the strike position, and watched the three people warily.

The woman looked like she was about twenty. A good twenty at that. The other man looked at Fin. "Don't eye Clair too much, pal, Fester might get offended."

Fester laughed. "Don't let on, Billy. Hey, you got a real treat meeting us. We're gonna be famous. We just robbed us a bank. Got a pretty good haul, too."

Fin glanced at the duffle bag. Rodent riddled and moth-eaten paper that may have once resembled money filled four bags to the brim. Fin pitied them all. A low moan drew his attention. The zombies weren't leaving any time soon.

"Okay good for you," Fin said. "Glad you robbed the bank, but you might want to move away from the opening your car just installed in my building."

Billy gave a quizzical look. "Why?"

Zombies outside shambled their way over to the exposed posse. Dead couples strolled. Rotting business men walked. Zombies shambled. The way of the world only now it was dead.

Fin sighed. "Well, see Billy. Zombies are outside there. You saw them, didn't you?"

Fin watched as a dumbfounded Billy looked at the group of shambling zombies. Billy looked right at them. There was no mistaking he could see them. "Where? I don't..."

Fin shot Billy in the leg. The buckshot made more noise than anticipated. Fin's ears rang loudly as Clair and Fester glared at him. Fester was about to charge at him when Fin shot him, too.

"We're leaving them for bait. If you slow me down, I'll kill you, too. You're all fucking insane. Doesn't anyone else see the zombies?"

Clair shook her head no.

Oh, she saw them all right, he thought. And if she didn't, then she saw Fin and his shotgun and what he'd done to her friends and that was enough. "Okay. I had a good thing going here, but you ruined it for me. So we'll just have to move up the road."

* * *

The car raced down the two lane highway. Fin tried to forget the chewing and gnashing sounds the zombies made as they fed on Billy and Fester's bodies, but knew he would need more than speed.

Clair's shock held steady as Fin dodged a stalled car, a nice Camaro at that, and threw her across the seats. The sun winked over the horizon, and Fin wished for that drink.

"Where are we going?" Clair asked.

"Don't know," Fin replied.

"Why'd you have to go and shoot Billy and Fester?"

The Arizona landscape eased past. Zombies stood here and there along the desert highway like drunks after a concert that had misplaced their cars. Just shambling about, forever wandering.

"I shot them because they were near the zombies and I needed a decoy. That's why if it makes you feel better. Coulda just as well been you. Was really nothing against Billy or Fester. Do I regret it? Not really. Why did you rob my bank?"

"Fester lost his job last week and we were in a bind. We didn't kill nobody. We just went in and got the money. Figured it was empty so nobody would get hurt."

Fin shook his head. Last week zombies reeked havoc, as they did the week before.

"What about the zombies?" Fin asked.

"Why do you keep talking about zombies?" she asked.

"What the fuck is that," Fin asked, hitting the brakes.

"I don't know, it shouldn't be there," she replied.

Fin shook his head as he slowed the car.

Someone had constructed a large fence across the Arizona highway. An eight foot concrete wall ran to the left of the highway and the chain-link fence, ten feet high with razor wire, blocked the entire road. Fin saw a man standing in a makeshift crow's nest on the left side of the highway, on the other side of the fence.

"Hello!" the man's voice boomed through a megaphone.

Fin searched for any signs of zombies, and seeing it was safe, opened his car door and stepped out. "Hello, yourself."

"What is it you want?"

"I'd just like to pass through, please."

The man shook his head. "I'm sorry. We couldn't risk contamination. You'll have to go around."

Go around, Fin thought. *Go around? Screw that! The fucking end of the world is upon us and this chump lays this bullshit line on me.*

Jumping back into the car, Fin stepped on the gas pedal, the car now headed straight for the chain-link fence. He broke through the fence and shortly after, the world flipped on its axis.

But it wasn't the world, it was the car, the vehicle having driven over a hidden land mine. The last thing Fin remembered before it all went black was a gang of teenaged boys running at him from the side and Clair crying out in fear.

* * *

The smell of a wood burning stove lightly tickled Fin's nose. He sat up too quickly and felt a huge, imaginary hammer slam into his forehead. He prayed for a hangover headache; there was so much pain it robbed him of his wits. He shook his head, but no wits rushed back in. Where was he?

He threw the covers off, feeling an ache behind his eyes as he opened them.

The first thought he had was that he was home on his bed and it had all been a terrible nightmare. But as the room came into focus, he saw he was definitely not home.

But where was he?

He stood up and crossed the room to the only door, opened it quietly, and crept into the hallway. His eyes adjusted slowly to the hallway's lack of light, and when he assured himself that the shadows were just that, he ventured down the corridor. He heard light music playing down the hall and to the right so he followed it.

The window he passed showed the deep blanket of night, and silhouettes of other buildings. He eased to the door the music drifted from, opened it, and peered inside. A lone crib sat in the middle of the room, and the coos of the crib's occupant could be heard over the light music. Fin's curiosity overrode his reasoning. He went to the crib and looked.

A tidal wave of understanding hit him full force. The zombies, his home destroyed, and the three wayward bank robbers. Looking at the baby, suddenly his will felt empowered and he knew that he could, would and had to save the world, if nothing else just for this little baby.

The headache grew worse when a woman shrieked behind him. The scream was like a drill as it bored with break neck speed into his head. He grabbed his ears and she rushed by him, snatched the baby from the crib, and ran from the room, taking her scream with her.

A male's voice boomed in the hall and soon a man appeared in the doorway. "Damn it, I knew I should've tied you up," he said, bringing a candlestick down on Fin's head.

161

Before Fin lost ties with the waking world, he thought, *My head can't take much more of this.*

* * *

Bound to a chair, his wits refused to abandon him this time. He knew what came before and feared for his future. He also felt the set of eyes that sheared his skin with their cold gaze.

"No use pretending you're asleep, buddy. I done saw you stir."

It was the same fellow from the hall. Fin opened his eyes and saw a shotgun pointed at him, *his shotgun.* The man was sitting at a dining room table, the candlestick madman operating the trigger end. Fin was seated across from him.

"Aspirin," Fin requested.

"Nope," the man answered.

"Who are you?"

"I'm the Sheriff of Nottingham."

"Of course," Fin replied. "Who else would you be?"

A nurse in a very short skirt entered the room carrying a platter. Following her, a built girl in a hooters outfit set plates before both the sheriff, and Fin. Next, a girl of playboy quality in a sexy bunny suit brought drinks for them. Fin guessed that all of the girls were about seventeen.

"Soon we'll be having Natalie for lunch," the sheriff said, sipping from his glass.

Fin took a drink and found that it was wine. "Who's Natalie?"

"She'll be along shortly. So tell me about the woman you were with? Was she crazy when you met her?"

"Most definitely. I shot her friends to distract the zombies coming for us."

The sheriff nodded. "Lost to the zombies, huh? When you say you shot her buddies, what do you mean exactly?"

"I had a nice place. Bank security and shit. Nice set up until the woman and her two friends plowed into the building to rob the bank. That was yesterday. Currency not being what it used to be, I took them for insane. So I shot the two men to distract the zombies and I took off with the woman."

The sheriff listened intently through the story. "So there was no other reason to shoot them. Self defense? Safety of another?"

"I did what I had to do. They broke into my place and wrecked it."

Yet another girl entered, this one wearing a bathing suit, and she sashayed past Fin, who watched as she placed a large platter on the center of the table.

Fin could no longer let it go, his curiosity getting the better of him. "So, what's with all the eye candy?"

The sheriff looked puzzled. "Eye candy?"

"The sweet looking honey's bringing in all the food."

"They're gonna help repopulate the earth one day. I made my home here where they used to shoot old westerns. Put the fence up ourselves."

Another door opened and a string quartet entered, composed of young girls in school girl uniforms. Plaid skirts, the whole bit. They struck up Green Sleeves. Three more servers came out, two with food for the sheriff, and one with a huge platter that she set next to Fin. They were also dressed to arouse the libido.

"So you're basically just one hell of a horny bastard," Fin summarized. A hush fell over the room, and the girls turned to see what the sheriff would do.

"We refrain from using the word *bastard* here. And I'll thank you to never say it again."

Fin picked up a piece of meat and chewed on it instead of dignifying the sheriff with an answer. Halfway through a mouthful of meat, Fin thought of something. "Hey, this Natalie. When will she be here? Shouldn't we wait for her?"

The sheriff nodded, finished his chewing, and wiped his mouth. "She's here already." He stood and removed the cover of the platter. A severed head rested there, and Fin's mind reeled. He'd thought it tasted a bit like chicken; of course he'd never had a Natalie so how would he know what one tasted like. But now he was gifted with not only the knowledge of the taste, quality, and texture of a Natalie going down, but also what one tastes like coming back up.

He bent over and began vomiting, the spasms causing his head to hurt once more.

"You sick fuck!" Fin shouted but the sheriff only smiled.

The sheriff picked up his walkie. "Guards, come in now, please," he said, then turned to Fin. "You're under arrest for murder."

"You cooked and ate a fucking girl. If anybody's a murderer, it's you."

Two boys of about fifteen came in and grabbed Fin's arms. They proceeded to speak every cliché they could remember. One told of how 'if Fin tried anything a can of whoop ass would be opened'. The other replied with the 'don't fuck with me 'cause when you do you'll be fucking with the best'.

The sheriff returned to his meal. Fin was about to vomit once more, but swallowed it back.

What a fucking week this is starting to be, Fin thought.

* * *

The door clicked as it locked. The two guards laughed about something and left Fin to defend himself from the invading silence.

"Fucking sucks don't it," a voice declared behind him.

To say Fin jumped would be like saying an atomic bomb goes boom. Fin spun and saw another boy lying on the lower bed of the jail's bunk. Fin, who'd never been to jail, relied on his movie watching experiences. "What're ya in for?"

The boy sat up. "Earl locked me up after I tried to defend Natalie."

"We never traded names, but I'm guessing Earl's the sheriff. By the way, name's Fin."

The boy stood up and held out his hand. Fin took it, imagining a world where this ritual used to take place all the time. "Mine's Jarrod. I screwed up. Did you see Natalie? Is she still . . ."

Fin nodded. "Oh, she's still," he replied regretting it after he said it. "He...well..."

"Ate her," Jarrod finished.

"I may have had a small bit, but it was just a little bit." Fin held his hand up and showed about a half an inch between two fingers.

"He's gonna cook them all now that I'm in here."

"Why?"

"The reason he cooked Natalie was she couldn't give him a child for his repopulation plan. The thing Earl don't know is he's shooting blanks. Since he set this thing up, nine children have been born, and every one of them can call me daddy. After he ate two girls who couldn't get pregnant, the girls started coming to me. Earl has four guards he's brainwashed thoroughly, and then me. I never went for his vision; guess you could say I was blind as a fucking bat.

Anyway they ask me to plant the seed so they could bare his child and not end up as supper. I believe Natalie just couldn't...you know, so when he told her the time had come, I fought him, but the other four guards protected him and I ended up in here."

Fin walked over to the bunk and threw the mattress on the floor. He then started toying with the box springs. "What're you doing?" Jarrod asked.

"That lock on the door. It's a knock-off . Any hard piece of metal will open it. Like this," Fin said, holding the metal piece he'd just worked off the box spring. "I'm guessing with props and stuff to keep up with already, the producers of whatever show was shot here didn't want the star locked up all night."

Fin bent the metal a bit and inserted it into the lock. A loud click later and he opened the door. Jarrod followed. "What now?"

Fin kept walking as he spoke. "We need a syringe, some zombie blood, and we need to retrieve Natalie's head. I'll trust you to take care of Earl's guards. Once me and Earl get started with our meeting, I don't want to be interrupted."

* * *

"I got my shotgun back," Fin told Earl's sleeping body. Fin waited for any signs of him stirring and when Earl refused to show any, Fin slammed the butt of the shotgun into his stomach.

Earl attacked like a man that had just gotten hit by the butt of a shotgun, and after the convincing performance, sat up stiffly. "How the fuck did you get out?"

"Resourcefulness," Fin replied.

Earl rubbed his stomach some more. "Well, what now, big shot? You holding all the cards, I reckon."

Fin rubbed his chin. "I'm not a bullshitter, Earl, so I'm gonna tell you straight. You've been found guilty of murder and cannibalism, and I'm fixing on sentencing ya in a moment."

"So you're gonna kill me?"

Fin nodded. "That's a given. I believe I may have hit the head on the nail when I called you a sick fuck. You know, I always like the fact that in countries other than the U.S., they cut your hand off if you steal. If you rape, they whack your pecker off. So in a moment I'm gonna give you exactly what you deserve. First, to hurt your ego, all them children you call son, or daughter—they all belong to Jarrod."

Earl's eyes grew to small slits, and hatred etched his face. "You're a fucking liar."

"Nope," Fin said, smiling. "Ya been shootin' blanks."

Earl seemed to ponder this as Fin set a cornhusk bag on the bed between the sheriff's feet.

"Now ever since I got the impression you were the sick fuck you are, inspiration hit me. My muse sang in ways you'd never dream of to come up with a punishment like this. Natalie's head here will bite you, and infect you. Beautiful ain't it? We found us a zombie just outside the gate, killed it, took some infected blood, and shot up Nat's head, and bam, Mrs. Pac man. Hungry, or better yet, Hungry, Hungry Hippos."

Earl stretched a finger out to Fin. "Well, just get it over with then."

Fin laughed. "Earl, Earl, Earl. Fucking retribution, buddy. She'll be biting you somewhere else. And she'll continue biting you there until you pass over to the zombie universe."

A look of horror crossed Earl's face as he finally got the picture. Fin lifted Natalie's head out of the bag and turned it to face Earl. Natalie's mouth continued to move like a baby bird reaching for the mother's offering. Earl's eyes grew in size, and kept getting bigger the closer Fin lowered Natalie's head between his legs.

As Natalie chewed and Earl screamed, thrashed, and acted like a man having his balls processed by a crazed zombie head getting its first bite to eat, Fin wondered what he would do next.

Jarrod would probably stay here. Fin, however, felt he needed to get moving. There behind his mind lay a plan of some sort, something he had to do. He would leave tomorrow.

Earl stopped moving and Fin shot Earl in the head and then the severed head of Natalie. He left them where they lay. Fin guessed maybe one or two honeys would be glad to see Earl gone.

Fin smiled widely.

What a way to turn a week around.

GETTING TO SAVANNAH

ROBERT M. KUZMESKI

Forests terrified Clay. For something so completely natural–
so utterly untouched by man–the woods seemed totally *un*natural
to him. Trees jutted violently out of the ground, their roots shred-
ding the soil and scarring the land. Years of dead leaves were at
their base, filling the air with the constant smell of decay. Green
moss and kudzu clung to rock, bark and soil, reflecting light and
casting a sick green pallor over everything.

Dying ferns brushed his legs as he ran, leafless branches raked
his face, and knotted bark stared at him with demonic eyes.

His brother Steven once told him that trees had souls. Not their
own; the souls of those that died within the woods. They took them
and absorbed them, twisting them into something monstrous.
Steven said the worst ones were the trees with white bark. He told
Clay that they held the spirits of the Indians that once lived off the
land. Now they haunted the bark, anger and revenge rotting the
wood from within. They could move, Steven said, and were known
to kill lost men that wandered alone.

Clay lived far from the woods. He called Savannah home and
would be there now if he could. He loved plantation life and missed
his family. His wife Ginny surely would have had the baby by now.
His mother probably had dinner waiting on the table for Steven,
Ginny and his father. She was a kind woman, even to the slaves
who worked the fields. She kept them fed better than most and
even stayed father's hand from lashing them a time or two.

That lifestyle was natural, Clay thought. Things were in order
there–everything was organized, scheduled and held a steady
rhythm day in and day out. The chaos of the woods unnerved him;
it contrasted with the life he was used to.

He would still be home if not for the War of Northern Aggression.

When the fighting started, he signed up for the Confederate
Army. He swore he'd die before letting a bunch of Yanks tell him
how to live his life and care for his family.

Now, running through the woods, it looked like he was going to make good on that vow. After piling victory upon victory, his regiment shattered in Atlanta against the might of General Sherman's men. The Yanks fought with renewed vigor when they hit the city. Clay still carried the soot of burning buildings in his nose and lungs.

Technically, Clay was a deserter. His entire unit was. They routed after an ambush and scattered in every direction. Somewhere, someone might be trying to rally them but Clay doubted it. If anyone was looking for them, it was probably Sherman's men. So Clay ran, even though he didn't know if anyone actually gave chase.

He didn't care if the Confederate Army caught up to him. What would they do? Put on trial his entire unit, perhaps the whole regiment, for deserting? He doubted it. Sooner or later his side would learn what he'd learned in Atlanta...the war was over and the Northerners had won.

All that mattered now was getting to Savannah, to his family. He wanted to see his firstborn and his wife. He wanted to taste family cooking. He wanted to get back to the life he used to lead. If he made good time, he'd be back in time for the holidays.

But first, he had to find his way out of the accursed woods. Every step he took made his heart beat faster. He'd kick up a pile of leaves or snap a fallen branch, and wonder if someone was out there, chasing him. Small creatures in the underbrush or birds fluttering in the tree reminded him that he was alone—completely isolated from other humans. There was no one to talk to and no one to help him if something went wrong. For a place reputed to be peaceful and teeming with life, he found his surroundings lonely and inhospitable.

When he stepped on a large branch, the loud snap of breaking wood echoed through the valley like a gunshot. The sound reminded him of Sherman's attack. That day, shots sounded and the battle went on in gentlemanly fashion, two armies fighting for a strategic advantage that would win the day. When night came, both sides broke off from combat. Clay's regiment drafted plans for the next day, discussing tactics they confidently believed would end the battle.

They never got the chance to employ them. As the men sat in the camp, cleaning their guns, eating their rations or just drinking themselves to sleep, the Union Army came.

The attack started with one horseman. He galloped through town on his black mare, swaying to and fro in the saddle in time with the horse's gait. Most of the men mistook the rider for one of their own—surely no Yank would be brazen enough to lead an assault on a Confederate camp alone and at night.

One soldier was quick enough on the draw to get a shot off, hitting the horse and dropping it to the ground.

"Someone run and fetch me a sawbones!" the man yelled. "We got us a prisoner!"

But the rider was dead. A doc arrived a few moments later and told everyone that the man had been dead prior to riding into the camp—a gunshot wound to the head had sealed his fate.

That's when everything went to Hell. Clay wasn't sure what happened and was convinced his eyes played tricks on him. Union men came slowly out of the woods around the encampment. They moved loosely, in a sort of skirmish formation. They carried no weapons and didn't charge when they were close to the Confederates. Instead, they walked slowly and purposefully, speaking only in guttural moans and primitive grunts.

Many of the Confederate soldiers hastily sought weapons; some even managed to fire off a few shots, but shooting them did no good. The Union soldiers just kept coming.

Some Confederate soldiers tried bayonets and found them to be equally ineffective. The enemy didn't even flinch when the blades burrowed deeply into their chests. The Confederate soldiers died painfully as the Yanks swarmed and literally ripped them to shreds.

Most of the soldiers were in such a deep state of shock, they did little to fight back. The attackers looked unnatural in the firelight. They were pale and sickly. Some displayed obvious wounds that would have fallen most men.

When Clay came face to face with one of the attackers, it was like death itself looked back. The man wore the tattered remains of a Union jacket, riddled with bullet holes. His mouth was crusted and stained with blood. He moved towards Clay, eyes locked on him. There was nothing in those eyes. No life. No soul.

Clay ran. All around him, he could hear the sound of fighting. He heard many of his fellow soldiers vomiting loudly, the rancid smell of these Union shock troopers filling the air with an odor not unlike an abattoir. He heard the screams of the dying, of men being torn limb from limb by a force that outnumbered them easily two to one. In his periphery, he could see other soldiers fleeing as well. He thought he even saw some of the attackers cannibalizing their victims, though he told himself it had to be a trick of the light.

He ran towards the colonel's tent, hoping the commander had a handle on the situation. Instead, he found several more of the savage Yanks attacking the officer, scratching at his face and tearing his clothes. The colonel fought valiantly but never had a chance. Just before he died, Clay saw the old man take a pistol to his head and fire...and still the attackers eviscerated him.

The sound of Colonel Winston's gunshot haunted Clay. Watching his leader commit suicide in camp said more than any orders ever could.

Go home, it told him. *There's nothin' to be done now. We've lost!*

He'd run ever since, bringing him to this godforsaken place. For two days now, he ran as much as he could, walking when he must. He rested infrequently and slept even less. He was hopelessly lost but had a rough idea of which direction the ocean lay. He planned to keep moving until he hit the water and then head south.

He kept going until the light grew too dim to see by. A thick fog shrouded the valley, bringing the day to a close much earlier than Clay had hoped. Failing to find shelter, he was forced to build a lean-to to hide him and protect him from the cold.

As he started dragging large branches to his camp, he thought he saw a hint of movement out of the corner of his eye. He stared hard into the darkness, hoping it was just his imagination. Convinced it was his mind playing tricks on him, he bent to start a campfire.

He heard the shuffling of leaves but his attacker was on him before Clay could react. A meaty arm wrapped around his neck, another around his mouth. He tried to fight back, imagining one of the crazed Yanks sinking their teeth into the side of his neck, tearing hunks from him like wolves from a deer. A few poorly-placed kicks to his assailant's legs and shins did nothing. This man was stronger and a much better fighter—Clay could do more than swing blindly at the man's head and land a few elbow jabs in his torso.

Finally, he stopped struggling and accepted his fate. If this was his moment to die, then he wasn't going to go out squirming and flailing. He'd die like a proper gentleman.

"You make a fire, you'll get yourself killed," a gruff voice whispered in his ear. "Probably the rest of us, too. We're on the same side, mister. If I let you go, you gonna be quiet?" Clay nodded and the man released him.

Clay turned to face his attacker, determined to berate him for the scare. Terror caused his heart to beat a mile a minute—only adrenaline giving him bravery. Though the man was at least half again Clay's size, Clay was ready to take him down a peg.

"Sorry 'bout that," the man said before Clay could begin his tirade. "Just want to make sure no one else gets hurt. Been enough bloodshed at Union hands without us stumblin' around and givin' them more bodies to feed on."

Clay paused for a moment. Had he heard correctly?

"Feed on?" Clay asked.

"Yep," the man replied. Then, he casually glanced over his shoulder and spoke to the trees. "Y'all can come on out now. He's one of us."

Three others emerged from the forest. The first to come forward was a pimply, skinny boy that looked like he had exaggerated his age on the enrollment form. He shuffled nervously from side-to-side, his eyes darting about like he was expecting something to burst out of the woods at any moment. Clay couldn't blame him.

Another man stood strong and proud, conveying wealth and aristocracy in the way he carried himself. His uniform showed officer's stripes, though it didn't fit him properly; Clay wondered if it was actually his. The last was a woman, a bit older than the men and somewhat wide around the waist. Her mismatched military uniform and the bag she had slung over her shoulder suggested she was a battlefield looter; a scavenger that picked upon the bones of the dead and sold anything of value at the nearest soldier camp.

They were all as nervous and jumpy as Clay, with the exception of the burly man that seemed to be in charge.

"Name's Luke," the man told him, holding out his hand to shake Clay's.

"Clay," he responded weakly, hearing the exhaustion in his voice.

"Why don't you come and sit for a spell?" Luke asked. "You look a might bit haggard. Bet you've been runnin' a while and could use a bite to eat." He motioned for Clay to follow.

Clay followed the rag-tag group to a particularly dense copse of trees, where they'd built a camp. Ropes hung from the trees, holding up canvas sheets as makeshift walls. Branches across the top created a patchwork ceiling, protecting them from the elements. The idea of being surrounded by yet more trees gave Clay pause and he almost didn't enter the hut. But they had bread, beans and some rabbit and he was very hungry.

He descended on the meat voraciously. Though it was charred and tough as boot leather, it was the best meal he'd eaten in days. The others joined him in silence, the few sounds they did make coming from spoons hitting bowls and the occasional belch.

Clay finished first, eating faster than usual. He pulled off his boots and socks to give his feet a rest and let them breathe. They were badly chafed from days of walking in wet wool socks with worn boots, much of the skin now blistered and raw. Now that he was sitting, he could feel just how much the rest of his body ached. He needed rest, even if it meant staying in the woods to get it.

When Luke finished eating, he introduced the rest of the group.

"The young'un there is James," he said, pointing at the pimply-faced boy. "This here's Edgar and our lady friend is Margaret. We all met up here in these woods a few days ago. We're holin' up here for a spell until Sherman's monsters are clear of the area."

"Monsters?" Clay muttered. "They certainly acted crazed, didn't they?"

"No, sir," James said. "They ain't actin'. They're monsters sure as can be."

"The boy's right," Luke added. "They ain't human. And I don't mean they act like animals. I mean they ain't like us."

Clay thought about what they were saying and decided not to believe it. "They're soldiers, is all," he said. "They just have different trainin'; different tactics."

Luke snickered while James and Margaret looked at one another uncomfortably.

"They ain't alive," Margaret explained. "I saw one of them get shot right in the chest by grapeshot. Know what he did? He stood up and kept on coming. Grabbed the nearest man and tore his throat out with his teeth. You think that's human, mister? You think the Yanks are trained to eat people?"

Clay tried hard to push back the memories of what he'd seen. Monsters weren't real. Still, he was nearly panicked just thinking about it. He knew spirits weren't real, either...but it still felt like the trees watched his every move.

"Balderdash," Clay muttered under his breath.

"Is it?" Luke challenged him. "What did you see? Not what you *think* you saw. Tell us what you *actually* saw."

Clay recounted everything he could remember from that night. When he was through, even he couldn't refute the horror of what transpired.

"So what are they?" Clay asked.

"The livin' dead," Edgar told him, drawing blank looks from everyone else. "Undead monsters...like in the book Dracula."

"Dracula?" Clay asked.

"Ol' Edgar here has a bit of schoolin'," Luke explained. "Even reads books for fun."

"Where do they come from?" Clay asked.

"We don't really know," Edgar responded. "My old regiment first ran across them just before they hit Atlanta. We heard lots of rumors about them before they attacked. They were sent to break our backs...to damage our supply lines and our morale so we wouldn't want to fight anymore. Sherman planned to live off the land, accordin' to the rumors, takin' our crops and grain. Turns out, there was more to it than that."

"I heard it all started in the Delaware Death Pen," James added. "The guys used to talk about how bad that place was. They say that men died real bad there, what with the starvin' and the dysentery. I reckon they died so mad, they refused to stay dead. So they just got up and started killin'."

"Dead men walkin'," Clay mumbled. "It's got to be somethin' else. Dead is dead."

Luke looked uncomfortably at the others, who shied away from his gaze. He grabbed a rifle and threw it to Clay.

"Get up," he said. "We're gonna scout around a little. See what you make of the whole thing."

Clay was reluctant to get up but didn't want trouble. These people had showed him whatever hospitality they could afford and it would be ungentlemanly to take advantage of them. Besides, if things turned contentious, he was outnumbered and outgunned. He put his socks and boots back on, ignoring the pain as best he could, and followed Luke out into the woods.

* * *

"What are we doin' here?" Clay asked once they reached the crest of a steep hill overlooking a large barn.

"Watchin'," Luke replied. "If what I hear is true, they keep them things in barns like the one down below until they're ready to unleash them."

"Then wouldn't we be in danger?" Clay asked.

"If I'm right about these things bein' monsters, we're in danger anyhow," Luke answered. "That's why I left the others behind. Someone needs to get the word out about this and if we don't make it, maybe they can let people know the truth."

Clay didn't care much for the explanation, but as he watched the barn below, he could see Union soldiers patrolling the area. Arguing with Luke didn't seem like the best course of action, given the circumstances.

He watched as the Yankees opened the barn door and began pulling out wagons. Near as he could tell with what little lantern light spilled out of the barn, there were only about five soldiers and an equal number of horses.

"Check out them wagons," Luke whispered.

Clay took a good look at the first one the soldier pulled out. It looked like a cage; something you would see holding the animals that pulled along in a circus train. His heart sank when he saw that the cages contained humans...not animals.

"War prisoners?" Clay asked.

Luke shook his head. "Pretty sure I see both sets of colors on those uniforms. Not likely they'd carry prisoners from both sides—especially not together. Let's take a closer look."

Luke moved through the tall grass like a snake. Clay didn't think going after him was a good idea but if he didn't, he'd probably get lost on his own. Luke seemed comfortable with the woods, and Clay needed that confidence, so he followed in step despite his reservations.

When they reached a better vantage point, he wished he hadn't. There was enough light now to see that Luke was correct...the creatures in the cage weren't human. Though they looked the part at first, they were too broken.

Some of them had gaping wounds in their chests and stomachs—cannon shot most likely. Others were pockmarked with dozens of bullet wounds. There were some with heads barely attached, some with torsos twisted backwards on their hips, and a few that lacked limbs but still managed to crawl along on the floor of the wagon.

"The livin' dead," Luke whispered. "No wonder we ain't able to stop Sherman."

They watched the scene unfold, too paralyzed by shock and fear to look away. The Union soldiers pulled a second cage out of the barn. They threaded rope through pulleys on the top of the barn, tying one end of the rope to the horse saddle and the other to one of the cage doors. Once they had the pulley system rigged, two of the soldiers mounted horses as the remaining three tied them into the saddle. The men shook hands and parted ways, the cavalrymen staying behind as the others moved out.

Just as Clay turned to suggest they head back to camp, the two mounted Yankees withdrew their pistols and shot their weapons into the air. The noise startled the horses and the frightened animals galloped off—pulling the cage doors open. Dead men poured forth from the cages, stumbling over each other to reach the humans.

Each soldier turned to cut their rope, freeing up the horses to run. With the bulk of the monsters on their heel, the soldiers then shot themselves in the head and the horses sped into the darkness.

Clay knew what would happen next. The horses would run through their camps, baiting the undead horde to follow. The men wouldn't stand a chance; they'd be attacked in the night, brutalized and maybe eaten. What he saw that night when first attacked was no trick of the light. It was reality at its sickest.

A few of the slower creatures lagged behind. They seemed to sense Clay and Luke, though neither man could guess how. When they started to move in their direction, Clay stood up to run.

Luke grabbed Clay by the collar. "We ain't lurin' these things back to our camp. We're killin' them here."

Clay counted eight of the things headed toward them. "We can't shoot all of them in time."

"Then we kill some by hand," Luke said, raising his rifle and firing. The shot jerked the first creature's head back and knocked it off of its feet. It stopped moving once it hit the ground. "See. Simple as that." He fired another shot, catching another one in the leg and hobbling it. He swore under his breath when he saw it still moving toward him.

The monsters were getting close enough that running didn't seem to be an option. Clay couldn't risk getting caught up in the trees with these things nipping at his heels, so he fired a shot as well, hitting one of them solidly in the chest. The creature staggered backward momentarily, but not enough to slow it down completely.

Clay fired again and heard a familiar dull clank—his Springfield had jammed! The creature closed the distance to Luke, catching him before he could finish reloading. It pummeled him with its fists, knocking Clay onto his back. It clawed and bit as Luke tried to roll and shove it off.

"Help!" Luke yelled, waking Clay from a moment of shock. Clay reacted, burying his bayonet into the creature's temple. It stopped moving at once and Luke threw the corpse off his prone body.

"Damn," the big man uttered when he looked up to see the remaining six creatures were on top of them.

Clay looked up just in time to see one of them lunging at him, teeth snapping. It bit a hunk of his cheek off before he could beat it away with the butt of his rifle. Another grabbed at his ankle, tearing into his flesh with its sharp fingernails. Clay used the bayonet to pin its hand to the ground.

He cast a glance at Luke and saw that the large man was faring no better. He hadn't regained his feet before the others reached him and now he was pinned to the ground.

When Clay saw a third creature lunge in Luke's direction, he knew the man's time had come and it was time for Clay to retreat. His fear became physical and a warm dampness spread down the front of his trousers. Instinct kicked in and he fled, ignoring Luke's screams of agony.

Clay knew only pain and fear as his legs drove him back into the woods. His cheek throbbed and warm blood dripped off his chin, to splatter the ground at his feet, and he could still smell the creature's fetid breath on his skin.

His raw feet stung mercilessly each time his heels struck the ground. Branches clawed at his face, tearing more flesh, each cut conjuring images of dead hands flaying his skull.

When his chest betrayed him, threatening to stop taking breaths, he had to stop running. It seemed like hours had past, though he was sure his body couldn't have endured more than a few minutes. He walked a few paces before slumping against a tree, letting it take his weight for a few moments. He listened for the clumsy creatures moving through the leaves and underbrush as they gave chase, but heard nothing. He was safe, but who knew for how long?

He tried his best to follow their earlier path, to use rocks and stumps as landmarks just as Luke had. It was hopeless. It all looked the same to him, the forest conspiring with the unnatural creatures to trap him and rip him to shreds. He pushed on, determined to get to James, Edgar and Margaret. He had to convince them to leave. With their help, they could get to Savannah and warn the troops about the coming doom.

All that mattered now was getting to Savannah, to his family. He needed to protect them and make sure they were safe.

He wandered the woods for hours, certain he was in the right area. He was tired and terrified, looking over his shoulder as much as he kept his eyes forward, so he didn't see the large branch that tripped him up. He hit the ground with a groan, rolling into a gully. No sooner did he come to a stop at the bottom of the gully, then he heard the sound of a gun being cocked.

"It's me....Clay," he said to the silhouette standing over him.

"Clay? Sorry, sir...I was just tryin' to protect us, is all," James said. The boy offered him a hand up and helped him to his feet.

Just as Clay stood, his knees buckled and he crumpled to the ground. He lay there sobbing, fatigue, fear and pain pouring out through his tears. James whistled quietly, signaling Edgar and Margaret over to lend a hand.

Together, they helped Clay back to the camp.

"What happened? Where's Luke?" Margaret asked as she filled a tin cup with whiskey. She handed Clay the cup and awaited an answer. They all sat in silence, waiting for him to discuss what had happened–what he'd seen.

Once he found some courage at the bottom of the cup, he told them about everything that happened. Even with the wound festering on his face, he found the story hard to believe. The group shifted uncomfortably as he told the story, especially when he talked about what happened to Luke. They assured him he did the right thing by running...that someone had to get word to the Confederate leadership about the disaster heading their way.

"So what happened to the monsters?" James asked. "How did you kill 'em?"

"I didn't," Clay said. "I lost them in the woods."

Margaret and James exchanged frightened looks before Edgar thrust a gun into James hand, the boy leaving wordlessly.

Edgar turned on Clay, anger flashing across his face. "You don't lose these things, you idiot. They don't stop. They just keep comin'. It's why the Union's usin' 'em against us. And now, you brought them right to us!"

Outside the tent, James screamed, the shrill cry of agony, fear and anger emphasizing Edgar's words.

Margaret and Edgar grabbed their guns and ran out of the tent. Clay heard a couple of shots, and then nothing.

"Margaret? Edgar?" he whispered after a few moments of listening to the wind blow through the trees.

The tent shook as if someone was coming in and then collapsed entirely.

Clay looked up to see Luke shoving his way through the debris as he made his way inside. Clay was confused at first, thinking the man had somehow survived and returned to help, but when he saw muscle and tissue hanging from Luke's mouth, he knew he was staring at death itself.

Clay tried to run but his body betrayed him. He'd made it about ten feet out of the camp before he fell to the ground. When his head hit the dirt, he found himself staring into Edgar's dead eyes. The monster that killed Edgar continued to feast on him, tearing chunks from his chest cavity and ravenously shoving them into its mouth. It stopped, looked at Clay and crawled towards him.

Sudden sharp pain in his thigh told Clay that something else had gotten there first. Luke had him pinned to the ground, his teeth ripping into Clay's flesh. Before he could release the scream in his throat, the other creature was on him; tearing out his windpipe.

Clay lingered for a few moments, feeling each bite cut into flesh, each hand tearing his muscles and sinew apart. He looked up at the trees, cursing them for his fate.

* * *

When the cage door opened, Clay stumbled forward. Pain drove him forward—the agony of having an empty stomach and a desperate need to eat. The horses in front of him had food atop the saddle; that much he knew by instinct. He followed them as quickly as he could.

He joined the massive horde of undead as they continued Sherman's March.

All that mattered now was getting to Savannah, to his family. Maybe then his hunger would be sated.

BASIC TRAINING

RICHARD MOORE

Fowler elbowed me out of the way and ran toward the woman. He struck her with the butt of his rifle and part of her chin disintegrated, covering the rifle butt in viscid black slime. He laughed and said, "Got me a wet one, boys!"

The woman stumbled backward and tripped over her feet. Her back crunched as she landed, and her head thumped against the carpet. Advancing into the apartment, Fowler twisted the M-16 in his hands and brought it to his shoulder; sighted and ready to fire. He scanned for foes.

"Clear," he called, and moved through to the bedroom. "Clear."

Mitch and I hadn't even made it through the doorway; the door was still swinging from when we'd kicked it open. The wild heroics were for Mitch's benefit. Answering the radio call, breaking protocol by coming to unknown territory with half a unit, and charging up the stairs and into the apartment; it was all so the new recruit would think Fowler was some kind of savior to the planet. It was pathetic.

Our orders were to drive to the training facility and pick up fifteen new recruits, then return to the base. The apartment could have had ten zombies inside. As it was, it just had the woman and her victim. But that didn't make Fowler any less of a jerk for risking our necks just so he could play war hero for Mitch, the only recruit who hadn't gone AWOL.

"C'mon in here and take at look at this, kid," Fowler called, locating what remained of the woman's victim in the kitchen.

Mitch looked at me for confirmation and I nodded. He entered cautiously, giving the woman a wide berth. She was lying on her back, trying to lift her head. Threads of black goop spilled from where her skull had whacked the floor. Every time she tried to raise her head, the tarry threads held it to the carpet, as though she were stuck in a pool of freshly squirted super glue.

I entered the apartment and squatted by her ankles to make an assessment. The woman was naked, and at a guess, in her mid-to-late-fifties. There were chunks of flesh missing from her legs and arms, and she was missing her right ear. I pressed the barrel of my handgun against her forehead. It was like pressing it into putty. A purple bloom spread, dark fluids welling up around the muzzle of the gun. The woman kept trying to lift her head, forcing the gun deeper. Pinpricks of white roved in her eyes, buried beneath layers of black-red crust.

At close range, the splatter effect could be fatal—my eyes, nose, and mouth all points of potential infection. I stepped away from the woman and took aim, ready to fire.

Fowler came back from the kitchen and said, "Well are you gonna fuck it or are you gonna stand there all day looking at it?"

"Christ, Fowler," I replied. "Give it a rest for once, would you?"

He ignored me and looked down at the woman. "Nice tits. Pussy looks a little runny, though. What do you think, kid? Feel like taking a dip?"

Mitch grimaced, not sure if Fowler was joking or serious.

"Why don't you take this one, Sarge," I said. "Show him how it's done."

Fowler grinned and grabbed his crotch. "Hey, man, mi casa kielbasa. Maybe I'll do just that."

"Well, then go for it, Sarge," I said. "Not like we don't got thirty seconds to spare."

Fowler turned on his hard-eyed stare, then grinned. "Better watch that lip, Johnny." He looked over at Mitch. "Hey, kid, you sure you don't wanna get you some head?"

"Right after you get yours, Sarge," Mitch said, playing along now that I'd given him the idea it was okay to give Fowler shit. It wasn't—not with Fowler. He was one of those guys who wanted to dish it out but couldn't take it when somebody gave it back to him.

"Oh, I'm gonna get mine," Fowler said. He looked down at the woman. She growled, pulling against the tarry threads. "Whaddya ya say, baby? Wanna give me some head?"

He grinned at me, then raised his boot.

I looked at him with pleading eyes. "Fowler, don't."

His grin didn't falter for a second as he jumped up on one foot and brought the other down on the woman's face. Her head came apart: skin, bones, brains, blood. Fowler slapped his thigh and stamped a beat with his foot. "They'll be coming round the mountain when she comes." *Stomp.* "They'll be riding six white horses when she comes." *Stomp, stomp.*

The kid stood in the corner of the apartment that passed for the kitchen, watching with huge horrified eyes as his sergeant danced, sang, and obliterated the woman's head.

Pantomiming exhaustion, Fowler dropped to the couch and wiped goop from his boot heel with a throw cushion. He lit a smoke and said, "Best damn head of my life."

I was tired of his antics. Fowler didn't care. He got the joke and laughed enough for both of us. I walked over to Mitch.

"Is he always like that?" Mitch asked.

"Fowler? Yeah, pretty much."

"He's crazy," Mitch said. It sounded less like criticism and more like admiration. A lot of guys were reeled in by Fowler's thuggish mentality. The man was either too stupid to be afraid or so insane he no longer cared—maybe both. But these naive, scared kids were all looking for somebody to follow now that everything they'd ever known about themselves and the world had ceased to exist. Fowler's bravado convinced them they were safe as long as he had their back.

The woman must have snacked on her victim's brain not long before we'd forced our way into the apartment. The linoleum was covered in dark sticky blood, and the man's head was cracked open like a hard-boiled egg. His fingers trembled and then his hand grabbed the recruit's ankle.

"Shit!" Mitch yelled. He pulled himself free and stumbled away.

The dead thing sat up, white eyes glimmering. Mitch freed his gun from its holster and aimed it at the zombie's head.

"Whoa, whoa, whoa!" Fowler called, waving his arms at the kid and running toward him. Mitch hesitated, looking confused. No matter what they're told in training, they always forget the first time they encounter a Reanimate.

"Lower your weapon," I said. "His brain's already been destroyed. You could empty your clip until there's nothing left of his head and he'd still be moving around."

Mitch lowered the gun. "Sorry," he said. "Sorry."

The victim incessantly moved what remained of his head—left to right, left to right, bubbles of dark fluid forming within the cavity where there should have been a brain.

"Remember," I said. "After you shoot one in the head and destroy its brain, you eliminate the threat. After that they'll stay down for around an hour. When they're about to return a second time, you'll see their fingers twitch. But a Reanimate isn't your enemy. You ever see ten Reanimates coming at you and one zombie, be sure to take out the zombie first and not waste all your ammo shooting what's never gonna lay down and die."

"Right," Mitch said, nodding.

I continued, "Once the flesh becomes reanimated, you're dealing with something that no longer has a brain. This thing is just cells that have life when there shouldn't be any. Think of them as earthworms in human form, but less than."

Mitch nodded. "I know what it is. It's just that I have a hard time thinking of them that way."

"You want my advice?" Fowler asked. "Get an ax and chop one of these things up into hundreds of tiny pieces. Then you watch them bits of innards, fingers and little body parts jumping around. After that you'll stop thinking of them as people."

Mitch grimaced. "That's gross."

Fowler laughed and slapped him on the back. "Hey, it worked for me!"

* * *

Our cargo bucked and thrashed in back, sealed inside body bags, knowing no purpose, and driving me half out of my mind with the constant *thump, thump, thump* as their limbs crashed against the floor. The radio was broken—it was one hundred and ten degrees outside, and we had no A/C. I was hot, bored, and irritated.

My thoughts looped. I'd think about my wife, then think about the dead, then about the army, about Fowler, about the new recruit, then wonder why I still cared about any of it. Then I'd ask myself if I really did. Then decide I didn't, only to keep catching myself thinking about the same things all over again.

Fowler was driving while taking occasional pulls from a bottle of Early Times. He handed Mitch the bottle. The kid took a swig and passed it along to me.

I decided to force down way more than I wanted just to piss off Fowler. The truth was, I'd never been much for hard liquor. But I could see Fowler getting agitated as I guzzled the whiskey, and that alone was worth fighting off the gag reflex.

"Hey, what the fuck, Johnny? Go easy there."

I swallowed what was in my mouth, took another long pull, then leaned over Mitch to hand the bottle back. As Fowler reached for it, I wagged my finger in his face. "Didn't your momma ever tell you, 'sharing means caring'."

Fowler glared at me. There was a time when a disapproving glance would have chewed at the inside of my mind, making me catalog all I could have done to warrant his disapproval. That was back when his good opinion still mattered to me, back when I looked up to him—*revered* him. But I'd learned to see through a man like Fowler and know what he was really all about. I knew him well enough now to know he wasn't worthy of my respect.

Fowler grabbed the bottle by the neck and yanked it out of my hand. All the years on his craggy face disappeared and he was a petulant four-year-old again, snatching back the toy he'd shared because the bribe hadn't bought the other kid's friendship. He breathed the word "asshole," then took a hefty swig of his whiskey and turned his eyes back to the road.

After a few minutes, some dirty joke must have popped into his head; he laughed to himself and started telling it to Mitch. I'd heard the joke a dozen times before, so I looked out the window, hoping to see something interesting enough to fade the drone of Fowler's voice. The only thing to look at was the desert, the highway, and a steady flow of trucks identical to ours passing in the opposite direction. Day and night the trucks journeyed from the base, going out into the world empty and coming back loaded with body bags containing dead flesh that refused to die. All the men inside the trucks knew they might not return. Others had already decided not to—knowing everything was going to Hell, and that the army was in the thick of it.

I kept looking, hoping to see a stray zombie I could shoot, but all I found were my thoughts— the same thoughts. My wife, the dead, the army, how much I hated Fowler—these were all familiar ground. Only Mitch, or more specifically the reason he hadn't bailed like the other draftees, was of any interest to me.

I'd long ago decided to keep my distance from the new guys, just as I did from the guys who'd been around a while. In my experience, soldiers fell into three categories; they were either killed in action, went AWOL, or turned out to be such ingrained jerks that it was better to know them superficially than to endure in-depth exposure. The men I had respected, the ones who'd been my friends, were either dead, or had chosen to protect the only country they could truly still believe in—that of their family.

I tried to speak to Mitch several times, only to find my mouth held nothing but silence. Overcoming my growing sense of detachment made genuine communication more difficult with every passing day. And so we rode in silence.

As the miles rolled beneath us, and the sun blazed against my face, I started to nod off. I'd just begun to doze when Mitch jerked in his seat, knocking Fowler's arm and making him momentarily lose the wheel.

"Easy there, kid," Fowler complained.

I looked at Mitch, annoyed that he'd woken me.

The kid clapped a hand over his mouth. "Jesus Christ! What in God's name is that?"

The stench of the pits was so ingrained in my flesh that I hadn't noticed it drifting into the cab through the open window. A few days exposed to the pits and the fumes seep so deep into your skin that the stink never washes off, no matter how long you shower, no matter how much soap you use, no matter how hot the water is. Before you know it, you acclimatize to what was once so unspeakably vile, that you forget it exists—there's no other choice.

That stench; imagine a city made up of fish markets and slaughterhouses; a city of garbage dumps and open sewers. Top it all off with the fumes of a thousand Meth labs. It was that very same acidy chemical smell of a zombie's breath. The stink of the pits was so bad civilians wouldn't stand within ten feet of a soldier who'd been sent to work the pits, so bad that if a crowd of us on furlough walked into a bar, three minutes later we were the only ones there.

But it was more than just the smell. You could see the fear in their eyes—the civvies. The government was lying to them. Civvies knew it, and we knew it, too.

Fit for active duty. What a crock.

Whatever messed up thing was making dead people run around and chow down on living people was eating at us, too. Only difference was, we were being eaten from the inside instead of the out. The pit soldiers all had the same look about them, a look that earned us the nickname 'skull-heads'. Pit soldiers were going AWOL faster than any other division, but even dressed in civvies, people still knew.

Out of uniform they might look like they had the big C or were slamming dope—but no matter how far they ran, they could never escape the way the pits had marked them.

When he first got into the cab at the training facility, Mitch grimaced and the color drained from his face. All the instructors at the training camp had been exposed to the pits, but not as recently as Fowler and I had. As the hours of the morning passed, Mitch gradually became a little more accustomed to our stink. But we were nothing compared to the real thing. The recruit went into a coughing fit, leaking tears.

Fowler inhaled deeply and grinned. "Mmm. Smells like home cooking."

Mitch dry-heaved.

"Better pull over," I said. "Looks like he's gonna puke."

Fowler sighed, his foot switching from the accelerator to the brake pedal. The kid held up his hand, indicating not to stop. He was determined to prove himself. He looked like hell—pale and sweaty and obviously needing to vomit, but as we drove on and the pit stink got thicker, he didn't make a sound of complaint; he somehow managed to hold onto his breakfast. That was better than

I'd done my first time out to the pits—Fowler too—and I could see respect in Fowler's eyes as he gave Mitch a pat on the shoulder.

The stench didn't make me want to puke, but that kind of lame camaraderie sure did.

If the stench of the pits didn't keep the civvies away, there was no shortage of signs warning them they were approaching a restricted area. Not that many came to look. They were trying to run from the things we took there, not get closer to them.

Three miles outside the base, we arrived at the checkpoint. Two bored looking guards inside a booth were the only chink in the armor. An eight-foot electrified fence topped with razor wire surrounded the entire compound. Airspace over the base was also restricted. Anybody who came within five miles received a command to turn back. At three miles, they would be shot down. The army didn't want the public seeing the pits. Rumors were one thing but photographic evidence that could cause a public outcry was something else entirely. Thankfully, nobody had decided to test the warning.

Yet.

Fowler pulled to a halt in front of the barrier arm. The guard inside the booth looked us over. Satisfied with two of the faces he saw, he raised the barrier, waving us through.

After another two miles of desert, Fowler turned off the paved asphalt that led to the base, and drove down a well-traveled dirt road. All the way to the pits, there were high mounds of earth on either side of us. Trucks like our own were backed up to the pits, soldiers emptying their cargo. Diggers were scooping earth from a fresh pit, making the total now seventeen of them. Each was half a mile across and two hundred feet deep.

As we approached one of them, I tried to imagine how this must have been for Mitch. The stink alone had turned his face a sickly yellow and he was dripping sweat. I imagined looking through his eyes at what was inside the pits. Some men had gone crazy the first time they looked inside those holes. Others took longer, over time.

"Oh my God," Mitch whispered. "God, God, God."

His first glimpse.

I could think of nothing to say to ease the horror of what we'd introduced him to.

Fowler swung the truck in a wide arc and reversed, backing up to the edge of one of the pits. He put the truck in park, pulled the brake, and opened his door.

"Time to take out the trash," he said.

"Maybe the kid's seen enough for one day," I said. "Why don't you sit tight, Mitch. We can take care of the two in the back."

"Suits me," Fowler said. "If he ain't up for it."

Mitch shot me an annoyed glance then turned to Fowler. "Who says I ain't up for it?"

"Atta boy." Fowler whacked him in the arm and then climbed out on the driver's side.

Knowing I might not get the chance again to be alone with him, and knowing the type of R & R Fowler and his boys liked to indulge in, I said to Mitch, "Just watch yourself around that guy. Don't let him talk you into doing anything you don't want to do."

"What do you mean?"

How could I explain? And if I did, would it really make a difference? I shook my head. "Never mind." I climbed from the cab and Mitch followed.

Approaching a pit and looking into it never got any easier. But it was impossible not to look. Mitch stood beside me, staring down into the hole. Fowler worked the deadbolt loose on the back of the truck and swung open the doors.

There were four other trucks backed up at various points around the rim of the pit. The squirming body bags were thrown in with a splash.

They wouldn't stay sealed long. The stuff in the pit had a corrosive effect that ate through the canvas and freed the bodies from their confinement. Without feeding on living flesh to delay the process of decomposition, the Reanimates liquefy in a matter of weeks. First their skin splits open and the black blood inside them spills out, then their limbs and innards come loose and drift away from the torsos. After that their heads fall off and they become part of the bubbling black sewage that flows inside the pits. It flows because it's still animated. Even the silt-beds, one hundred feet beneath the surface, are somehow still alive. To me, the pits looked like pools of crude oil with dead things moving in them; thousands of body parts that had once sustained human life now living independently.

Below us, a headless torso broke from the inky blackness and went under again, a rope of intestines twisted around it. Upside-down legs went by, feet kicking. A face peered up at us from a body bag that had started to split open. A hand rose from below the surface and skittered across the bag, moving over the face, then dropping back into the blackness and disappearing from sight. On the other side, the same thing was happening in a thousand different places simultaneously—a black stew comprised of moving body parts and internal organs.

Mitch ran screaming, or tried to. His legs carried him a few feet away from the edge, then buckled. He fell to his knees. Vomited then sobbed.

Fowler tossed one of the body bags from the back of the truck, and it landed on the ground, stirring up dust. He looked over at me. "Least he didn't jump in. Saw a man do that once." He clucked his tongue, remembering, then ducked back inside the truck.

I went to Mitch and squatted beside him. He turned to look at me, a thread of vomit hanging from his chin, his eyes begging me to make it all disappear, to make the bad dream go away.

I put a hand on his shoulder.

"This is insane..." Mitch whispered. "Insane... Why don't we just burn them like they do everywhere else? Why?"

I knew the answer but wasn't about to say what it was. Not so soon after seeing the pits. So I said, "A soldier's job is to follow orders. Not to ask questions."

The pits were an experiment and so were the soldiers exposed to them. That much was obvious. The Government wanted to know what happened when the things decomposed. They tested the air, took samples from the pits. They ordered us to undergo weekly physicals and give blood, urine, and stool samples to determine the effects of exposure to the gasses the pits released.

Or at least, that's how it was until about three weeks ago. There'd been no testing or physicals since then. The experiment seemed to have been abandoned. Civilization was falling into chaos. The enemy's numbers were multiplying with every passing day. We were losing the war. But until we were told to destroy the pits and start burning bodies, all we could do was follow orders and wait.

But Mitch needed to hear something—*anything*. "What's in those pits isn't human," I said. "It doesn't think or feel or understand what it is or what's happening. It's just tissue that refuses to die—just confused DNA that's trying to resemble something it used to be."

Fowler tossed the second body bag from the back of the truck. He jumped down and dragged a bag over to the edge of the pit, then rolled it in.

There was a soft splash, and the kid looked up, watching Fowler return for the other one.

Fowler winked at Mitch. "Don't you worry about losing your breakfast, kid. Soon as we're through here, I'll treat you to lunch. Maybe even a few beers to go with it."

Mitch forced a smile and wiped the vomit from his chin.

Looking at Fowler's grinning face, knowing the son-of-a-bitch had a hidden agenda, I blurted, "And later on, if you'd like, you're welcome to come over to my house for dinner. My wife's making spaghetti. Best I ever tasted. The recipe's so closely guarded that her mother threatened to kill me when she caught me reading it over her shoulder."

Mitch managed a smile.

My wife's mother lived in Los Angeles and my mother and father were in Atlanta. I didn't know if they were still alive and didn't want to think about it. Their phones still rang, but no one ever answered. The messages we'd left on their answering machines was never returned.

"Your wife lives with you here on the base?" Mitch asked.

"Sure," I said. "There are families here, too. There's even some families with daughters about your age. Maybe I'll introduce you to a few."

That was an outright lie. The families were long gone, transferred when requests were approved, AWOL when denied.

"Thanks," Mitch said. "I'd like that."

Fowler didn't. Not one bit. He kicked the dirt and chewed his bottom lip.

In a hushed voice I said, "And remember what I said about watching yourself around that guy."

"Roger that," Mitch whispered. "Actually, he seems like he's kind of a psycho. But he's my sergeant, you know?"

"Come on," Fowler called out. "Let's go, before I die of thirst out here."

"I'll write down the address and directions before we drop you at your barracks. Four o'clock sound okay?" I asked him.

"Sounds great, Johnny," Mitch replied.

What was I doing? I'd seen so many of my friends killed. In all likelihood, Mitch would be killed, too. To keep my sanity, I'd vowed to never care too deeply about the fate of another soldier. And now here I was, doing it again.

* * *

What I'd told Mitch about my wife's spaghetti being the best I'd ever tasted was true. But my wife wouldn't be cooking it. She'd been gone for close to four weeks. I didn't want anyone to know. So I kept coming back to my house—my army provided accommodation—making like she was still there when anyone asked about her, making like everything between us was fine. She had left no note. All I had for a goodbye was our *last* conversation. I refuse to say final. I keep telling myself that one day I'll wake up and she'll be there beside me in our bed. Or that I'll walk into the living room and she'll be there, on the couch watching her soaps, or cooking in the kitchen, everything the way it was before the entire world went to hell.

I got a beer from the fridge and walked to the bedroom. The bed was empty. That was where it had happened—where she'd said it out loud instead of feigning sleep, or a headache, like she had those last two months.

"I can't, Johnny," she'd said. "I can't. God, I can't stand it when you touch me. Rubbing that stink all over me. I can't even stand to kiss you—I can taste it on your mouth. And when I look at you... God, you look like a cancer patient. You all look like cancer patients. Do you know what people call you? They call you skull-heads. *Skull-heads.* Do you think I want to end up the same way?

192

You wouldn't want me to become what you've become. You wouldn't want that. Not if you love me, Johnny. Not if you love me."

I finished my beer and worked my way through another two while I made spaghetti sauce. I had no idea what I'd tell Mitch about my wife not being there; but I'd invited him to dinner and planned to make good on my offer. When it was done, I got a spoon from the drawer and let the sauce simmer. It tasted okay. Just not the same as when my wife made it. I tried another mouthful. Savoring it, I remembered how my wife would always give me hell for using a metal spoon and scratching away at the non-stick coating on the pan. The memory was all the persuasion I needed to crack a fourth beer and head for the couch. I nodded off halfway through a news report on the TV about a mass exodus of civilians to Alaska.

When I woke up, it was ten after five. If anybody had knocked I would have woken. I sat there in silence, telling myself Mitch could take care of himself, that if Fowler talked him into doing anything, then Mitch was to blame for listening in the first place. The argument wouldn't sell. Two minutes later, I was headed out the door for the clubhouse.

* * *

I parked my jeep out front and entered the clubhouse. The bar was already packed, but there was no sign of Mitch or Fowler. The grunts were doing their best to escape the terrors they'd encountered that day, drinking too fast and talking loudly. There were no women—only men. I tried not to look at them too closely. Tried not to notice their deep sunken eyes and skin; it looked too much like wax paper. I ordered a beer, took a deck of cards, and sat at an empty table to play solitaire.

Fowler and his boys came in an hour or so later. I saw the usual faces: Fowler, Hodges, Jones, and Hayden. They pushed through the throng to the bar, swapping friendly insults with the soldiers on their way. Mitch was with them. I tried to push what that might mean from my mind. Tried again to tell myself whatever happened was none of my business. They were drunk. My guess was that

Fowler had treated Mitch to a liquid lunch and all thoughts of his dinner engagement at my house had gone right out of his mind. He looked pretty rough—his hair mussed, his uniform rumpled. Like he'd been asleep on his bunk until they'd gone to rouse him from his barracks.

I watched Fowler, looking for the telltale signs that would confirm my deepest concerns. For an hour they drank, laughed and told jokes, and I thought for once Fowler would do nothing worse to the kid than get him drunk.

But then it started. Nudges and winks, whispers and grins. Mitch was completely oblivious to the plotting going on around him. It made me feel nauseous. Fowler said something to Mitch. Who looked back blankly, unable to keep his body from swaying. Fowler repeated what he'd said and Mitch nodded.

When they headed out the door, I stood and followed, catching up outside. I grabbed Mitch's arm and spun him around. He looked at me bleary eyed.

"Hey, Johnny," Mitch slurred. "How you doin' man? We was gonna go play some cards. You wanna come play some cards?"

"Don't do it, Fowler," I begged as he grinned at me. "It's a mistake."

"Don't do what?" Fowler asked, the grin growing wider.

"You know damn well what. Just let him go."

He shrugged. "We ain't gonna hurt him. Just gonna show him a good time."

"Not this kid," I said. "It's not what he wants."

"How d'you know what he wants?" Fowler looked at Mitch, draped an arm over his shoulder. "Hey, kid, you wanna have a good time with me and the rest of the boys, doncha?"

Mitch grinned. "Sure, man. Let the good times roll." Something occurred to him. "Aw, shit. You invited me for dinner, Johnny. Sorry, man, I forgot all about it."

"Trust me," I said, taking Mitch's arm. "You won't enjoy what these guys have in mind."

Fowler slammed into me, knocking me to the ground. The rest of his boys moved in, boots drawn back, set to give me a kicking.

Fowler whistled. "Hey! Quit it!"

His dogs obeyed and backed away. Mitch swayed, confused.

"Just chill, Johnny," Fowler said. "It's time this boy became a man. Ain't that right, soldier?"

One look at Fowler and Mitch was grinning. Even now the kid still trusted him.

"S'right," Mitch said. "Let the good times roll."

I watched Fowler lead him away as I got up and followed at a distance. I knew where they were headed. Some called the place 'The Woodshed', others 'The Shed'. For years it was a disused gymnasium, until it was unofficially reopened for other purposes.

Mitch was led through the door. I waited thirty seconds or so before following them inside. They were leading him somewhere I knew he wouldn't want to go. If I was wrong, then all well and good. But if I was right, and they tried to coerce and bully him; to me that made it no different than rape.

I entered The Shed and shivered. Outside it was still ninety degrees, but The Shed was kept almost as cool as a refrigerator. I found them looking down at a 'Toy' that was strapped to a cot.

Mitch just stood there, mouth hanging open, eyes uncomprehending. The rest of them were grinning down at the thing they'd brought him to see.

"Pretty sweet, huh, kid?" Fowler asked. "Bet you never had a piece of ass that fine before."

"She..." Mitch said. "She don't got a head," he stammered.

"None of them have heads," I added, coming up beside him. I could see my breath as I spoke. "It was decided they shouldn't look too human, so none of us would forget that they were only Toys."

"Like blow up dolls," Hodge said. "Only better. Cause they still get wet down there."

Mitch shivered and I didn't think it was because of how cold it was. There were fifty cubicles like the one we stood in. Each had a drawn shower curtain in front of it. Soldiers' boots were set outside many of the closed curtains to let everyone know those Toys were taken. Groans and grunts came from inside the occupied cubicles.

The headless thing on the table was strapped at the wrists and ankles so she couldn't move. From the neck down, it was the body of a supermodel. It had remained that way for a few days until the rot set in. But there were plenty more where this one came from—millions.

And more with every passing day. The only sign of disease was on the corpse's left shoulder, where a zombie had sealed the headless woman's fate by taking a chunk of her flesh. It had been cauterized and was now a lump of scar tissue.

"Course you gotta wear a rubber," Fowler said. "Cause there's a chance the virus gets passed that way. Me, I always wear two. But it ain't so bad once you get used to it."

He grinned, the skin on his cheeks pulling so taut that his cheekbones looked like they'd rip right through. He looked like a living skull. They *all* looked like living skulls, except for Mitch. I suppose I must have looked like one, too.

"But she...she ain't got a..." Mitch looked at Fowler, appalled. "You have sex with these things?"

Fowler said, "Might seem kind of strange. Seemed that way to me at first. But think of it like this. You pay a hooker for sex—you're buying the use of her flesh. But there's still a person inside. These days, times being what they are, that just don't seem right. But this way, you're using flesh nobody wants and nobody owns."

"When you think it over, Mitch," I said, "you'll see it's better to put these bodies to good use than just toss them in the pit. And we only use them for a few days. Until they start to fall apart. And you're under no obligation to lie down with them, Mitch. It's something we do by choice. Don't think for a second you have to do it if you don't want to."

The Toy pulled against its restraints, its thighs opening, revealing pink meat.

Mitch reeled back in disgust and pushed past us. He took off across the gymnasium, heading for the door. As he ran, his arm snagged one of the shower curtains, snatching it back. A soldier was on a cot screwing one of the Toys. His chin was set on the cauterized stump of her neck. His pants were around his ankles. His ass rose and fell as he hammered away. He'd freed her ankles from their straps and her legs were wrapped tightly around his ass.

Mitch screamed. The sound echoed throughout the gymnasium, becoming one with the grunts and quiet moans and *KY-slap-slap-slap* as soldiers claimed what little reward they could for risking their lives and sanity in a world where every civilian saw them as symbols of death and madness.

Mitch spun around, looking for an exit.

"Happy now?" I asked Fowler.

Fowler shrugged. "The kid had to learn sooner or later."

I found out then what I'd wanted to know for longer than I remembered. I wanted to know how my fist would feel slamming into Fowler's jaw. It felt as good as I'd imagined. Better, because this was the real thing. Fowler fell easy for a man his size. As I looked down at him, I regretted waiting for so long to do it. Fowler looked up at me, dazed, rubbing his chin, uncertain if what had just happened could possibly be real.

"If it had been later, after he saw how real women treat us, he might have been okay with this," I said. "You ever pull a stunt like this again, I'll fucking kill you. You got that, Fowler?"

He didn't nod. Just lay on the floor looking up at me like he was the one who'd soon be doing the killing.

Mitch had pushed his way through the door and disappeared into the night.

I set off to look for him and to hopefully make him understand our madness.

* * *

Mitch ran as fast as he could back toward the barracks. I wondered just who he intended to tell. I set off after him, keeping him in sight but gaining no ground on his lead.

Back at the clubhouse, I got into my jeep. Knowing he couldn't outrun me now, I kept my distance and watched to see what he intended to do. Every so often he'd slow to a jog and look at the buildings he passed. He didn't enter any of them. He must have realized The Woodshed had to be sanctioned for it to exist. That meant anybody he might tell already knew about it. Poor bastard, there was nowhere he could turn.

He looked back and saw me following. When he started down the road that led away from the base, I knew he intended to go AWOL. He would never get past the guardhouse; not on foot. And there was no way over the fence. Mitch seemed to realize this and at the entrance to the pits, he turned and walked onto the dirt road that led down to them.

My headlights found him standing at the edge of the first pit, staring down into it. I turned off the engine and climbed from the jeep. When I reached him, he was sitting on the edge, crying, rocking back and forth. I squatted down beside him.

"I thought nothing could be worse than this," he whispered, gazing into the pit.

"It's a lot to take in," I said. "The question now is what you intend to do about it."

His voice trembled as he spoke. "That back there, all those bodies—that's evil. Evil, Johnny. It's an offense in the eyes of God."

"More of an offense than this?" I asked, gesturing toward the pit. "If there is a God, then to allow what's down there to exist when He has the power to make it stop—that's a crime far worse than any we've committed."

"I joined the army to help people and to fight for the ones who can't," he said. "Not to become a part of some sick and twisted little club. How can you guys...how can you..."

I sighed. "There's no good and bad guys here, Mitch. There never were. That's something you learn with age. There's just people doing what they need to do to get by. I keep telling you they're not human but just body parts that won't lie still. All we did was find a way to utilize some of them. Don't us guys deserve that much, given what we do every day?"

Mitch looked at me. "You think I can just forget all that shit back there, man? Think I can act like I saw nothing? Just say nothing?"

I shook my head. I knew what had to be done.

Mitch would never leave the base again. The order would be given to silence him, and the thugs sent to do the job wouldn't just have their fun; they'd also take their time about it. I'd seen it before.

It occurred to me that we could get in my jeep and run the checkpoint. I could save the kid's life, even salvage what little sense of decency I had left.

But then I had a terrible self-realization.

Just like the body parts inside the pit, I was trying to resemble something I used to be—trying to recapture a time when I was a better man.

Before everything went to hell, it was easy to convince myself that an unshakable sense of decorum guided my every thought and action. But now a new truth had emerged—I really didn't care. I'd gone out on a limb to protect Mitch, but only because I'd been looking for an excuse to exorcise my long-standing hatred for Fowler.

Mitch said, "What am I gonna do, Johnny? I can't..."

He didn't expect me to do it, never saw it coming. One second he was sitting on the edge of the pit, trying to make out my face in the dark, the next I hoisted him up from behind and tossed him into the darkness. I heard his body tumble down the rocky embankment, heard a splash as he landed in the foul blackness below, heard his scream as the dead things unwittingly claimed his life, dragging him down below the surface.

I stood listening, waiting—making sure.

It had to be done.

What if he'd somehow made it past the checkpoint? What if he went to the press, and The Woodshed closed? Then what? The bodies gave me a reason to exist. There was no way I was going to jeopardize that. I was a pariah to my wife, dead to every woman I'd ever encounter from here on out. There was nothing left for me except the Toys.

I returned to my jeep and headed back toward the base. I wondered if the Toys would always be enough to satisfy the needs of the rest of the men. Or whether, as time went on, they would start to return with different toys—the kind that were still alive.

I guess in the end, it really didn't matter.

ABOUT THE WRITERS

David H. Donaghe lives and works in the high desert of southern California. In 1995, he took the First Place prize in the California Writer's Club short story contest with his Western short story, Blind Justice. His short story, Some Call it Madness appeared in Nocturnal Ooze, an online journal in 2009 and he has three other stories published with Living Dead Press. He invites you to come join his readers network at:
http://www.authornation.com/MCRIDER
He is currently enjoying life and working on his next novel.

Daniel Fabiani is a 22 year old kid from NYC with the accent to prove it! He loves romance languages and cooking; the written word is sewed to his soul. His most favorite achievements are his inclusion various print anthologies, as well as the completion of his first novel. Credits include House of Horror, SNM, Pagan Imagination, Living Dead Press and others. His website is http://danfabiani.webs.com

Anthony Giangregorio is the author and editor of more than 40 novels, almost all of them about zombies. His work has appeared in Dead Science by Coscomentertainment, Dead Worlds: Undead Stories Volumes 1-5, and Wolves of War by Library of the Living Dead Press. He also has stories in The Book of Cannibals, End of Days: An Apocalyptic Anthology Vol. 1 -3, the Book of the Dead series Vol. 1-4 by LDP, and two anthologies with Pill Hill Press. He is also the creator of the popular action/zombie series titled Deadwater.
Check out his website at www.undeadpress.com.

Dane T. Hatchell grew up in Baton Rouge Louisiana and has lived there all his life. In his youth he was a fan of old school horror movies, and a collector of magazines such as Creepy and Eerie. Now in his early fifty's, he is devoting his free time to writing to satisfy a lifelong passion. The inspiration for "Love Prevails" comes from the evacuation of New Orleans during Hurricane Katrina. There were many stories of uncontrollable mobs attacking neighborhoods, committing unspeakable acts against humanity. He promised his wife now of thirty-two years, that he would be there to save her.

Robert M. Kuzmeski lives with his family and a menagerie of pets in his home state of Massachusetts. He writes in a variety of genres with a focus on science fiction, horror and modern dark fantasy. He's published several short stories and has multiple novels in the works. When not writing, he can usually be found playing role-playing games, doing photography or dabbling with music.

Jonathan McKinney lives in Winchester, KY with his wife, Charla, and their three children. His story "Shiny Eyes" appears in the anthology Close Encounters of the Urban Kind. He also writes reviews and upcoming news for Examiner.com. http://www.examiner.com/x-12963-Lexington-Suspense-Fiction-Examiner

Kevin Millikin, born in Northern California, now calls Portland Oregon home. He has previously spent time as a music journalist and aspires to be a screenwriter. The Scent of Rot is his first (of many hopeful) forays into the world of fiction.

Rick Moore, originally from Leicestershire, England, moved to the U. S. ten years ago and now lives in Phoenix, AZ. Rick's fiction has appeared in numerous zines and anthologies, including The Undead: Flesh Feast, History Is Dead, The Beast Within, Cthulhu Unbound, Harvest Hill, Dark Animus, the 2009 Stoker nominated Horror Library 3 and Bound For Evil (his inclusion in which still regularly sends Moore into a geekified frenzy of frothing at the mouth fanboy excitement as the collection also contains fiction by two of his childhood heroes, H.P. Lovecraft and Ramsey Campbell). To earn his daily crust, Rick works for the Arizona State Hospital as a Mental Health Specialist. Visit him online at http://www.myspace.com/zombieinfection

Gerald Rice has been a horror fanatic ever since he was little. He saw movies inappropriate for his age, such as The Howling and Creepshow when he was in kindergarten and has been writing professionally for the last ten years. Gerald has a BA in English from Oakland University and he lives in Rochester, MI with his wife and daughter.

His first novel, "The Ghost Toucher", will be published this year. Visit his website at www.feelmyghost.webs.com

DEAD RAGE

by Anthony Giangregorio
Book 2 in the Rage virus series!

An unknown virus spreads across the globe, turning ordinary people into bloodthirsty, ravenous killers.

Only a small percentage of the population is immune and soon become prey to the infected.

Amongst the infected comes a man, stricken by the virus, yet still retaining his grasp on reality. His need to destroy the *normals* becomes an obsession and he raises an army of killers to seek out and kill all who aren't *changed* like himself. A few survivors gather together on the outskirts of Chicago and find themselves running for their lives as the specter of death looms over all.

The Dead Rage virus will find you, no matter where you hide.

CHRISTMAS IS DEAD: A ZOMBIE ANTHOLOGY

Edited by Anthony Giangregorio

Twas the night before Christmas and all through the house, not a creature was stirring, not even a. . . zombie?

That's right; this anthology explores what would happen at Christmas time if there was a full blown zombie outbreak. Reanimated turkeys, zombie Santas, and demon reindeers that turn people into flesh-eating ghouls are just some of the tales you will find in this merry undead book. So curl up under the Christmas tree with a cup of hot chocolate, and as the fireplace crackles with warmth, get ready to have your heart filled with holiday cheer. But of course, then it will be ripped from your heaving chest and fed upon by blood-thirsty elves with a craving for human flesh! For you see, Christmas is Dead!

And you will never look at the holiday season the same way again.

BLOOD RAGE

(The Prequel to DEAD RAGE)

by Anthony Giangregorio

The madness descended before anyone knew what was happening. Perfectly normal people suddenly became rage-fueled killers, tearing and slicing their way across the city. Within hours, Chicago was a battlefield, the dead strewn in the streets like trash.

Stacy, Chad and a few others are just a few of the immune, unaffected by the virus but not to the violence surrounding them. The *changed* are ravenous, sweeping across Chicago and perhaps the world, destroying any *normals* they come across. Fire, slaughter, and blood rule the land, and the few survivors are now an endangered species.

This is the story of the first days of the Dead Rage virus and the brave souls who struggle to live just one more day.

When the smoke clears, and the *changed* have maimed and killed all who stand in their way, only the strong will remain.

The rest will be left to rot in the sun.

THE BOOK OF CANNIBALS
Edited by Anthony Giangregorio

Human meat . . . the ultimate taboo.

Deep down, in the dark recesses of your mind, can you honestly say you never wondered how it might taste?

Honestly, never wondered if a chunk of thigh tasted like chicken or pork?

Or if a hunk of an arm was similar to steak? And what kind of wine would be served with it, red or white?

Would a human liver be no different than one from a cow, or a pig?

For all we know, human flesh is as tender as veal, better than the finest tenderloin. And that is what the stories in this book are about, eating each other. But be warned, after reading these tales of mastication, you may just become a vegetarian, or at the very least, think twice before taking your first bite of that juicy steak at your local restaurant.

DEADFREEZE
by Anthony Giangregorio
THIS IS WHAT HELL WOULD BE LIKE IF IT FROZE OVER!

When an experimental serum for hypothermia goes horribly wrong, a small research station in the middle of Antarctica becomes overrun with an army of the frozen dead.

Now a small group of survivors must battle the arctic weather and a horde of frozen zombies as they make their way across the frozen plains of Antarctica to a neighboring research station.

What they don't realize is that they are being hunted by an entity whose sole reason for existing is vengeance; and it will find them wherever they run.

VISIONS OF THE DEAD
A ZOMBIE STORY
by Anthony & Joseph Giangregorio

Jake Roberts felt like he was the luckiest man alive.

He had a great family, a beautiful girlfriend, who was soon to be his wife, and a job, that might not have been the best, but it paid the bills.

At least until the dead began to walk.

Now Jake is fighting to survive in a dead world while searching for his lost love, Melissa, knowing she's out there somewhere.

But the past isn't dead, and as he struggles for an uncertain future, the past threatens to consume him. With the present a constant battle between the living and the dead, Jake finds himself slipping in and out of the past, the visions of how it all happened haunting him. But Jake knows Melissa is out there somewhere and he'll find her or die trying.

In a world of the living dead, you can never escape your past.

DEAD MOURNING: A ZOMBIE HORROR STORY
by Anthony Giangregorio

Carl Jenkins was having a run of bad luck. Fresh out of jail, his probation tenuous, he'd lost every job he'd taken since being released. So now was his last chance, only one more job to prevent him from going back to prison. Assigned to work in a funeral home, he accidentally loses a shipment of embalming fluid. With nothing to lose, he substitutes it with a batch of chemicals from a nearby factory.

The results don't go as planned, though. While his screw-up goes unnoticed, his machinations revive the cadavers in the funeral home, unleashing an evil on the world that it has not seen before. Not wanting to become a snack for the rampaging dead, he flees the city, joining up with other survivors. An old, dilapidated zoo becomes their haven, while the dead wait outside the walls, hungry and patient.

But Carl is optimistic, after all, he's still alive, right? Perhaps his luck has changed and help will arrive to save them all?

Unfortunately, unknown to him and the other survivors, a serial killer has fallen into their group, trapped inside the zoo with them.

With the undead army clamoring outside the walls and a murderer within, it'll be a miracle if any of them live to see the next sunrise.

On second thought, maybe Carl would've been better off if he'd just gone back to jail.

ROAD KILL: A ZOMBIE TALE
by Anthony Giangregorio
ORDER UP!

In the summer of 2008, a rogue comet entered earth's orbit for 72 hours. During this time, a strange amber glow suffused the sky.

But something else happened; something in the comet's tail had an adverse affect on dead tissue and the result was the reanimation of every dead animal carcass on the planet.

A handful of survivors hole up in a diner in the backwoods of New Hampshire while the undead creatures of the night hunt for human prey.

There's a new blue plate special at DJ's Diner and Truck Stop, and it's you!

DEAD THINGS
by Anthony Giangregorio

Beneath the veil of reality we all know as truth, there is another world, one where creatures only seen in nightmares exist.

But what if these creatures do actually exist, and it is us that are only fleeting images, mere visions conjured up by some unknown being.

Werewolves, zombies, vampires, and other lost things that go bump in the night, inhabit the world of imagination and myth, but all will be found in this collection of tales.   But in this world, fiction becomes fact, and what lurks in the shadows is real. Beware the next time you sense you are being watched or catch movement in the corner of your eye, for though it may be nothing, it might just be your doom.

INCLUDES THE DEADWATER STORY: DEAD GRAVE

THE DARK

by Anthony Giangregorio
DARKNESS FALLS

The darkness came without warning.

First New York, then the rest of United States, and then the world became enveloped in a perpetual night without end.

With no sunlight, eventually the planet will wither and die, bringing on a new Ice Age. But that isn't problem for the human race, for humanity will be dead long before that happens.

There is something in the dark, creatures only seen in nightmares, and they are on the prowl. Evolution has changed and man is no longer the dominant species. When we are children, we're told not to fear the dark, that what we believe to exist in the shadows is false.

Unfortunately, that is no longer true.

SOULEATER

by Anthony Giangregorio

Twenty years ago, Jason Lawson witnessed the brutal death of his father by something only seen in nightmares, something so horrible he'd blocked it from his mind.

Now twenty years later the creature is back, this time for his son.

Jason won't let that happen.

He'll travel to the demon's world, struggling every second to rescue his son from its clutches.

But what he doesn't know is that the portal will only be open for a finite time and if he doesn't return with his son before it closes, then he'll be trapped in the demon's dimension forever.

SEE HOW IT ALL BEGAN IN THE NEW DOUBLE-SIZED 460 PAGE SPECIAL EDITION!

DEADWATER: EXPANDED EDITION

by Anthony Giangregorio

Through a series of tragic mishaps, a small town's water supply is contaminated with a deadly bacterium that transforms the town's population into flesh eating ghouls.

Without warning, Henry Watson finds himself thrown into a living hell where the living dead walk and want nothing more than to feed on the living.

Now Henry's trying to escape the undead town before he becomes the next victim.

With the military on one side, shooting civilians on sight, and a horde of bloodthirsty zombies on the other, Henry must try to battle his way to freedom.

With a small group of survivors, including a beautiful secretary and a wise-cracking janitor to aid him, the ragtag group will do their best to stay alive and escape the city codenamed: **Deadwater**.

DEAD END: A ZOMBIE NOVEL
by Anthony Giangregorio
THE DEAD WALK!

Newspapers everywhere proclaim the dead have returned to feast on the living!

A small group of survivors hole up in a cellar, afraid to brave the masses of animated corpses, but when food runs out, they have no choice but to venture out into a world gone mad.

What they will discover, however, is that the fall of civilization has brought out the worst in their fellow man.

Cannibals, psychotic preachers and rapists are just some of the atrocities they must face.

In a world turned upside down, it is life that has hit a Dead End.

BOOK OF THE DEAD 2: NOT DEAD YET
A ZOMBIE ANTHOLOGY
Edited by Anthony Giangregorio

Out of the ashes of death and decay, comes the second volume filled with the walking dead.

In this tomb, there are only slow, shambling monstrosities that were once human.

No one knows why the dead walk; only that they do, and that they are hungry for human flesh.

But these aren't your neighbors, your co-workers, or your family.
Now they are the living dead, and they will tear your throat out at a moment's notice.

So be warned as you delve into the pages of this book; the dead will find you, no matter where you hide.

ANOTHER EXCITING ADVENTURE IN THE DEADWATER SERIES!
DEAD SALVATION
BOOK 9
by Anthony Giangregorio
HANGMAN'S NOOSE!

After one of the group is hurt, the need for transportation is solved by a roving cannie convoy. Attacking the camp, the companions save a man who invites them back to his home.

Cement City it's called and at first the group is welcomed with thanks for saving one of their own. But when a bar fight goes wrong, the companions find themselves awaiting the hangman's noose.

Their only salvation is a suicide mission into a raider camp to save captured townspeople.

Though the odds are long, it's a chance, and Henry knows in the land of the walking dead, sometimes a chance is all you can hope for.

In the world of the dead, life is a struggle, where the only victor is death.

INSIDE THE PERIMETER: SCAVENGERS OF THE DEAD
by Alan Spencer

In the middle of nowhere, the vestiges of an abandoned town are surrounded by inescapably high concrete barriers, permitting no trespass or escape. The town is dormant of human life, but rampant with the living dead, who choose not to eat flesh, but to instead continue their survival by cruder means.

Boyd Broman, a detective arrested and falsely imprisoned, has been transferred into the secret town. He is given an ultimatum: recapture Hayden Grubaugh, the cannibal serial killer, who has been banished to the town, in exchange for his freedom.

During Boyd's search, he discovers why the psychotic cannibal must really be captured and the sinister secrets the dead town holds.

With no chance of escape, Broman finds himself trapped among the ravenous, violent dead.

With the cannibal feeding on the animated cadavers and the undead searching for Boyd, he must fulfill his end of the deal before the rotting corpses turn him into an unwilling organ donor.

But Boyd wasn't told that no one gets out alive, that the town is a death sentence.

For there is no escape from *Inside the Perimeter*.

DEADFALL
by Anthony Giangregorio

It's Halloween in the small suburban town of Wakefield, Mass.

While parents take their children trick or treating and others throw costume parties, a swarm of meteorites enter the earth's atmosphere and crash to earth.

Inside are small parasitic worms, no larger than maggots.

The worms quickly infect the corpses at a local cemetery and so begins the rise of the undead.

The walking dead soon get the upper hand, with no one believing the truth. That the dead now walk.

Will a small group of survivors live through the zombie apocalypse?

Or will they, too, succumb to the Deadfall.

LOVE IS DEAD: A ZOMBIE ANTHOLOGY
Edited by Anthony Giangregorio
THE DEATH OF LOVE

Valentine's Day is a day when young love is fulfilled.

Where hopeful young men bring candy and flowers to their sweethearts, in hopes of a kiss...or perhaps more. But not in this anthology.

For you see, LOVE IS DEAD, and in this tome, the dead walk, wanting to feed on those same hearts that once pumped in chests, bursting with love.

So toss aside that heart-shaped box of candy and throw away those red roses, you won't need them any longer. Instead, strap on a handgun, or pick up a shotgun and defend yourself from the ravenous undead.

Because in a world where the dead walk, even love isn't safe.

ETERNAL NIGHT: A VAMPIRE ANTHOLOGY

Edited by Anthony Giangregorio

Blood, fangs, darkness and terror...these are the calling cards of the vampire mythos.

Inside this tome are stories that embrace vampire history but seek to introduce a new literary spin on this longstanding fictional monster. Follow a dark journey through cigarette-smoking creatures hunted by rogue angels, vampires that feed off of thoughts instead of blood, immortals presenting the fantastic in a local rock band, to a legendary monster on the far reaches of town.

Forget what you know about vampires; this anthology will destroy historical mythos and embrace incredible new twists on this celebrated, fictional character.

Welcome to a world of the undead, welcome to the world of Eternal Night.

BOOK OF THE DEAD
A ZOMBIE ANTHOLOGY VOL 1
ISBN 978-1-935458-25-8

Edited by Anthony Giangregorio

This is the most faithful, truest zombie anthology ever written, and we invite you along for the ride. Every single story in this book is filled with slack-jawed, eyes glazed, slow moving, shambling zombies set in a world where the dead have risen and only want to eat the flesh of the living. In these pages, the rules are sacrosanct. There is no deviation from what a zombie should be or how they came about. The Dead Walk.

There is no reason, though rumors and suppositions fill the radio and television stations. But the only thing that is fact is that the walking dead are here and they will not go away. So prepare yourself for the ultimate homage to the master of zombie legend. And remember... Aim for the head!

REVOLUTION OF THE DEAD

by Anthony Giangregorio

THE DEAD SHALL RISE AGAIN!

Five years ago, a deadly plague wiped out 97% of the world's population, America suffering tragically. Bodies were everywhere, far too many to bury or burn. But then, through a miracle of medical science, a way is found to reanimate the dead.

With the manpower of the United States depleted, and the remaining survivors not wanting to give up their internet and fast food restaurants, the undead are conscripted as slave labor.

Now they cut the grass, pick up the trash, and walk the dogs of the surviving humans.

But whether alive or dead, no race wants to be controlled, and sooner or later the dead will fight back, wanting the freedom they enjoyed in life.

The revolution has begun!

And when it's over, the dead will rule the land, and the remaining humans will become the slaves...or worse.

KINGDOM OF THE DEAD
by Anthony Giangregorio
THE DEAD HAVE RISEN!
In the dead city of Pittsburgh, two small enclaves struggle to survive, eking out an existence of hand to mouth.

But instead of working together, both groups battle for the last remaining fuel and supplies of a city filled with the living dead.

Six months after the initial outbreak, a lone helicopter arrives bearing two more survivors and a newborn baby. One enclave welcomes them, while the other schemes to steal their helicopter and escape the decaying city.

With no police, fire, or social services existing, the two will battle for dominance in the steel city of the walking dead. But when the dust settles, the question is: will the remaining humans be the winners, or the losers?

When the dead walk, the line between Heaven and Hell is so twisted and bent there is no line at all.

RISE OF THE DEAD
by Anthony Giangregorio
DEATH IS ONLY THE BEGINNING!
In less than forty-eight hours, more than half the globe was infected.

In another forty-eight, the rest would be enveloped.

The reason?

A science experiment gone horribly wrong which enabled the dead to walk, their flesh rotting on their bones even as they seek human prey.

Jeremy was an ordinary nineteen year old slacker. He partied too much and had done poorly in high school. After a night of drinking and drugs, he awoke to find the world a very different place from the one he'd left the night before.

The dead were walking and feeding on the living, and as Jeremy stepped out into a world gone mad, the dead spotting him alone and unarmed in the middle of the street, he had to wonder if he would live long enough to see his twentieth birthday.

THE CHRONICLES OF JACK PRIMUS
BOOK ONE
by Michael D. Griffiths
Beneath the world of normalcy we all live in lies another world, one where supernatural beings exist.

These creatures of the night hunt us; want to feed on our very souls, though only a few know of their existence.

One such man is Jack Primus, who accidentally pierces the veil between this world and the next. With no other choice if he wants to live, he finds himself on the run, hunted by beings called the Xemmoni, an ancient race that sees humans as nothing but cattle.   They want his soul, to feed on his very essence, and they will kill all who stand in their way.   But if they thought Jack would just lie down and accept his fate, they were sorely mistaken.

He didn't ask for this battle, but he knew he would fight them with everything at his disposal, for to lose is a fate worse than death.

He would win this war, and he would take down anyone who got in his way.

THE WAR AGAINST THEM: A ZOMBIE NOVEL
by Jose Alfredo Vazquez

Mankind wasn't prepared for the onslaught.

An ancient organism is reanimating the dead bodies of its victims, creating worldwide chaos and panic as the disease spreads to every corner of the globe. As governments struggle to contain the disease, courageous individuals across the planet learn what it truly means to make choices as they struggle to survive.

Geopolitics meet technology in a race to save mankind from the worst threat it has ever faced. Doctors, military and soldiers from all walks of life battle to find a cure. For the dead walk, and if not stopped, they will wipe out all life on Earth. Humanity is fighting a war they cannot win, for who can overcome Death itself? Man versus the walking dead with the winner ruling the planet. Welcome to *The War Against Them*.

DEADTOWN: A DEADWATER STORY
BOOK 8
by Anthony Giangregorio

The world is a very different place now. The dead walk the land and humans hide in small towns with walls of stone and debris for protection, constantly keeping the living dead at bay.

Social law is gone and right and wrong is defined by the size of your gun.

UNWELCOME VISITORS

Henry Watson and his band of warrior survivalists become guests in a fortified town in Michigan. But when the kidnapping of one of the companions goes bad and men die, the group finds themselves on the wrong side of the law, and a town out for blood.

Trapped in a hotel, surrounded on all sides, it will be up to Henry to save the day with a gamble that may not only take his life, but that of his friends as well.

In a dead world, when justice is not enough, there is always vengeance.

END OF DAYS: AN APOCALYPTIC ANTHOLOGY
VOLUMES 1 & 2
Edited by Anthony Giangregorio

Our world is a fragile place.

Meteors, famine, floods, nuclear war, solar flares, and hundreds of other calamities can plunge our small blue planet into turmoil in an instant.

What would you do if tomorrow the sun went super nova or the world was swallowed by water, submerging the world into the cold darkness of the ocean? This anthology explores some of those scenarios and plunges you into total annihilation.

But remember, it's only a book, and tomorrow will come as it always does. Or will it?

  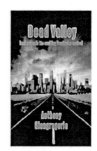

Breinigsville, PA USA
01 November 2010
248458BV00004B/68/P